MEET YOUR NEW PARTNER

The Elaki was deep grey, with pinkish hues toward his middle where the brain was located. David thought Elaki looked like huge stingrays walking upright. They averaged a height of seven feet, but they were no more than a couple inches thick—thin and flappy. Their oxygen slits made a happy face pattern at the midsection.

David caught the light lime smell of the Elaki. Someone had told him once that to an Elaki, humans smelled like strong cheese.

"Look at the ID," Mel said, under his breath.

The Elaki had a departmental badge hanging under his breathing slits. David wondered how it stayed on.

The Elaki slid close.

"I am from family of Puzzle Solvers. Which of you is from the David Silver?"

David realized he was looking at the happy face pattern of breathing slits on the belly. He raised his gaze to the Elaki's eyes, housed on two pronglike sections at the top.

"I'm Silver."

"Please. I am your Elaki adviser."

"We don't need any goddamn advisers."

"Not only are Hightower's aliens truly alien—her cops are actually human! A high-spirited and spooky new *Silence of the Lambs* with otherworldly overtones."
—Terry Bisson, Nebula Award–Winning Author

Alien Blues

Lynn S. Hightower

ACE BOOKS, NEW YORK

For Scott, who helps run interference when I'm working, because he swears I am dangerous when disturbed. And who doesn't mind (or do you?) dropping everything to discuss the latest idea.

And for Alan, Laurel, and Rachel, who played Authors & Editors when they were little, instead of Cowboys & Indians, and who are all wonderful storytellers (sometimes when they shouldn't be).

And for Matt, who is terrific to work with and a good pal, and who has the endearing habit of calling and asking after my characters as if they were family. Which they are.

This book is an Ace original edition
and has never been previously published.

ALIEN BLUES

An Ace Book / published by arrangement with
the author

PRINTING HISTORY
Ace edition / January 1992

ISBN: 0-441-64460-0

Ace Books are published by The Berkley Publishing Group,
200 Madison Avenue, New York, New York 10016.
The name "ACE" and the "A" logo
are trademarks belonging to Charter Communications, Inc.

PRINTED IN THE UNITED STATES OF AMERICA

10 9 8 7 6 5 4 3 2 1

PROLOGUE

THE OLD WOMAN FELT A HAND ON HER SHOULDER, AND THE faint tickle of a kiss on her cheek. She opened her eyes reluctantly; it still felt like the middle of the night. She clipped her hearing aids on and eased her legs over the side of the bed.

It was dark out. Storm coming? Nothing better than hot coffee on a rainy day. She took a deep breath, but didn't smell coffee. She was puzzled. Earl never woke her till the coffee was hot.

She looked at the clock. Three forty-two. No storm coming, it *was* the middle of the night. And Earl had been dead three years. Her eyes moistened with tears.

A loud squeak came from the kitchen, followed by a groan. The old woman trembled. There was no mistaking that noisy kitchen window. Someone was breaking in.

She stood up. Her legs were shaky and stiff—they never worked good in the morning. She glanced at the phone, but decided that calling for help would take too long. She needed to get upstairs, between the intruder and the children.

She took a step, then hesitated. There was no need for the stairs—the children were grown and gone. Wake up, she told herself. Wake up.

She heard the kitchen faucet smack into the wall and the clunk of dishes on the counter. She considered hiding in the closet, curling up small and tight. She'd read that possums didn't really play dead when they were scared; they passed out. She had laughed when she'd read it, but she believed it now.

She didn't have much to steal. Who would break in and bother an old woman?

All kinds of people, she guessed. The world being what it was.

1

The old woman folded her arms across the sag of her tired breasts. She had nothing on but cotton underpants and a blue nylon gown that didn't quite reach her knees. The news disk was full of Machete Man bulletins, but Saigo was a large city. Why would that killer pick her out of all these people?

Because you're old, said a nasty inner voice. Because you're helpless. He likes them helpless.

When she'd had children to protect, she hadn't been helpless. Once a neighbor's dog had gone crazy during a storm, and run into the yard after her daughter. She had streaked from the house like lightning, beating the dog with a broom, screaming for her little girl to get inside. She still had the scars on her hip and calves where the dog had bitten her open.

She heard footsteps in the kitchen, and then in the hall. Get out, she thought. Get out, get out. She stumbled and fell into the dresser, wincing at the crash and tinkle of her lipstick tubes, perfume bottles, and picture frames. A sweet puff of spilled powder smoked the air. The light in the kitchen went out.

The old woman held her breath and listened. The footsteps had stopped. Whoever it was had stopped to listen, too.

She took a breath and waited for her eyes to adjust to total darkness. She let go of the dresser and walked forward, hands outstretched. She felt for the doorjamb and crept into the hallway.

Someone stood just outside the kitchen. The darkness was denser there. And she smelled him—a rank animal odor of urine and sweat. She heard a small intake of breath, and a footstep, and felt the surge of another human being heading her way.

Her legs were working now, and she ran forward, veering left into the living room. The front door was locked up tight—three dead bolts all solidly in place, two of them requiring keys.

No, not keys. Her grandson had put the voice activator in a week ago. Bless Dennis, dear Dennis, the Good Lord bless his heart.

"Open locks!" Her voice was shrill. She heard the creak of the old wood floor as the man tried to find her in the dark.

Her hands were slippery on the doorknob, but it turned—thank you, God—and swung wide when she yanked it. Warm humid air rushed through the screen door, and the porch light sent a shaft of brightness into the room. Had she latched the screen? Oh, damn, oh, God, her fingers were shaking badly. The latch bit into the ball of her finger, and she slid the metal clamp aside. She jammed the handle and opened the door.

He was in the living room now, right behind her. Impossible to resist turning to look.

He was startled by her gaze. His eyes were sleepy-looking and red around the edges. She gasped and stumbled out the door—three concrete steps, and then she was in the yard. The grass sagged with dew, wet and cold on her bare feet, and chill bumps emerged on her arms, legs, and back. She ran across the lawn, the thin blue nightgown billowing out behind her.

ONE

DAVID WONDERED HOW LONG ROSE WOULD BE GONE THIS time. He ran a finger inside his shirt collar, and wondered what he'd feed the kids for supper. It was too hot to cook.

Maybe hot dogs? A fine thing for a half-Jewish guy to be feeding his children. But the pickles would be kosher.

David stood up and stretched. His partner, Mel Burnett, sat at the desk butted in front of his. Burnett yawned and scratched the back of his neck. His hair was brown, thick, and wiry; badly in need of a cut. He was short, but solidly built, barrel-chested. His face was burnished by heavy sunlight, and his eyes were blue. Like Rose's.

"You going already?" Mel said.

"Rose is going out of town again. Got to get home so she can make her flight."

"Another animal rescue, huh?"

David shrugged, aware that Della Martinas was listening.

"Don't she give you the details?" Mel said.

"Somewhere in California." He glanced at the glassed-in office in the corner behind his desk. Captain Halliday looked up, caught his eye, and grinned with the usual psychotic cheerfulness. How the man could be consistently upbeat in the gloomy precinct room was puzzling.

The air was thick with the faint hum of printers, and the light was harsh and bright. Marks and dents in the floor were proof that the desks had stayed in perfectly spaced rows for many years, but the precinct's days of symmetry were long gone. Desks were clumped together haphazardly, making hash of available space.

The building was done bunker style, built when they were still putting up offices hand over fist. The floor was white linoleum with black flecks, the walls grey concrete block. And there were no windows.

David wondered how cops could think without windows to stare out of.

4

Mel rubbed his stomach, right over the belly button. "I'm hungry."

"Come to the farm," David said. "Have supper with me and the kids."

"Naw, I don't feel like fooling with the brats tonight."

"Go ahead, flunk unclehood."

"They'll swarm, and I'm beat." He rubbed his eyes and looked around his desk. "Hey, where's my Coke? Della!"

A dark-skinned woman looked up. She was pretty, with a rich, smooth complexion and long, wiry black hair plaited in corn rows. She took a slow swallow from a can of Coke.

"What you want, Burnett?"

"Nothing, Della girl. Just looking for the can I was using as an ashtray."

Della smiled. "You don' smoke, sweetheart. Maybe you should take it up. Soft drinks aren't good for you—too much sugar."

The phone rang. Mel picked it up.

"What." Mel grimaced. "Hell, yeah, this is Homicide Task Force. Don't you know who you're calling?" He grinned at David. "Naw, Silver ain't here. This is Burnett." Mel listened for a moment and grabbed a pencil. His voice changed.

"Give me that address again."

David went back to his desk.

"Got it." Mel looked up. "Another one."

David's stomach felt odd. "Machete Man?"

"Looks like. Victim's alive."

"What?"

"She got away."

"When?"

"Last night."

"Last night?"

"Didn't know it was our boy. DNA match just came through." The printer purred and started up.

"That'll be our report," David said. He bent close to his terminal. "Message, Rose. Crime scene at . . ." He leaned over his desk to look at Mel's scratch pad. "Twenty-three eighty-nine Spenser. If you can't wait, bring the kids in. Leave them in a priority car with a uniform. Sorry, babe."

David glanced at Halliday. He was reading the report and a look of dark malevolence flitted across his face. So much for good cheer.

The parking garage was hot and humid. Sweat popped up along David's forehead and across his shoulder blades. He hated the way the city smelled and felt at the end of a hot day. A humid breeze blew trash across the buckling sidewalks and into the gutter. This time of day the colors were bad—shades of dirt, all the dingy hues.

Even the people were dingy. Lately he saw them as formless grey hulks, with dark holes where there ought to be faces. He had to look hard to find the faces. In the morning he could find them easily—at the end of the day, not so easy.

The car was hot inside, and it smelled like cigar smoke and old plastic. David steered them into the road grid and hit the priority vehicle switch. Like magic, traffic flowed out of his way.

Mel rattled the report. "Looks like they had it down as B and E. Guy scraped his head getting in the window—they got hair root and blood."

"An embarrassment of riches."

"Says here the victim—a Millicent Darnell—got away clean."

David opened his window. The vendors were closing down and the city smelled like a fairground at the end of a run—old greasy food, sweat, hot metal. A man packed up displays of cantaloupe, watermelon, and strawberries.

David wanted to get the kids some fresh melon. He started to push the pause command, then changed his mind. Money was a little tight this week. He ought to leave everything in the account, in case Rose needed something.

She never did. When she hired out to the animal activists, she didn't work cheap. She never took anything with her, money or clothes. She'd leave in a worn pair of jeans, nothing more than a purse slung over her shoulder. And a day or two after she got back, a deposit was made in her personal account. Those deposits had bought them the farm.

"Where is the Darnell woman?" David asked.

"Next door. Residence of a Mr. and Mrs. Roderick Pressman. He made the call."

Traffic was heavy with commuters heading out of the city— the Friday exodus. It was still light out. David shut his window. The air conditioner battled the hot, stale air.

In a few hours the signs would be lit, and the broken pavement thick with predators. Up and down the streets, innocents would weave their way in and out, unaware and vulnerable.

The car slowed and paused. A new BMW with an adapted roof eased into traffic ahead of them.

"*What!*" Mel glared out the window. "Since when did those bellybrain Elaki bastards get priority over a police vehicle?"

David chewed his lip. He could see the faint grey shimmer of the Elaki behind the wheel. Their Ford slid in behind the BMW. They seemed to be headed the same way.

"Assholes are like horses. Never sit—not even to sleep. Ever hear of a horse driving a car? They ought to be hauled around in vans." Mel rubbed his stomach.

The car bore right and David swung the wheel.

Commercial areas gave way to residential. Small houses, old and deteriorating, lined both sides of the street. The trees were large and the shade pleasant. David steered the Ford right again, and then left. The BMW stayed ahead.

A two-story wood-frame house had the yellow-green crime stamp glowing on the door. David checked the address—2389 Spenser.

The BMW pulled into the driveway. David stopped the Ford in front of the house.

A guy in blue jeans and a grey cotton sport coat stood in the front yard. His hair was blond and long, and a bald spot was spreading from the back of his head. He wore sandals, his shirt was pink and yellow, and an earring swung from his right ear.

Cheerful, David thought.

The man turned, looked at the BMW, then grinned at David.

David walked over curiously, noting the ID clipped to the man's belt.

"David Silver." He offered a hand.

"I know." The man's grip was firm. "Nice to meet you, Detective. I'm Vern Dyer."

David frowned. He knew that name.

"Oh, yeah," Mel said, shaking hands. "You work vice, don't you? I heard of you."

"Been inside?" David asked.

Dyer smiled and flicked his ID with a broken thumbnail. He was tan, his face lined and tired. His eyes were brown and intelligent—bloodshot at the moment.

"No authorization. Can't get through the seal. If you don't mind, I'd like to go in with you. Take a look around."

"How come?" Mel asked.

Dyer shrugged. "I'm on my own time, following a hunch. Something related to another case. Probably nothing."

The door of the BMW flipped up, and they watched as an Elaki slid out of the front seat. He turned from side to side, balancing on a broad-based fringe that was covered by muscled scales. The Elaki teetered forward in the breeze, poised like a toe dancer, fringe folded backward. He rippled across the grass toward David, the fringe scales contracting and releasing like the belly plates on a snake.

Sunlight glinted in the tiny jewellike scales that made up the outer skin.

A light breeze ruffled David's hair and rippled the Elaki.

The Elaki was deep grey, with pinkish hues toward his middle where the brain was located. David thought Elaki looked like huge stingrays walking upright. They averaged a height of seven feet, but they were no more than a couple inches thick—thin and flappy. Their oxygen slits made a happy face pattern at the midsection.

David caught the light lime smell of the Elaki. Someone had told him once that to an Elaki, humans smelled like strong cheese.

"Look at the ID," Mel said, under his breath.

The Elaki had a departmental badge hanging under his breathing slits. David wondered how it stayed on.

The Elaki slid close.

"I am from Family of Puzzle Solvers. Which of you is from the David Silver?"

David realized he was looking at the happy face pattern of breathing slits on the belly. He raised his gaze to the Elaki's eyes, housed on two pronglike sections at the top.

"I'm Silver."

"Please. I am your Elaki adviser."

"We don't need any goddamn advisers," Mel said, staring into the Elaki's midsection. David put a hand on Mel's arm.

The Elaki waved winglike fin tips in something like a shrug.

"Captain Halliday should have explained for advance knowledge. I will study with you this case."

David looked at Dyer, who was staring at Mel's feet. No help there.

"I understand that there have been Elaki assigned to administrative areas within the department," David said. "But this is an active investigation Mr., um, Puzzle. Perhaps if you'd return to your . . . office, or whatever, we can straighten this out later. I'll be glad to give you a call tomorrow."

The Elaki's left fin tip flowed into a shape resembling three thick, short fingers. He raked them across the ID, making a staccato of taps. David was reminded of an elephant scooping peanuts with a ripple of his trunk.

"There is no mistake, Detective Silver."

"I think there is," Mel said.

The Elaki headed for the front door, the grass flattening under him.

David shrugged. "Let's see if he can get in."

The Elaki swarmed up the cracked concrete steps and opened the door.

"Looks like he's got authorization," Dyer said.

"I'm calling the captain." Mel headed for the Ford.

"Mind?" Dyer asked.

David wondered what vice wanted with Machete Man. Dyer didn't seem to want to share his thoughts, but he didn't look like a thrill seeker either.

David waved him on. "Please."

TWO

IT WAS STUPID, DAVID THOUGHT. EVERYBODY ELBOWING THEIR way inside, clomping through the tired old house. But there was always the need to see for yourself.

The car door slammed.

"Talk to the captain?"

"Not there," Mel said tersely. He charged up the steps.

David felt sorry for Mel, and a little sad. Mel's father, a gifted software analyst, had been crowded out of a high-level job, thanks to the Elaki. The aliens' infiltration of fieldwork was something David had been dreading.

The Elaki had come to Earth with slightly superior technology, and vastly superior mastery of the "soft" sciences. They were a strange mix of benevolent arrogance, eager to help with what interested them, but keeping their own society separate. Still, they had cured the myriad manifestations of schizophrenia, rescuing a lot of people from the streets and making David's job easier. And they were well on the way to curing eating disorders.

They had taken over a lot of businesses, too, because they were better at them. An Elaki doctor was more compassionate, much more competent, and much less likely to withhold treatment due to the status of national health accounts, or an unwillingness to shake the status quo. And they had wonderful ointments for the uncomfortable and disfiguring rashes people sometimes suffered after AIDS.

They seemed to be advising everywhere—national politics, local politics, in the AMA, the NHO, Amnesty International, Literacy For All, the Educator's Forum, even the Police Benevolent Association. They also worked with numerous agricultural groups, and had found a way to control Japanese beetles.

And now police fieldwork.

David concentrated on the house. Was there something about it that would draw the twisted attention of Machete Man?

The victims were certainly an eclectic bunch. No real similarity, other than the usual one—vulnerability. And this killer had spread from young women and men to the aged, *and*, most unusual, was killing interracially. The last victim had been Oriental.

The house looked lonely, but David knew that was not an objective opinion. If a house did not have a bike in the driveway, or a stuffed animal abandoned in the grass, to him, it was lonely.

He didn't want to go in. It would be hard to concentrate under the eye prongs of the Elaki, and in the swell of hostility emanating from Mel.

He went to the house next door and knocked. There was a yellow ceramic heart on the door, with "The Pressmans" lettered in green.

The door sensor buzzed. "Good evening, sir. This is the residence of Ron and Sybil Pressman. Please state your business."

David held his ID up to be scanned. "Detective Silver. I'm here to see Mrs. Darnell."

The door opened. The man peering out was heavy and short. His hair was oily and mussed, and his shorts were rumpled khakis with mud stains on the front. David smelled beer on the man's breath.

"I'm Ron Pressman." He opened the door. "Come on in. We're sitting out back. Peeping over the gate at you fellas. Hey, you see that Elaki? What's he up to?"

"Mr. Puzzle is assisting in the investigation."

"Puzzle, huh? Those people got funny names."

Pressman led him down a dark hallway. David saw a formal living room off to the right—dusty and unused. Pressman led him through a den where the TV played. The computer terminal was dark. Newspapers were scattered on the floor, and there was a bowl of soggy cereal on the coffee table.

The house smelled musty, but it was cool, and David was sorry to follow Pressman out the back door. The yard was small, enclosed by a six-foot privacy fence. Sunflowers, yellow-brown and heavy, lined the back and sides of the fence. The yard was tiny, but David counted eight trees and four flower beds, in addition to a huge vegetable garden. The tomato plants were tall. David spotted the deep red of ripe tomatoes. He wished his looked that good.

Two women sat in metal rocking chairs. The chairs were green and had heart-shaped backs. One of the women was dumpy, fiftyish, with unlikely blond hair and a worn pink complexion. She had on shorts and a loose overblouse. Her feet were bare, the toenails painted a deep violet. Her legs were flabby, lined with blue varicose veins.

She held up a glass of beer. "Hi there. Get you something?"

"No thanks."

The other woman was old, and she watched David warily. This must be Millicent Darnell. The victim. Her eyes were soft brown and alert, and she wore a pink belted house robe that had cotton knobbles on it. Her arms rested on the rails of her chair. Her fingers were shaking.

David took off his coat and tie.

"Beautiful," he said mildly, waving his hand at the backyard. In all honesty, the profuse greenery pressed him—like standing in a crowded floral shop with no elbow room. Stainless-steel shears and a heavy pair of cotton gloves rested on a table by the chairs. Pressman had been gardening through the worst heat of the afternoon.

"Those are wonderful tomatoes," David said. "Mine aren't near that big, and I'm just now getting some ripe ones."

Pressman beamed. "Here, sit. I'll tell you my secret." His chair creaked as he leaned forward. "*Grass clippings*. Put them right 'round the base, makes wonderful compost. And always keep them pruned. Make 'em stay in the cage."

David nodded.

The old woman started to rise. "I guess it's me you want."

"Mrs. Darnell? How do you do, I'm Detective Silver. Please, don't get up."

The woman sank back down. Her hair was white and tangled in the back. She wore heavy stockings, rolled down below her knees. The skin of her arms was loose and thick, freckled with age.

"They tried to get me a doctor. But I'm not hurt."

"I'm very glad to hear that."

"I s'pose some pretty bad things could of happened. They said you'd want to talk to me at home. At the scene, they called it." Her lower lip trembled. "Darn shame, isn't it? When an old woman's afraid to go home. I've lived in that house for forty years."

"Forty years?"

"Forty years. I'm ready, though, you want to go over there. Been worrying over it all day, but Ron says, you got to cooperate, so the . . . the police can find this fella. So I'm ready."

"Please, relax, Mrs. Darnell. We need to talk, but you should be comfortable."

"She had a rough night," Sybil Pressman said.

"You want us to leave?" Ron Pressman stood up.

"Don't let me run you out of your garden." David studied the old woman. Still rattled. "Would you be more comfortable inside?"

His shirt stuck to his back. He smiled at her hopefully.

"I just as soon be out here, if it's okay, then. I don't have to go back to the house?"

"Not now, no. Why don't you tell me everything, from the beginning. Assume I don't know a thing."

"She loses her train of thought," Mrs. Pressman said. "If you interrupt. Those others, last night. They kept interrupting and never did get the story straight."

Millicent Darnell looked annoyed. "That's just police business, Sybil. That's how they work." She looked kindly at David. "I see that notebook behind your leg. Don't dangle it down in the dirt. Go on and take your notes."

David smiled and waited.

Her eyes narrowed and she stared at her toes. "Well, now, I was asleep. Sound asleep. And I woke up, and looked at my clock. It said three forty-two. I got my aids off the table." She pointed to her ears. "Don't hear too good without them, and I ain't a good risk for surgery." She patted her chest. "Heart. I take the aids off at night because they rub. Anyway, as soon as I put them on, I hear something funny . . . A kind of squeak and crack. And then I remember, that's the noise that old kitchen window makes when it opens.

"Boy, that scared me! Oh, I can't tell you how scared. It hit all a sudden, and I go out of my bedroom . . . I can't run. My legs don't work so good when I first get up. And I bumped into my dresser, and it made an awful noise, all my knickknacks rattling.

"I figured he'd be on me in a minute, but he must of stopped to listen too. And I go through the hall—dark, you know. I didn't turn on no lights. And I go into the living room to the door, when I hear footsteps. He's coming to get me." She took a breath, her eyes full of tears.

"I used to have a hard lock to open on that door, but a while ago my grandson—Lord bless his heart—he put in that voice-activator thing.

"I told the door to open, and it opens. And I heard him. I know he was in the hall, but I was afraid to turn and look. I went down those steps and . . . I ran. Across that grass in my gown and nothing else, but I ran, and I don't think I done that since I was fifty, and my grandson fell in the pond."

David pictured it—the dark night, the killer in the house, the old woman running in her nightgown.

"I banged on their door something awful," she nodded at the Pressmans. "Confused hell out of the sensor, but Ron let me right in. Sybil tucked me up in her robe, and held my hand till the police come."

"Who called the police?"

"I did," Ron Pressman said.

"Did you see anything?"

"Well, I came out here in the garden, to watch for the cops. And I watched the house to see if he'd come out."

Lucky he didn't see you, David thought.

"I didn't see him, but I saw a light go on in Millie's bedroom."

"Oh my," said Mrs. Darnell.

David looked at her. "What woke you up?"

Millicent Darnell twisted her hands in her lap. "What?"

"In the middle of the night. What woke you up?"

"I don't know. I guess maybe I heard something."

"But you weren't wearing your hearing aids, Mrs. Darnell."

Sybil Pressman sighed. "Go ahead, Millie. Tell him what you told me."

This, thought David, would be it. The stray piece of information that helped break the case.

"Earl got me up."

David blinked. "Earl?"

"My husband."

"Where is Mr. Darnell?"

"I . . . he . . . I'm a widow, Mr. Silver. My husband's been dead for three years. Hard to believe—three years without Earl. We were married a long time."

David scratched his head, and Ron Pressman shifted in his seat.

"Earl didn't sleep so good." Millicent Darnell smiled faintly. "He liked to sit up late and read. Sat in that old brown recliner in the living room, and read military history books.

"But he was always up making biscuits at six every morning, no matter how late he went to bed. And he'd come in after breakfast was fixed, and lean down, and kiss my cheek and pat my back. I'd wake up, put in my hearing aids, and go in for some coffee while he scrambled the eggs."

David peeled the cuticle back on his left thumb.

"Anyway, it was *Earl* got me up last night." She looked defiantly at David.

"It's okay. Tell me."

"I was sound asleep. I felt Earl kiss my cheek and pat my back. It was just like every morning before he died. I put in my aids and tried to smell the coffee. Then I remembered Earl was dead. I looked at the clock, and it was the middle of the night. That's when I heard the noise in the kitchen."

David felt the hair stir on the back of his neck.

Tears rolled down the old woman's cheeks. "I wish it had been Earl. I wish it had been Earl, and coffee, and biscuits, and eggs. I wish Earl were here." She pointed to her house and her hand shook. "They say . . . they say that man did awful things in my bedroom. Me and Earl's bedroom. I want to go over there. I want to see what that fella did."

Sybil stood up and patted her shoulder. "Now, Millie, we agreed that after the police were done, I'd go over and clean up first. You can stay with us tonight, and Dennis will come get you tomorrow."

Millicent Darnell stood up. "I want to go home."

David studied her. What would be best? For her—he was not sure. But she might remember something if they went over it again.

"I'll take you. Just one minute." He stood up. "Mr. Pressman, can I use your phone?"

He called and told Mel to clear the house. Dyer, the Elaki, and Mel should wait out front—he and Mrs. Darnell would go in through the kitchen.

He took Mrs. Darnell's arm, and they made their way slowly out of the backyard, while Ron and Sybil Pressman watched them go.

The Darnell yard seemed bigger, though it probably wasn't. The grass was dry and heat-scorched, and there was a shade tree by the side of the house. They walked along a path of hexagonal concrete steps. David searched the grass for footprints or a stray wallet. No such luck.

"Who put that on the door?" Mrs. Darnell pointed.

"That's a seal—we put it on all crime scenes. Keeps everything secure."

"Maybe so, but it's turned that panel of glass green. Will it come off?"

"Yes ma'am, it sure will."

The back door opened into the kitchen—a small dingy room, the floor tile a battered reddish-maroon. The countertops had yellowed with age and were crammed with greasy appliances. The refrigerator hummed. There were snapshots on the door—babies, and men and women, many of them tending to fat. A family, David thought, that would benefit from Elaki research on eating disorders.

The kitchen window was shut. David opened it. It squeaked and groaned.

"That what you heard last night?"

The old woman nodded. "Yep. It's a noisy window. Been trying to get someone in to fix it. Good thing I didn't."

"Mrs. Darnell, do you notice anything different about the kitchen? Anything missing?"

She folded her arms. "He seems to have left a mess."

He wondered how she would know, then squelched the thought. His house didn't look much better. He remembered his mother's kitchens—the blank, gleaming counters, meticulously organized cabinets, garbage stashed out of sight. Lavinia Silver would do without food, rather than have it on the counters. In Little Saigo, they'd had to scrape together every leftover, but once they got out, she'd said eat it now or toss it. It wasn't till he met Rose that he discovered the peculiar improvement of meatloaf after a night in the fridge.

"Where exactly, Mrs. Darnell?"

She pointed. A knot of cups from Burger Bazaar were strewn across the worn wood table.

"I think those were left by my colleagues." David scooped up the trash and stuffed it into the recycle compacter. "Anything else?"

She shook her head. She peeped out the kitchen door.

"Would you like to look through the living room first?"

"Yes." She frowned. "No. I want to see."

She led him down the dark hallway. The bare floorboards creaked. David could smell the faint acrid odor of the nano machines that had been run through the house to collect minute evidence. A lot of effort for a B and E. What had gotten them to put on the heat?

Sunlight poured in the bedroom window. Mrs. Darnell paused in the doorway, shoulders rigid.

"Oh my."

She turned a white face to David. He leaned forward and caught her before she hit the floor.

THREE

DAVID SURVEYED THE BEDROOM. HE SHOULDN'T HAVE brought Mrs. Darnell here. But at least he knew why the uniforms hadn't treated this like a typical B and E.

A drawer full of panties and old cotton bras had been dumped on the bed, then hacked to pieces. The blade of the machete had bitten deep into the mattress. The semen-stained bedspread had been removed by the lab tech.

CATCH YOU LATER was scribbled on the wall in bright pink lipstick. Who was the guy talking to—cops or Darnell?

The closet door had been yanked so hard it wobbled off the hinges. Mrs. Darnell's floral dresses lay in shreds over her shoes. David squatted down and looked at them. Shoes not touched— no foot fetish. Men's clothes hung undisturbed at the back of the closet. Earl's? Probably. Machete Man hadn't been interested.

David wondered why the clothes were still hanging there three years after Earl's death. He thought of his mother's apartment— still locked up and unattended to. He hadn't been particularly close to his mother. It would be hard for Millicent Darnell to dispose of a husband she had loved for so many years.

He checked his watch—seven P.M. The kids needed to eat, poor babies, he hoped they'd had a late lunch. They'd been sitting out front in a priority car when he went out to see Rescue off. Mrs. Darnell had been conscious and complaining, but the EMT hadn't liked her vitals, and had taken her to a clinic for observation. She had cried a little. David felt bad about sicking the meds on her, but she definitely looked shocky.

Della Martinas and Pete Ridel would start tomorrow morning, going through Mrs. Darnell's things, getting the make on the victim. Somewhere must be a connection. David thought about the window. Small—hard to get through. Guy was slender, or agile anyway. He'd hit his head. He was professional enough to get around the sensor alert, but he'd missed his victim. Must have made him mad. He was cool or crazy, taking the time to chop up the bedroom and jack off with the police on the way. The uniforms

17

must have come close to getting him.

David thought of the last victim, lying spread-eagled on the bed. His hands and feet had been cleanly severed and placed on his abdomen, then Machete Man had hacked the stomach to putrid gore, and masturbated over the whole mess.

David remembered when he was a uniform, and dicky wavers used to upset him.

Five victims. Darnell was number six, and she had gotten away. Thank God. Thank Earl. David rubbed the back of his neck. He was tired, and his girls were waiting. It was too hot to wait.

It was carnival time out on the lawn. Ron Pressman had the Elaki backed up next to his car.

"Okay," Pressman was saying. "If they're not Japanese beetles, what kind are they? Do a hulluva lot of damage whatever they are."

David smiled. Dyer had spread his sport coat on the hood of David's car, and all three girls were perched on the coat, swinging their legs and eating candy bars. They were deep in conversation with Dyer, Mel, and a uniformed patrolman, and they barely noticed when he walked up.

Kendra carefully wiped the chocolate from her hands onto Dyer's coat.

"Kendra!" David knew he was blushing. "Sorry, Dyer. Let me have it cleaned."

Dyer grinned. He looked young when he smiled. "Don't sweat it, pal. It'll wash. Serves me right for giving them sweets before supper."

"Juice boxes too!" Lisa smiled and waved a box of apple juice. "Mommy said wait for you. And *not* to go in the street. We seen the ambulance. Somebody dead?"

"No, honey. An older lady didn't feel well. She should be all right by tomorrow."

Kendra gave him a worried look. "Uncle Mel said we could take the candy. Mr. Dyer gave it to him, and he gave it to us, so it wouldn't come from . . . you know. Stranger."

"And absolutely right, too," Dyer said.

The patrolman folded his arms and grinned. "How *old* are these girls, anyway?"

David patted their heads as he reeled off their ages. "Seven, five, and three."

"Boy, the stuff they been telling me. You don't really have a three-legged dog and eight crippled rabbits?"

"Not anymore."

"What about the chimp?"

David glanced at Mattie and saw her lip quiver. "I'm afraid he died."

"Your wife a vet?"

"No, we just . . . have a farm. These things seem to come our way sometimes."

Mattie's eyes filled with tears. "Po' Benny."

"Well, hey," Dyer said loudly. "You ladies going to give me back my jacket?"

Kendra jumped down.

Lisa pointed at his earring. "What's that?"

"Got a unicorn on it." Dyer bent close. "See?"

The girls crowded next to him.

"It has a blue eye!" Kendra said.

"That's turquoise. My girlfriend brought it back from Mexico last year. Said my gold hoop was a bore. It's my good-luck charm."

"Mama won't let me get my ears pierced." Kendra gave David a stern look.

David noticed the BMW drive off. Pressman was gone. Dyer had a packet of wipes and was cleaning chocolate off the girls. David stepped forward to help, but Mel and the patrolman beat him to it, one man to a girl.

Rose had left him a car seat, and he strapped Mattie in while Kendra belted herself. He remembered a time when they'd had three car seats to do. The back seat of the car was littered with broken crayons, scraps of paper, and a stuffed bear. Mattie held her blanket and sucked her thumb.

Lisa was still in the yard, handing out pictures. David strapped Mattie's seat and bumped his head on the door frame.

"Too hot!" Mattie squirmed and kicked her feet.

"Come *on*, Lisa," David said. He made a mental calculation. Just enough cash on him to pick up supper from the Burger Bazaar, if the girls shared a big drink and he waited to eat.

The patrolman waved a piece of yellow paper with pink crayon on it. "Bye bye, Lisa."

"Bye, Fred."

David picked Lisa up. He saw chocolate behind her ear and wiped it away with his handkerchief.

"Need one of these?" Dyer held up a wet wipe.

"I got it. How many kids you got, Dyer?"

"Me? None."

David cocked his head. "Come on. You got candy, juice, wipes . . ."

Dyer shrugged. "I work vice. Run across a lot of kids in vice. Nice, sometimes, to be able to give them a little something." He waved at Lisa, and at Mattie and Kendra. "Bye, girls." Dyer slung his jacket over his shoulder and headed for his car. "Thanks for the look see, Silver."

"Anytime."

Mel put a hand on David's shoulder. "Your daughter's quite an artist. But she oughtn't give this stuff to a guy works vice."

David took Mel's picture.

"What's it look like to you, David?"

The drawing looked very like a penis. David frowned and handed it back to Mel.

"Mushroom, of course."

FOUR

THE CRY BROUGHT DAVID UP FROM A DEEP SLEEP. HE STUM-
bled out of bed and into the hallway. The cry came again, and
he went into the girls' room, impaling his big toe on a plastic
horse. Too many toys and too many girls in one room.

Kendra and Lisa were sound asleep in their bunk beds. He
checked Mattie's bed and found his daughter buried beneath a
pile of stuffed animals, her security blanket wound tightly around
her tiny fist.

David swept the animals to the end of the bed, and shifted
Mattie so her head was on the pillow. Her eyes opened to slits,
then closed. He unwound the blanket and tucked it next to her
head, then covered her up.

He was awake now, and aware that Rose hadn't been in bed
beside him. He went out in the hall and tripped over Dead Meat.
The dog yelped and hung her head.

David scratched her ears. She was a mutt, some kind of collie
mix, no more than a couple years old—one of Rose's new acqui-
sitions, along with a large black rabbit. The rabbit was blind, bare
of fur on one side, the tender exposed skin red and scabby. Rose
had come home late yesterday, both animals in tow.

The dog had been rescued whole and healthy. Rose had been
unable to leave it in a cage with the ominous notation Dead Meat on
the tag. David felt a moist nose in his crotch, and he crouched down
and patted the dog's back. She licked his unshaven cheeks.

She was a sweet dog, eager to please, timid. So far, very gentle
with the kids. He closed the door to the girl's room.

"Sorry, dog." He refused to call her Dead Meat, though it was
the only name she'd answer to. "Can't sleep in there till I know
you better."

Dead Meat walked three circles in front of the door and lay
down, head on paws.

Rose was asleep on the couch, a fine film of sweat over her
forehead. A pile of newspapers rested on her stomach, and the
T-shirt she wore rode up on her hips, giving David a view of

her white bikini panties. She was a small woman—fine-boned, blue-eyed, with long, very black hair. An empty wineglass was turned over on the floor, and a few drops of red wine had soaked into the carpet.

Should he wake her? She did not sleep well, but those cries he heard meant nightmares. She'd had bad dreams all the time when they first got married, a holdover, she'd said, from her years with the Drug Enforcement Agency. Whenever he asked her what she dreamed, she said she didn't remember.

It had been a long time since she'd cried in her sleep. She hadn't said anything—she never did—but he could tell this last job had been a bad one.

He touched her shoulder and her eyes opened. She blinked and sat up.

"Hi, David."

"What you doing in here?"

"Couldn't sleep." She rubbed a hand over her face and hung her head. "God, what a dream. And that rabbit."

"You were dreaming about rabbits?"

"No. The one I brought back. I hope they're okay."

"They? You just brought one."

"I meant the girls."

David sat down beside her and let his mind drift. He was too tired to talk to Rose. It took too much concentration to follow her grasshopper mind.

He put his arm around her and yawned. "Can we go to bed?"

"Sure."

They stumbled arm in arm down the hall. Dead Meat whimpered when they closed their door, leaving her alone in the hallway. Rose curled up against David's back.

"We need a new name for the dog," David said, drifting to sleep.

The phone rang.

"God damn it." He heard Rose fumbling.

"What." She paused. "Of course I'm home. Listen, Mel, would you like a cuddly black rabbit to curl up . . . don't call *me* in the middle of the night and cuss. All right, he's here. David. It's *Mel.*"

David took the phone and listened. His heartbeat picked up.

"Dyer did? Okay, I'm on my way. Hell yes, get him up. Sounds like Dyer's in trouble."

Rose turned the lamp on and watched David pull on a pair of jeans.

"Who's Dyer?"

"A cop in trouble." David loaded his gun and put it in the holster. "Bye, sweet."

"Be careful. And call when you can!"

David ran to the barn. It was dark out, and a haze of humidity hung in the air. The car started immediately, the headlights illuminating the black rabbit, cowering at the back of its cage. He didn't want the chill of the air conditioner, so he slid the windows down, then backed the car into the drive.

Gravel and dirt crunched under the tires, and he gave the car his full attention. His farm was off the beaten path, and the roads were plain roads until about twenty miles out of town.

The clock on the dash said two A.M. There was still traffic—the world never slept now, even in the remote rural parts. As soon as he guided the car onto the track, traffic picked up. He pushed the priority switch, took his foot off the gas, and eased his grip on the wheel.

Mel had been working late when the message came through. John Q. Citizen had been driving Highway 18 and run across a wrecked car in the middle of the road. He got out to help, and some crazy guy, blood streaming down his forehead, had commandeered his car in the name of the law.

Man was obviously crazy—rumpled, dirty, flashing a phony badge. The man had told him to call the cops, and ask for Detective Silver in Homicide Task Force. Tell him officer needs assistance. Name of Dyer.

Mel had gone to talk to John Q. David, being so far out of town, was on his way to Highway 18.

The car was ditched by the side of the road—same little orange Datsun Dyer had been driving the other day. David parked and left his lights on. Mosquitoes danced in the glare, and a fat green beetle whizzed by his head. The breeze was cool, but the humidity made him sweat.

The front end of the Datsun was smashed. David looked up and down the roadside, wondering what the car had hit. No big trees or guardrails. Nothing likely.

He squatted down in front of the car, shining his penlight. The front bumper was a mess. David saw traces of dark paint. He scratched a piece off with a fingernail, and looked at it closely. Dark green.

He shined the light on the tires. The rubber was cut up, so Dyer had been bumping on and off the track. David stood up.

The windshield was starred—gunshot. Three or four. What was Dyer into, and why had he wanted David?

The door on the driver's side was smashed and stuck shut. More dark paint streaked the sides. David went to the passenger side and slid in. He hated little cars. Dyer must have been miserable in this tiny bucket—guy must be six-foot-two and David was only five-eleven. Jewish six feet, he called it.

There was blood on the dash and the driver's seat. Dyer was hurt, and it was worse than a little cut on the head. A pack of wet wipes had been ripped open. He found a wad of them on the floor, soaked with blood and smelling soapy. The blood was dry.

David slid behind the wheel and pushed a switch on the steering column.

"Datsun here," a voice said. "V.I.N. number 007298864YBX2. My fuel tank is low. I am in need of repair. I am not operable. May I suggest a garage?"

"Datsun, please give me a rundown on what happened tonight—the, um, the time and the details of your damage."

"At eight fifty-eight P.M. I sustained tire damage, right front, left front, right rear, left rear. My rods have been abused with excessive speed and would benefit from lubrication. At nine-fourteen my left front fender was smashed by another vehicle."

"Would you recognize the vehicle, if I showed it to you?"

"Yes. Do you wish me to continue the report?"

"Please."

"My windshield has been punctured and cracked in three places. This was done at nine-eighteen P.M. And my oil pan and axle rod were scraped and bent at nine-nineteen P.M. My radiator hose burst at nine twenty-one P.M., at which time I ceased to operate." The voice paused. "That is a full account of my recent damages. However, there are some long-standing problems I would be happy to—"

"No thanks."

"Preventative car maintenance is—"

"No."

"May I suggest a garage?"

David flipped the switch.

He opened the glove compartment, finding a battered pair of sunglasses, car registration, spare computer disks, condoms. He punched the personal memo button on the terminal. It didn't work. Neither did the radio.

He searched the back seat, and found a dirty pair of socks, a pair of old tennis shoes, and a cool box full of candy bars and juice boxes. He got a crowbar from his own car and forced the trunk of the Datsun.

David shined his light, illuminating a pair of water skis, an oily toolbox, three canisters of instant tire, a piece of rug, and a woman's bikini top rolled in a mildewed towel.

David shook his head. The last thing he'd rolled up in a towel in his trunk was a dirty diaper he couldn't find a place to dump.

He got back in the front of Dyer's car. Come on, Mel, he thought. Dyer's bleeding somewhere.

David ran his hands in the cracks between the seat, pulling out old napkins and getting gunk under his fingernails. Dyer ate a lot of fast food in the car. Stakeouts.

David leaned across the seat and ran his hands between the driver's seat and the smashed car door. His fingers closed over a plastic handle. He fished it up. It was new and clean and looked like a toothbrush with the bristles in the middle. It would have fallen out if the driver's door had been opened, so Dyer had probably dropped it tonight.

David put it in his pocket and listened to the cicadas.

FIVE

THE REARVIEW MIRROR CAUGHT THE GLINT OF THE EMERGENCY lights on the patrol car. David heard the groan of brakes as a large wrecker stopped by the Datsun. The flashing yellow light blended with the red one. He stuck his head out the window. Mel was pointing and talking to the uniform.

"Mel! I'm going!"

Mel ran to the car, a white bag clutched in his hand. He got in, and David had the car moving before the door was shut.

"Coffee?" Mel asked.

"Thanks." It was hot—cream, no sugar, double size. "Hey, it's good."

"Came from that café down on West. Sent the uniform for it, while I squeezed this Arnold Yeager."

Night air blew in the windows. David smelled cut tobacco. A shiny green June bug splattered on the windshield.

"Yeager uncooperative?"

"Boy howdy. Worried about his car. Dyer got himself a brand-new Yamaha All-Terrain. I'd be worried too, it was my car, but I didn't tell Yeager that. I threatened to hit him with obstruction—he bitched about the car. Told him I'd sic my kid sister on him—he bitched about the car."

"He doesn't know Rose."

"Yeah, the dumb butt. Told him we had a cop in trouble needing immediate backup. He says the badge looked like a fake. Man, I wanted to kick his balls so bad, my feet were twitching."

"What'd you do?"

"Told him the only chance he had of getting that car back was to tell me everything he knew. Cooperate, I told him, and it's more likely I'll find the car. Don't help me out? Then when we do find it, if we ever do, I'll have it impounded and tied up as evidence. And I'll see it gets caught in a program bug that'll take a lifetime to straighten out. Next time he drives it, going to be an antique."

"You dirty cop, you." David took a big swallow of coffee. "Hey, check the map, okay? Make sure there really is a Possum Head Lane. This ain't Tennessee, you know. Makes me nervous when the nav program won't take it."

"I already checked 'fore I left. Made Yeager show me on a map. I mean really—Possum Head? It's there, though. Dead ends, Yeager said."

"What else he say?"

"From the top?"

David nodded.

"Guy lives in a townhouse—upscale. Brawny fella, but most of it's soft. Fisherman too, had a marlin on the wall. Anyway, he's coming home from a fishing trip down Deer Lake, buzzing along Highway 18, kind of dozing. Car starts to slow down, and that wakes him up, and he sees this car blocking the road. Car's pretty bashed up, so he gets out to see if he can help. Dyer's right there by the door, flashing a badge and screaming for the guy's access code."

"Screaming. That you talking, or Yeager?"

"Yeager. Said the guy was bleeding, looked banged up and scruffy. Very excited. Dyer says, 'I'm a police officer, this is an emergency, and I am commandeering your car.' "

"I've always wanted to do that," David said.

"Me too. Anyway, Yeager don't like it, and says so. Dyer grabs him and throws him against the hood. Says he's taking the car. Says he's following some people and they turned off 'bout a half mile down, he saw the taillights. Wanted to know if Yeager knew the area, knew where the road went.

"Yeager says yeah, that's Possum Head Lane. Dyer must of had the same reaction I did, but Yeager swore that's what it was."

"Yeager know what's out there?"

"Nothing, he says. Maybe some turnoffs. Anyway, Dyer tells Yeager to get to a phone as fast as he can—pretty funny cause the guy's on foot—and call Homicide Task Force. Ask for Detective Silver, tell him Dyer's in trouble and heading down Possum Lane."

"Why me?" David asked. "Why not his own people?"

"He's working maverick, David. Only explanation. Our case, too."

"What could this have to do with Machete Man?"

"God knows. Maybe he's tracked him."

"Why not wait for backup? He's hurt. What's the hurry?"

"He's hot, David, I don't know."

"What time was this?"

"Yeager said a little after ten P.M."

David checked his watch. It was five forty-seven.

"Damn."

SIX

THE SKY WAS BEGINNING TO LIGHTEN, BLACK FADING TO GREY.
David eased the car along Possum Head Lane, looking for turnoffs
they'd missed in the dark. There was no track for the car, and
hadn't been since they'd turned off Highway 18.

"There. Look, David, stop. Told you I thought there was something."

A narrow dirt road snaked through a cornfield. The corn was
tall and green.

"Tire marks?" David asked.

"Can't tell. Tried everything else, though. Let's follow it."

Yeager had been right, Possum Head Lane had dead-ended in
a field. They had followed two turnoffs—one leading to an empty
broken-down barn, the other petering out in front of a blackened
chimney and a rubble of brick.

Corn stalks whacked the car doors, and dew-laden leaves collect-
ed on the side mirrors and the sills of the windows. The car's chassis
scraped over weeds growing between the ruts of the turnoff.

"This isn't even a road," David said. "This would flunk driveway."

"No wonder we missed it in the dark."

They went slowly—five to seven miles per hour.

"I'm hungry," Mel said. "You hungry?"

"Yeah."

"Stop a second."

David slowed the car. Mel helped himself to a couple of ears
of corn, ripping the damp stalk and silks away.

"Got to fight the worms for it," Mel said.

The corn was whitish yellow—just ripe. Bits of silk clung to
the crevices between the kernels. David took a bite. The kernels
popped between his teeth and juice ran down his chin. The corn
was sweet and starchy.

"More," he said.

They ate and drove. The corn thinned out and quit, the road
leading them through overgrown pasture.

"Hope to hell we don't get shot in somebody's old marijuana patch."

"Yeah, it hurts getting shot in the old marijuana patch." David slowed the car. "Look at that."

The road stopped in front of an old farmhouse. Weeds grew thickly. David took out his handkerchief, wiping corn juice off his mouth and silks off his shirt. The corn sat uneasily on his stomach.

The house listed to the left. The roof had holes, and the glass in the windows had been broken out years ago. The front door was boarded shut, but a window on the porch gaped open.

Lair. That was the word that popped into David's mind. Had Dyer been on the trail of Machete Man? David's finger twitched. He had a sudden urge to call for backup.

He listened, hearing nothing but the breeze stirring the weeds.

The sky was bright now, streaked with pink and yellow. But the house was grey and ugly, weathered and forlorn. David got out of the car, leaving the door slightly ajar so it wouldn't slam. The house had come on them too quickly. Better to have come quietly and on foot, leaving the car a half mile down the road.

Too late now.

Out of the corner of his eye, David saw Mel disappear into the weeds. David's steps were loud on the porch. The wood was soft, rotten.

He knocked, feeling like a fool.

"Hello? Anybody?"

David peered in the empty window frame. The inside was little more than a ravaged shell. Warped splintery sheets of plywood made up the floor. The dry wall was crumbling, sporting huge holes. A bright cardboard bucket from Kentucky Fried Chicken sat in a pile of napkins and squashed beer cans. Whoever had been there drank Miller Lite. Was Machete Man counting calories?

David climbed in the window, catching the seam of his jeans on the sill. The wood was grungy with the withered crumbling bodies of dead insects, and David felt the sticky hairs of a spiderweb brush his face and neck.

A breeze blew through the house. The napkins swirled, and a beer can rolled across the floor. David shivered. He looked inside the chicken bucket. Bones and skin were piled in the bottom, and he could smell the greasy meat. Someone had been there in the last few hours.

Finger lickin' good, Machete Man?

David heard movement in the back of the house. He crept softly into the gloom of the hallway, glancing back over his shoulder. Weeds crowded the side windows, blocking the sun. David saw a piece of yellow cardboard and a plastic tie. The tie was red, shiny and new—the kind that came with large garbage bags. He pocketed it and headed for the back of the house.

Mel was in the kitchen, staring at the walls. David stared too.

The splatter of blood had fanned upward. David wondered what had caused it—a major artery spouting? A chair sat in front of the bloodstained wall. It too was covered with dried brown blotches. The floor was surprisingly clean—only a few smears, here and there. David smelled stale cigarette smoke.

"Wonder where the body is," Mel said.

David took a long, slow breath. "Get on the radio. Let's take this place apart."

SEVEN

A HOT SHOWER WAS NO SUBSTITUTE FOR SLEEP, BUT IT HELPED.
David pulled his jeans back on and rubbed a towel in his hair. He ran
a hand over his chin, rasping the sandpaper stubble of beard.

He opened the bathroom door.

"Mel? I borrow your razor?"

"Razor?" Mel's head appeared around the corner. "Sure." Mel
was eating something. "Borrow the comb, too. Look like you
stuck your finger in a socket."

David wiped condensation off the mirror and squinted through
the streaks while he lathered his face.

The comb had several teeth missing and the end was broken
off. David smoothed his hair back and put his shirt on. He stepped
over the pile of underwear and jeans that blocked the doorway,
and headed for the kitchen.

Mel sat at the table, flipping through his mail.

"I smell coffee," David said. Bad coffee, he thought, but coffee.

The kitchen was tiny. The appliances had originally been white,
but were yellowish-looking now. The counters were sticky with
coffee rings. A trash can next to the refrigerator overflowed with
auto-hot packaged meals and beer cans. An empty ice-cream carton
hung over the edge of the counter, the spoon in the bottom giving
it enough ballast to keep it from slipping to the floor.

Mel rinsed a plastic mug. Henly Garden Center was stenciled
on the side. As soon as the coffee hit the mug, a tinny jingle of
music sounded from the handle.

"The Henly Garden Center will give you a green thumb! Seed-
lings, EPA-sanctioned fertilizer, all natural pest con—"

David broke the handle off the mug, slopping hot coffee over
the back of his hand. The music stopped.

"Shit."

He opened the freezer, got a piece of ice, and rubbed it across
a widening red spot on the back of his hand. Mel smeared peanut
butter on a bagel and offered it to him.

"I *hate* bagels."

"You do? Didn't know that. If I'd known that, I'd have gone and gotten some grits."

"You never ate a grit in your life."

"David, you don't say 'a grit.' They don't come singular. *Don't* open that!"

David pulled the handle of the refrigerator. "I just want some milk for my . . . *Christ*, Mel, what happened in there?"

"It wasn't cooling right. 'Member I told you, it wasn't cooling right? Stuff was going bad."

"I told you to get Rose to look at it, not . . . what *did* you do?"

"Sent for a repair kit. Not just parts either, I sprung for a nano machine kit to grow the thing back together right."

"They sent you the wrong kit."

"I *checked* it. Said it was for the fridge, right model number and everything."

"Wonder what it was really for."

"Looks like the inside of a dishwasher to me—all those plastic prongs and stuff. See over there—like a place for silverware."

"But why does it *smell* so bad?"

"It got meshed up with the food."

"Jesus, Mel, you didn't clean it out first?"

"Directions said I didn't have to."

David slammed the refrigerator and it rocked back and forth, then steadied. "Fine, I'll drink it black."

"Naw, I got these." Mel rummaged in a drawer full of bank receipts, pencils, and small tools. "Here." He put a few plastic packets of non-dairy creamer on the table. "Picked them up at that KP restaurant. One down the street."

David emptied a packet of creamer into his coffee and the liquid turned greenish brown. He put a hand in his pocket and brought out the hard plastic brush he'd found in Dyer's car. He brushed crumbs off a spot on the table and set it down. Mel looked at it and chewed his bagel. A smear of peanut butter appeared on the left corner of his mouth.

"What's that?"

David thought about the café on West Main and the taste of their coffee. On his mind particularly was the way they made blueberry muffins.

"David? What is that?"

"You tell me."

Mel picked it up. "Looks like the kind of brush comes with an electric razor. Just bigger. And the bristles are in the wrong place."

"Found it in Dyer's car, between the door and the seat. Looks like it fell down the crack last night."

Mel gave it a second look. "Maybe it's some kind of artist's brush." He turned it over in his hand. "No writing or anything on it."

"Let's take it down to the precinct. Maybe somebody down there knows what it is." David dropped it back in his pocket. "Mel?"

"Yeah?"

"Dyer's got to be dead, don't you think?"

EIGHT

DAVID AND MEL STOPPED AT THE CAFÉ ON WEST MAIN, AND were late to the staff meeting. Della Martinas, Pete Ridel, and Dawn Weiler, the FBI liaison, were already at the oval table in the captain's office. An Elaki stood between the table and the wall.

"That's *him*." Mel grabbed David's sleeve. "The one that crashed our crime scene."

"Shhh." David peeled Mel's fingers off his wrist. "Take it easy, will you? This is a different one. Pinker in the middle—see?"

"What's he doing at a staff meeting?"

"Hell, I don't know."

"I ain't working with that guy."

"You won't have to. Halliday wouldn't just spring something like this."

David opened the door and Mel followed him into the office.

Dawn Weiler was talking. David nodded at her, smiling gently. Mel stood behind his chair, looking from the Elaki to the captain. Halliday frowned at him. Mel sat.

The Elaki swayed ever so slightly back and forth. David wished it would be still.

He tried to concentrate on what Dawn was saying. She was a slender brunette, freckles across her nose, green-eyed. Her fingers were long and bony, and she tended to wear longish skirts and tailored blouses with Peter Pan collars. She absently twisted a strand of hair around a pencil.

"Maybe it's just me. *No*. Something's way off. This one is atypical weird." She frowned and wrinkled her nose.

Halliday smiled. His teeth were very white. He had high, sharp cheekbones and a thin, angular face. His hair was lank and brown, and his clothes studiously nerdy.

"Dawn, can you get a little more specific?" Halliday glanced at the Elaki.

Dawn Weiler blushed. "Okay. What we know. The killer is white and male. Well, big deal, most of them are. What bothers me?" She chewed the pencil eraser. "The last attack was an old lady. Caucasian. Before that—male, Oriental, early twenties. Before that—young woman, Caucasian. The other two victims— black man, fifties. White woman—forties. *Absolutely* no pattern whatsoever. That's so frustrating. Even Henry Lee Lucas . . ."

"It's the same guy doing it," Ridel interrupted. "DNA match on all sperm samples."

"Oh, I agree," Weiler said. "Same guy. But he absolutely won't type out. These killers fall in two groups."

The Elaki edged forward, closer to David than he liked. Mel blew air through his teeth. Dawn frowned at him.

"First bunch," Dawn said, "is stalkers, planners. These are the older ones, the smarter ones. Twenties, thirties. They like to control and torture—they're sexual sadists. Then there's the impulsive ones. Usually they kill quickly, because they feel threatened. Then they mess around with the corpse. Sometimes they cover it up, like they're ashamed. Usually they're younger, often live near the victim.

"This guy we got—he stalks, gets absolute control. Then kills quickly, first blow. The victims are dead before he takes off the fingers and hands, et cetera, et cetera. That surprises me."

"I think for the best they are dead first."

Everyone looked at the Elaki.

"Sure." Dawn looked annoyed. "It just bugs me. I mean you add that to the incredible range of victims. And there's no pattern to when he hits. He does the first three in a two-week period. Bizarre. Then he stops for three months! Then another, six weeks later. Usually, these things build. Start slow and work their way up. That two-week blitz—that kind of stuff usually happens when a guy is spooked and on the run. Nothing to lose."

"Maybe he was in jail during those three months," David said.

Della shook her head. "I've run the known felons, misdemeanors . . . only a few likelies and we interviewed those."

Dawn shrugged. "Normally I could say to you, hey, this guy is twenty-three to thirty-three years old. He probably works in a hospital, has a girlfriend, lives with his mother, et cetera. Your boy, I don't know. I'm afraid to type him. I don't want you looking one way, when you should be looking another."

"Please explain the significance of typing him. You say that twice. Type people? This is to be desirable?"

"See," Mel said. "There used to be this thing called a typewriter. Started out little, so they could fit on a desk, but some genius cop gets the idea to roll the perps on the platen, kind of like tattooing— you know what tattoo means?"

"Mel, I want you to stay after the meeting," Halliday said. He looked at the Elaki. "What Detective Burnett means . . ."

David tuned Halliday out. He rubbed his eyes. This was going to be a bad one, very bad. Careers would make or break on this one. Most sociopathic killers were caught by accident, a lucky break. David wasn't feeling lucky. And meanwhile, Machete Man was going through a lot of people.

The phone rang and Halliday picked it up.

"Halliday. Yeah, Mark. No, I've never been to one of them places. I don't suppose you got any idea which? How about the blood? All right. You know about Dyer. You know what we're dealing with." Halliday hung up.

"That brush you found, David. Came from an Elaki restaurant. They give 'em out—Elaki get crumbs embedded in their skin—"

"Scales," the Elaki said.

"What?"

"Scales. Not skin."

"Whyn't you just wear a bib?" Mel said.

"What is the bib?"

"Oh, see . . ." Mel said.

Halliday looked at him.

"We'll talk about it later," Mel promised.

"Sounds like Dyer was off on something else entirely," Della said glumly. She gnawed a blueberry muffin. David glanced through the glass walls of Halliday's office to his own desk. The bag from the café was gone.

"What you got on the break-ins?" Mel asked.

Della wiped crumbs off her mouth. "Guy is a pro."

"Ex-cop maybe?" Ridel said.

Dawn shrugged. "That, or worked security. Lots of these boys are police groupies. Take a look at the ones who tried to hire on with the police, but got turned down. Or maybe ones who got fired after a few months on the job. Particularly if they've got a rent-a-cop background. And look for past enrollment at EKC—anywhere there are law enforcement classes. Or law school. Mainly the ones who didn't make the grade, or didn't stick with it."

"Pete," Halliday said. "Cover that, okay? Della, you stay on method of B and E, account for things missing. He may take souvenirs—a lot of them do. Keep trying on some kind of connection between the victims. Maybe they all order from one pizza place, I don't know. Might be a good idea for you and Pete to go back through arrest records, right when that three-month calm started.

"David, you and Mel stay with this Dyer business. It may be a whole other case, but check it out."

"And how may I assist?"

"Pardon?" Halliday said.

"I would be pleased to help."

"Mr. String, your offer is appreciated. But your function is strictly advisory. You'll leave the investigation to experienced professionals."

The Elaki swayed backward and sagged. "If as you say."

Mel grinned and licked his finger, chalking "one" in the air.

"Captain," David said. "We could use some uniforms on the legwork. Help cover the Elaki restaurants."

"Sorry, David. Wish I could."

"Could have a cop killing here."

"Confirm it and I can swing the people. Until then, no. Dyer was working maverick and his people are pissed."

The Elaki inched closer to David. "You said *Elaki* restaurants. I would be valuable there. To help in this work of legs."

Halliday spread his hands. "I don't think—"

"You ain't got legs," Mel said.

Halliday glared at Mel and took a deep slow breath. "You know, Mr. String, I appreciate your being willing to help out. I think you might be a big asset in this area of Elaki restaurants, and I think Detective Burnett in particular would be glad of your help." He stood up and stacked papers. "Okay, people. You got work to do."

Chairs scraped across the floor and loud conversations broke out. Mel followed Della out of the office, admiring the bracelet on her wrist.

Pete Ridel was talking to Dawn Weiler and David waited for them to finish. He had a question for Dawn.

"David?" Halliday motioned him over. "Hey, Pete, shut the door on your way out, okay?"

Pete and Dawn walked out into the squad room. David saw Dawn laugh, then head out. Damn. He'd call her later.

Mel stuck his head back in the door. "I forget, Captain. You said stay around?"

Halliday leaned back in his chair. "Sit down, Burnett."

Mel shut the door, but did not sit. He held up a hand.

"Look, Captain, you don't got to apologize about the Elaki. I already know what you're going to say—you know what I'm going to say. Let's just cut to the chase and consider it said."

Halliday scratched his chin. He looked tired.

"Anything else?"

"No, Burnett."

Mel slammed the door shut behind him.

David leaned back in his chair. "You're lucky he decided to be big about this, Roger."

Halliday smiled.

"It may be a mistake, you know." David stared at the wall.

"What?"

"Letting that Elaki in on the staff meeting. Sending him out with me and Mel."

Halliday shrugged. "He's not hurting anything. He's only on the edges of the investigation, something I have no choice about, so neither do you. We have to make sure nobody can accuse us of not cooperating. We got sensitive information to discuss, the Elaki won't be at the meeting."

"Why send him out with us?"

"He might be able to help on Elaki turf. The restaurants."

"I don't understand his interest, Roger. That worries me."

Halliday nodded. "Okay, David, that's a point. I don't understand his interest either, and the official justification is crap. Take him along and watch him. See if he helps, or gets in the way. Give you a chance to check him out."

"Something comes up I don't like, I'm ditching him."

"Your call, David."

"I won't jeopardize Dyer."

"Point taken."

David stood up, but Halliday waved him back to his chair. David sat. He didn't like Halliday's look of concern.

"I just want you to know, I appreciate the work you been putting in on this Machete Man. You didn't take your week when your mother died. How are you doing, by the way?"

"I'm fine."

Halliday leaned back in his chair. "See, here's how it works. You're supposed to get a week, compassionate leave. When you don't take it, the computer red flags the department shrink, not to mention the union guys."

"Captain . . ."

Halliday held up a hand. "It's just procedure. Machete Man isn't exactly a thing you leave behind to clear up after vacation. I know that. I have no problem that you didn't take the time. In fact, I appreciate it. You want to catch this boy and so do I. I'm just letting you know, I fielded all the bureaucratic horsecrap for you. That way, if anybody approaches you, you'll know what's going on. You tell me, and I'll take care of it."

Halliday rocked back and forth in his chair. "You know how they watch cops. Seems like the whole system is set up to hassle the ones who do a good job. And listen, after this is over, you can have a week of compensatory. Whenever you want."

"Not necessary. Look, I can see it's a sin not to be totally broken up here, but frankly, my mother and I were just not that close."

"Fine. Whatever. But think twice about that time off. You might take those girls of yours fishing."

NINE

THEY WERE HEADING FOR THE THIRD ELAKI RESTAURANT AND
David's feet were hurting. Mr. String did not seem tired. And
he was still talking. His voice was muffled because he was folded
into the back seat.

"So the whole family and many friends were to go there."

Mel yawned. "To this river?"

"Yes."

"With the beautiful waters," Mel said. "Like red eye gravy."

"Yes."

"What you do there, get drunk?"

"Perhaps."

"Eat?"

"Very much."

"Take a dip in the lake?"

"A dip?"

"Swim," Mel said.

"Certainly *not*."

"Don't swim? I mean, it's hot, the water looks good. Thought
that was the big thing at Elaki gatherings."

"*Fringe* wetting only. Elaki do not swim. I suppose, if there was
much drink, it could happen in private corners with lower types,
but *my* family—"

"Sorry, hey."

"May I finish the story?"

"There's more?"

"I am getting to the amusing section. When my pouch-sib is
swearing by the blue maker."

"Who is the blue maker?"

"Must you be interruptious?"

Mel shrugged. "Trying to make sense out of this."

"The blue maker is an idiomatic term for the one God who does
not exist. It is used as term of great and vicious vulgarity. Illegal
reference, in strict communities. And here is my pouch-sib, sitting
on back of the lika—"

"The what?"

"*Lika*. It is similar to a . . . a . . . car-wagon. And it is blue maker this, and blue maker that." String stopped talking and his belly rippled. "And the Mother extrudes and knocks him off the lika, into the red dirt."

"You're right, that's funny."

"*Not* yet. So, my pouch-sib gets up slowly, hurting, and gets back up in the lika, and we start up again, and he says—'What, honored Mother, by the blue maker did I say?' "

David and Mel exchanged looks.

"Quit encouraging him," David said.

String peered over the back of the seat at their bellies.

"You do not find this amusing?"

David parked by the curb. He opened the back door of the car. The Elaki looked at him sideways.

"Can I . . . give you a hand?"

"It would be best, I think, for the back to turn."

"The back of what?" Mel asked.

"Of us," David said.

"Oh, like, for the dignity to be preserved. We're going on in, Gumby. Meet us inside."

David heard a thud.

"No. Please, wait . . . there. I am with you now."

The Elaki owner was friendly, but not helpful. He eyed String curiously.

"But you do have people—*humans*—come in here for dinner?" Mel asked.

"Not very often, no. They don't care for our menu."

"Really?" David said. "Somebody's cooking something back there, smells pretty good."

String nodded.

The Elaki seemed pleased. "It is a new item, we trying it out on our lunch crowd. We are very fond of Cajun cooking."

"Oh yeah?" Mel said. "I like Cajun. What is it?"

"Muskrat."

"You kidding?"

"It is not difficult to prepare. Simmer the muskrat in salted water, along with onion, garlic, bouquet garni. The secret is to simmer until the meat is so tender it falls from the bone. For the sauce, you use mustard, pepper, sherry, a little egg yolk—and some of the stock, of course. Perhaps you would care to sample?"

"God, no," Mel said. "Muskrat? Only Elaki would eat something like that."

The restaurant owner turned his body to Mel. "You think so? Essentially *all* of our recipes are local. Our people come here to try Earth food. And muskrat, I must tell you, tastes very like cow. Indeed, it is better than rabbit. You eat rabbit, don't you? Southerners eat rabbit, is my understanding."

"My sister offered me one just last night."

"There, you see. But your reaction is typical. Few humans will eat here. And yet I see many balding men and I understand the loss of hair is mentally painful. These men would do well to come in and eat stewed cane rat, maybe once a week. I would not mind more human clientele."

"Stewed cane rat grows hair?"

"It is the rat meat. In fact, we serve a very nice grilled rat bordeaux every other Wednesday."

David handed the Elaki a picture of Dyer.

"You see this man yesterday, last night?"

The Elaki studied the picture. "I . . . I do not think so. We do not get many humans—and usually those for the novelty of coming in. But I must admit . . ."

"We all look alike," Mel said. "Yeah, Mr. String here tells me that all the time. I don't believe I introduced him. Mr. String is aiding in our investigation."

"Unusual," the owner said.

"Good for human/Elaki relations," String explained.

"Sure is," Mel said. "Get to know one another, all that. String's promised to take us swimming."

The Elaki restaurant owner scooted backward. String arched his back.

"The human is joking you."

"By the way," David said. "You give out those little brushes, you know, for crumbs? Kind of a souvenir for my daughter. She's very interested in Elaki things. Collects them."

The Elaki's eye prongs swiveled. "You see, Detective, this is a family restaurant. We encourage our clientele to bring their young ones and we try to keep our prices down. We could not afford to hand out such things, and with the young ones it would be like trying to hold water. We do not worry for crumbs."

David held up the brush he'd found in Dyer's car. "You know of anyone who gives these out?"

The Elaki looked at it. "Surely. The Ambassador, on Short Street. But they are not open this early and . . . they do not encourage humans. It is unlikely your man was there. But if he was, they will remember him."

"Thanks," David said.

Out on the sidewalk, String stopped in front of the car.

"I cannot face to fold myself into the back again. I also must return to my work. Regret that I will be unable to further help. Good of the day." He glided away down the sidewalk.

"He seem upset about something?"

"Get in the car, Mel."

The double doors leading into the Ambassador had been redone to accommodate Elaki height. They were also locked. Mel beat on the glass. The inside was lit and David could see a man running a vacuum cleaner. An Elaki female came to the door. She wore a short plaid vest—one of the few Elaki David had ever seen wear clothes. Perhaps it was a habit for the rich and trendy.

"We're closed," the female said. Her side pouches were smooth and almost closed. No children, David decided.

"How about reservations for tonight?" Mel said.

"I'm sure we're full."

"Next week?"

"Perhaps if you call and check tonight. I am afraid we book most quick."

David looked at Mel. "You done?"

"Yeah."

David flashed his badge. "I'm Detective Silver, Ms. . . ."

"Cook," she said.

"Ms. Cook. May we come in, please? I need to ask you a few questions."

She unlocked the door and let them in. A phone rang.

"Excuse."

She headed for the hostess station and they followed.

"Yes?" She tapped an inquiry into a terminal. "Yes, the private arrangement can be made. Would the seven-fifteen be okay? Good. For many? We do look forward to seeing you."

"I thought you were booked for tonight," Mel said.

"What for you gentlemen need?"

There was a stack of brushes next to the terminal.

"Those brushes," David said. "You give those out?"

"Of course."

"Just to Elaki? Or your human clientele?"

"I'm afraid we do not cater much for the human palate. Most of our patrons work in the government. They come here for relax, be among their own kind."

"You cooking rats in the kitchen?" Mel asked.

The vacuum cleaner shut off.

"Thank you, Claude," Ms. Cook said. "Please see for the floor in the kitchen."

"No!" Someone was shouting into a microphone.

David looked up. Two Elaki were on a small raised stage. Rehearsing?

"You use yours from the right," said one of the Elaki on stage. He wore a tie and nothing else. "I use mine from the left."

The Elaki produced fake hands and shook hugely, a parody human handshake. Ms. Cook's belly rippled. She looked back at David.

"We do not cook rodents. We specialize in seafood."

David pulled out the photo of Dyer. "This man come in here last night?"

The Elaki studied the picture. "No. We had no humans in last night."

"I see." David picked up one of the brushes. Exactly like the one he'd found in Dyer's car. "Mind if I keep this? Souvenir?"

"Feel free."

Mel tapped the counter. " 'Course you weren't on duty all night."

"I took a couple of breaks, but mostly . . ."

"How about your waiters?"

"They are off duty. Except Mr. Slyde."

"Where's he?"

"In the kitchen."

Mel headed toward a pair of folding doors. "Let's see what he has to say."

Ms. Cook was annoyed, or so David thought. It was hard to tell with Elaki.

The kitchen had white tile floors, stainless-steel sinks, and microwave ovens. Two Elaki, wearing white chef hats, argued in low murmurs over a simmering pot.

A voice—human, David decided—came from behind a closed door.

"Not your problem, *Peanut*."

David heard a low mutter, then—

"Just stick to your cooking. Everything else is taken care of." The mutter again.

David gave Mel a look. Mel turned to one of the Elaki who stood over the boiling pot.

"What you making?" Mel asked.

David edged closer to the door. Storeroom?

"Shark curry."

The muttering stopped.

"Smells pretty good. Which one of you guys is Mr. Slyde?"

The door opened. A small Elaki came out. "I am . . . Slyde. Who be looking for me?"

David pushed past Slyde. The storeroom was small, the floor dirty, the shelves laden with tablecloths, utensils, cans. The walls were red brick, the light supplied by one dimming fixture. There was no one there, but a door on the left wall hung ajar. David pushed it open.

He looked outside, to a narrow alley. Green garbage lined one side of a white cement gutter. There was a strong sweetish-sour smell. And no one in sight. David went back to the kitchen.

"You on duty last night?" Mel was saying.

"Who are you?"

Ms. Cook slid down the floor toward David, her eye stalks on the entrance to the storeroom. David was aware of her cool lime scent. He wondered if she was bothered by his human cheese smell. He shifted weight from one foot to another.

"These are policeman, Mr. Slyde," Cook said. "They are looking for a human. They do not seem to understand they are looking in the wrong place."

"Is it Claude they want? He's taking out garbage, but will soon be back."

David held up his picture of Dyer. The Elaki's eyes were on Ms. Cook, not the picture.

"Look at it," David said. "You don't get too many humans in here. Surely you'd remember if he came in."

"No, Detective. I did not see him."

"You're certain?"

"I am certain, yes."

David did not like the feel of the Ambassador, or the waves of contempt that emanated from Cook and Slyde. More so than the usual reaction? Could he blame them for not wanting cheesy people in their restaurant?

"How about your other people—the ones who worked last night?"

"Serve and Tend will be on duty at eight o'clock."

"We'll be back," Mel said. "Put us in your book."

David headed back into the dining room. The comedians were gone. The tables were shoved up against one wall. There were no chairs. Claude would be back soon, to finish the floor. David glanced at a table in the corner.

A grey sport jacket was wadded on the top. David walked over and picked it up. There were dark chocolate stains across the sleeve. David checked the pockets—empty, except a slip of paper in the inside pocket. David opened it up, finding a mushroom drawn with a pink crayon.

TEN

THE ELAKI NAMED PUZZLE SOLVER HAD AN OFFICE IN THE Museum of Human Behavior. David and Mel had to come in through the back door—front entrance for Elaki only—and were left waiting in front of the exhibit on eating disorders.

Behind the red velvet ropes, a lifelike woman was posed in front of a kitchen mock-up. The woman, wearing an old-fashioned three-piece suit, stood in front of a refrigerator and held up a brief-case, fending off a giant Barbie doll dressed in a red swimsuit. A placard labeled the exhibit, but it was written in Elaki.

Puzzle Solver slid toward them from the other end of the hall. "Detective Silver? Detective Burnett?"

David nodded, feeling awkward because Elaki didn't have hands to shake.

"Please. We can talk in my office."

Mel started down the hall.

"Wait," David said. "What does the sign there say?"

Puzzle bent over the exhibit. "It say, 'Why does this woman think she is fat?' "

"Oh."

They followed him down a wide corridor. The floor sloped upward. Their footsteps were silent on the thick grey carpet. David shivered. It was cold in the museum, and quiet. The hot noisy city outside seemed miles away.

They went past a display of a tenement room. A junkie lay "dead" on the floor. The door to the apartment had been kicked in and a soldier in a Drug Enforcement Agency uniform was half in and half out of the room. The uniform was familiar. Rose had one, packed away in the back of their bedroom closet.

Puzzle's office had a computer terminal mounted on a high glass table. It was a late-model setup—very expensive. Along the side of the wall was a moving file of poster-sized pictures. The pictures showed street scenes, and there were people in all of them.

"Shall I have some chairs brought in for the sitting?"

"No, that's okay." David didn't want the Elaki towering over him. "What I'm interested in, Mr. Puzzle, is your fascination for my case."

"Machete Man?"

"Yes."

"I would not use term of fascination."

"No? I've looked into it a little. You aren't a police adviser, Mr. Puzzle. The Elaki assigned to tag along with us, String— he really works for you, doesn't he? And you're an Elaki sociologist."

"A laiku, if please. Your term, sociologist, has some very primitive connotations for my people."

"Machete Man appeals to the primitive," Mel said.

"Mr. Puzzle, you pulled favors to get access to my case. You get reports as soon as I do—maybe sooner. You have authorization to go over crime scenes. I want an explanation."

"Detective Silver, you are knowledgeable officer of the law. You know Earth cities are on verge of a drug problem the likes of which have not been seen since the 1980s."

"It's not *that* bad," Mel said. "And it won't be."

"Please, I hope not, Detective. But I think you would find the historical cycle of cocaine usage most extremely interesting."

"The Drug Enforcement Agency has a lot more teeth, now it's part of the military."

"Indeed," Puzzle said. "There are many of us who think the corruption problems in your military stemmed from combining military corps with drug enforcement."

David blushed and Mel grew quiet.

"Mr. Puzzle," David said. "You do me the courtesy of being frank, and I'll show you the same consideration. One of my colleagues is missing—Detective Vernon Dyer. He was working on this case, and he's disappeared. The last night he was seen he spent some time at an Elaki restaurant called the Ambassador. You know it?"

"I have heard of such establishment."

"I want the connection," David said. "I want to know why Elaki keep showing up in a simple case of a sexual sadist on a death spree."

"Detective Silver, if you were not so serious, I would think you were mocking. What is simple about sexual sadism?"

"That's beside the point, isn't it, Mr. Puzzle? Help me out. Help me catch this man. Help me find Dyer."

"Your colleague Dyer is likable human. I wish I could be help to you. I am afraid I cannot. My interest in the case lies purely in most clinical, academic sense."

"If that were true, you could just study the files," Mel said.

David roamed around the office and stopped in front of the pictures. "You mind?" He didn't wait for permission. All of them had a vaguely familiar feel, and he realized they all showed drug buys being made on the streets.

"Mr. Puzzle, are you on the Horizon Project?"

Puzzle turned his body toward David. "What do you know, Detective, about Project Horizon?"

"Just rumors, Mr. Puzzle, cops hear things. Think you can cure us of our addictions?"

"It would be a goal of worth."

"Make our job easier," Mel said. "How come you bel . . . Elaki give a rat's ass, anyhow?"

"Detective Burnett, I have worked on many projects. Horizon is one. I am deeply involved in work on human eating disorders. I helped with cure for schizophrenia—and still do much work as adviser for those effecting the cures."

"What a great guy," Mel said. "He—it is he, isn't it? He's got advice for everybody. Except us."

"The only advice I give you, Detective, is for to cut back on fats and oils, and eat more regularly."

"This from a guy eats rat? You tried the shark curry over at the Ambassador lately?"

"Gentlemen, I cannot help you, and have work to do."

David headed for the door, but Mel leaned close to the Elaki.

"I think you're holding back on me, pal, and to my way of thinking, that makes you dirty." Mel headed for the hall, then turned. "I got a lot of patience. I'll get you sorted."

Puzzle's office door closed behind them. Mel looked at David. "Where did you hear about this Horizon Project?"

"On a file on his desk." David headed down the sloping floor. "Helps to read upside down."

Mel grinned, his voice booming through the corridors. "You know how Elaki screw, Detective Silver? They stand in a line, boy-girl, boy-girl, passing the sperm along. Line copulation, biologists call it. Makes you want to know what they got in their pockets."

"Mel, would you please just shut up? At least till we get out of the building?"

"Sure." Mel scratched an unshaven cheek. "Makes you wonder, though, what they'd say to a rhumba."

ELEVEN

IT HAD BEEN AGES SINCE HE'D MADE IT HOME BEFORE DARK. David rubbed the back of his neck, trying to keep his attention on the road. He turned in the driveway and stopped. A bullfrog squatted in the center of the gravel drive and glared at him.

David struck his head out the window. "You again?" He honked the horn. The frog made a rude noise. David drove around him.

The sun was still bright and hot. The grass around the house needed mowing, and neither he nor Rose had gotten around to putting flowers in the beds out front.

Still, the house looked good.

It was small—a two-bedroom ranch house on thirteen acres of fairly useless woodland. It was a haven from the city, a good place to raise children, and a far cry from the Little Saigo tunnels, where David had spent seven dark miserable years.

Rose sat out front in the porch swing, one leg tucked under her, the other dangling. She watched him stoically. David chewed his lip. He waved a hand and pulled the car around back. A familiar mud-spattered Jeep was parked next to the barn.

Kendra and Lisa were under the ash tree, squatting on the ground, absorbed. David put the car in the barn. The black rabbit wasn't in the cage. David frowned, taking off his jacket and tie.

"Hi, girls."

Kendra looked up. "Daddy! C'mere."

He walked to the ash tree.

"Watch!"

Kendra had tied a piece of string to the leg of a gigantic, iridescent green June beetle. She threw the beetle into the air and it flew in a circle around her head.

"See?" She held tight to the end of the string. "Better than a kite."

"My turn now," Lisa said.

"Get your own."

"I can't tie the knot. Daddy!"

David tied a piece of string to the leg of Lisa's beetle.

51

"Mommy been in the swing all day?"

Kendra gave him a look. "Since this afternoon. After we found the package on the porch."

"Can we have a jar, Daddy?" Lisa said. "We're training these beetles. We're going to keep 'em."

"Later, kiddo. Where's the munchkin?"

"In the house."

David went through the back door into the kitchen. There were bowls on the cabinet from breakfast, and lunch dishes on the table. A box of cereal was overturned on the floor, but nothing had spilled. David picked it up. Empty.

"Daddy!" Mattie ran into the kitchen, followed by Dead Meat.

David picked his daughter up, and tried not to stumble over the dog that wound her way in and out of his legs.

"Daddy? Do spidos have tails?"

"Spidos? Spiders?"

Mattie nodded.

"No tails."

"Whew!" Mattie wiggled out of his arms and ran down the hall to her room. Dead Meat barked and ran after her.

David passed through the living room, picking his way over sofa cushions, broken crayons, and video cartridges. A loaf of bread was open on the rocking chair, several slices scattered on the floor. David closed the package and turned off the television. He heard the porch swing creak as Rose shifted her weight.

Mattie ran back into the kitchen.

"Daddy!"

"In here, munchkin."

"Daddy, the wabbit died. It went asleep las night and din get up this morning." Tears streaked down Mattie's plump, babyish cheeks. "Mommy said it was too sick."

David gathered Mattie up and rocked her. "Sorry, baby."

"Just like po' Benny."

"Yeah. Benny was a sweetheart. But you have a dog here. And this dog needs a new name."

Mattie scooted out of his lap.

"Where you going, munchkin?"

"Ask the dog what he wants for a name." She ran down the hall.

David went out front. He sat beside Rose, his weight bringing the wood swing to a halt.

"Hi, honey. I'm home."

Rose smiled absently.

"Saw the Jeep out back. Where's Haas?"

"Doing an errand for me."

"What kind of errand?"

Rose was quiet.

"Mattie told me about the rabbit," David said. "She took it bad?"

"Pretty bad."

"The other two?"

Rose shrugged. "Hard to tell."

The silence grew awkward.

"Mel called," Rose said.

"Oh?"

"Not coming to dinner after all."

"How come? We were going to work."

Rose shrugged. "Kendra told him I'd been in the swing all day. He said he'd come sometime when I wasn't so depressing to be around."

"Sometimes your brother is a jerk."

Rose shrugged.

At least, David thought, when she's down I can follow her conversation. What there was of it.

"Sorry about the rabbit," he said. "I'll go fix supper. Got anything in mind?"

Rose shook her head. "Why don't you do the packages?"

"Home cooked is best. I assume Haas is staying? Anything sound good?"

"Nope."

David got up, started in the door, then stopped, hand on the latch. "Rose? What was the package you got today? The girls said somebody delivered a package."

The swing stopped. David turned and looked at his wife. Her eyes filled with tears. He felt a chill on the back of his neck.

"What was it, Rose?"

"Video. Taken at a lab. I'm not sure which one, it's been bugging me all day. But I know I've been there. I think it was this last job."

"What was on the tape?"

"It was a nasty little thing, David. A lab tech, woman, I don't think she knew she was being filmed. She was slamming a rabbit into a table—it wouldn't be still. I'd bet she broke its back."

David swallowed.

"It brought back . . . you know, I never told you this . . ."

"Mom!" Kendra appeared at the door. Her face was flushed with heat, and she pushed hair out of her eyes. "We're hungry."

"There are Oreos in the pantry," David said.

Lisa crowded in the doorway beside Kendra. "Mom won't let us."

"Go ahead," David said. "Eat them. Watch your TVs. Go."

The girls disappeared.

David sat back down on the swing. His palms were wet. He wiped them on his pants.

"What were you going to say, Rose?"

"Have you never wondered why I left the DEA?" Rose asked. She took his hand, running a finger up and down his thumb.

"You said it was corrupt, and dangerous for a straight soldier. You said you got sick of it."

"True. I also . . . I had a partner I worked with. Manolo Deloso. We worked together a long time. He saved my ass . . . I saved his. You know how it is when you work close like that. Like you and Mel."

"I understand."

"We were trying to set up a dealer. Guy had ties to the Colombians, the IRA—he was very bad. Then Deloso disappeared. And somebody dropped a video into my food box. I was in town then. I had delivery."

"Here?"

"No. Miami."

"What was on the tape? Deloso?"

Rose nodded. "The things they did to him . . . defy the imagination."

Mattie burst through the door. "Lisa and Kendra are eating cookies!"

"You can have some too," Rose said.

Mattie went back in the house.

David heard footsteps on the gravel drive. Haas came around the side of the house and up on the porch.

He was a big man, broad-shouldered—blue eyes and pale blond hair. He had a strong jaw and an animal grace that made David uneasy. Guys built like that, he had always told himself, were invariably stupid.

Haas wore loose khaki shorts and a white cotton shirt, sleeves rolled up over tan, muscular arms.

"Hello, David."

"Haas." He found the slight German accent grating, mainly because Haas always smiled when asked about it, and swore he was born in the U.S.A.

"Rose, I saw nothing you didn't spot already. And I have buried the rabbit—in back of the barn, by Benny."

"Thanks."

David frowned. "Mattie said the rabbit died in its sleep."

Haas raised his eyebrows and looked at Rose. She shrugged.

"The rabbit was strangled," Haas said.

Rose folded her arms. "Somebody broke into the barn last night and killed it."

David looked from Rose to Haas. "Somebody want to explain what's going on?"

"We really don't know," Rose said. She looked at Haas. "Stay for dinner."

Haas glanced at David. "I think not. I have a horse ready to foal, anyway. I like to be around."

He shook David's hand, apologized for the dirt that rubbed from his palms to David's, and headed around the house to his Jeep.

David listened till the engine started and gravel spurted from under the tires. Haas waved as he drove the Jeep down the driveway.

"David," Rose said. "Get dinner together, okay? I need to walk. We'll talk tonight, after the girls are in bed. Try not to worry. I'll take care of things."

David went in the house to clean up the kitchen.

TWELVE

DAVID SAT ON THE COUCH UNDER A PILE OF LITTLE GIRLS— all of them in cotton nightgowns, their hair damp from their baths. He read from a tattered storybook in a voice that sounded deep and froglike. Kendra sat at his feet, reading a book of her own, half an ear on the story he read. Lisa snuggled under his arm and Mattie leaned against his side, eyes half-closed, thumb in her mouth.

In the kitchen, the dishwasher groaned rhythmically. The air was pungent with the dinner smell of wine, garlic, and chicken. He heard a cabinet slam. Rose was doing the dishes—a good sign.

While dinner cooked, he had straightened the living room and made up the beds—he hated tucking the girls into beds that hadn't been made. He felt better with the house in order. Things were beginning to return to normal.

He closed the book.

" 'Nother one," Mattie said.

"Nope. Bed. Mommy? Watch Mattie brush her teeth."

"On my way."

"Kiss me good night, girls. I'll tuck you in later."

The phone rang. David heard Rose's voice from the kitchen. She sounded chirpy all of a sudden.

"David?" Rose said. "Ruthie's on the line."

David made a slit throat motion and Rose glared at him.

"Ruthie? Can I have him call you back? He doesn't seem to be in the house. Probably poking around in the barn. Yeah, I think the girls would love to. I could drive them up . . ."

David shook his head vigorously.

" . . . but let me check first and make sure David doesn't have any plans. You know how it is with a cop in the family—we do everything on the spur of the moment, if we do it at all. What? That's good of Howard, but I don't think David would enjoy that kind of work. Yes, I'll tell him. Bye, Ruth."

Rose put the phone down. "David, why do you *do* that? They're *your* relatives."

56

"They weren't my relatives when my mother and I lived in the tunnels. They never came calling in Little Saigo."

"Fine. Hold a grudge."

David's jaw was tight. It was not so easy to dismiss the tunnels, when you'd spent seven years of your life buried alive.

"She want the kids again?" David asked.

"Yes. What's so bad about it, David? She also wants to know if you've gone through your mother's things."

"Nosy old bat. Why? She want something?"

"Their synagogue is putting clothes together for tornado victims, and she thought—"

"*Jewish* tornado victims, I'm sure. She won't touch anything of Mama's."

"*Fine*. Don't yell at me about it."

"Anything else she want to know? Like the details of our sex life?"

"What's to tell, lately?"

"Is that a complaint?"

"Yes. I demand my conjugal rights."

"You're the one who keeps falling asleep."

"Why don't you ask me when I'm awake?"

"You're never awake."

"How would *you* know, you're never home."

"Rose . . ."

She held up a hand. "David, I want to make a point, before we get way off the subject. The rent on Lavinia's apartment is coming due again. We can't afford to keep paying it. I haven't wanted to press, but we need to get her things squared away. Would you like me to do it? I don't mind."

"I'll do it. I'm her son, I should do it."

"We'll go together."

"No. I'll go. It's not that big a deal, Rose. We just weren't that close."

Rose looked sad. "Whatever you say, David."

He went to his workroom—a small cubby, off the kitchen. The previous owners had called it a mud room.

"This is David," he said to the computer. "Code Shalom. Come up please." He fished his glasses out of a drawer and put them on.

The terminal hummed and beeped. The screen lit up.

"Shalom, David."

"Simulation of the Darnell case."

He sat in a battered brown easy chair and watched the screen.

The image was very like an "exploded" blueprint. David had an aerial view of the killer at work—an angle he hated.

"Cut to face-on simulation."

"As you wish. Accuracy sixty-eight percentile."

David watched Machete Man ravage Millicent Darnell's underwear.

"Input entire caseload Machete Man to Darnell case."

"As you wish."

David drummed his fingers.

"Ready," the computer said.

"Face-on simulation of Darnell case."

"As you wish. Accuracy eighty-one percentile."

The computer had given Machete Man a mustache—that was new. The face was bloated-looking, the eyes sleepy. David felt a hand on his shoulder. He jumped.

"Machete Man?" Rose asked.

"Yeah. Look familiar?"

"Kind of like Mel."

"I'll tell him you said so." David squinted at the screen. Rose rubbed the back of his neck. He sighed deeply.

"Everybody does so much work at home now. So you're never *home* at home anymore."

"Gives us more opportunity to fight," David said.

"Speaking of which. You weren't nice to Haas tonight, David."

"I was too."

"So why didn't he stay for dinner?"

"You heard him, Rose. His horse is having a baby."

"You create an atmosphere, David."

"What the hell kind of complaint is that? I create an atmosphere? Maybe Haas saw the mess in the kitchen, and that's why he didn't stay."

"I thought you'd gotten over being jealous of him."

David rubbed his chin. "I am not jealous. I admit I don't like it when the two of you have secrets."

"We work together sometimes, David. Please remember that we're the only family he's got."

"Just why is that?"

Rose shrugged.

"More secrets," David said.

"You and Mel have secrets. You damn near talk in code."

"Mel doesn't look like Haas."

"Truer words were never spoken."

David turned his chair around and faced her. "Time you told

me what's going on, Rose. I need to know if you and the girls are safe out here. Right now, I'm afraid to leave you."

"Okay, David." She turned a chair backward and straddled it, giving him all of her attention. It was like being spotlighted, after sitting in the dark.

"The last job out was a bad one. Haven't seen one like that in a long time. Lately, you know, I've been thinking my job is obsolete, as far as the labs go, anyway. The laws on animal research are pretty tough now . . . and public opinion can pressure a sloppy operation. Turn it around. Most places use simulation models anyway, they're more accurate. There's really no *point* to these labs anymore. But there's always a few diehards. Usually, legal channels are all we need."

"But when that doesn't work, they call you. What do you do, Rose?"

"You're a cop, David."

"I know that."

"Then don't ask me what I do. I'm an enforcer—professional harassment."

"My wife is hired muscle?"

"Put it any way you want. Why is that funny?"

"Rose, you're such . . . I'm sorry. You just don't . . . I better shut up."

Rose smiled lazily.

"What do you do, Rose? What kind of enforcement?"

Rose shrugged. "Usually it doesn't take much. You get through somebody's security, and let them know it—let them know what could happen to their research. That's all it takes. They've gotten radical, they leave booby traps. Usually very amateurish. Most of the time I could do this job in my sleep."

"But not always."

"No. Not always."

"Rose, I always wanted to ask you. That lab in New Jersey, the one that blew up. Did you . . ."

"If I did, I wouldn't admit it."

"You *did*, didn't you? The whole *town* was overrun with mice. And what about that zoo where the gorillas disappeared?"

"David, you're a police officer. It is your job to uphold the law. Don't ask me things that will cause us both problems."

David leaned back in his chair and stared at his wife. "What now? What is it with the rabbit?"

"A joke, a message—the gauntlet." She propped her chin on the back of the chair. "This last job did not go well. There was more going on there—areas I didn't penetrate. Santana was waiting for me."

"Santana?" David narrowed his eyes. The way Rose said the name was unsettling. "Who is this Santana?"

"Someone from the old days. Hires out."

"Like you."

"Not like me. But I will have to go back. And Santana knows that. So, I'd like to send the girls to Ruthie, in Chicago."

"You think they'll be safer there?"

"The safest place for the girls is with me. But they'll be all right in Chicago."

"You're leaving then?"

"Not yet. I need to work out a little, firm up. Job's been too easy, and I'm soft."

"I like you soft."

Rose sat in his lap and put her arms around him. "Can I be on top tonight?"

David kissed her ear. "Good night, Machete Man. Hello, Rose."

THIRTEEN

THE BEDROOM WAS LIT BY SUNLIGHT—TOO MUCH SUNLIGHT.
David rubbed his eyes and looked at the clock. He reached for
Rose, but found cool empty sheets.

"Looking for me?" Rose leaned against the doorjamb.

David stretched and yawned. "Where you been?"

"Just checking. The girls are okay. No visitors last night." She
slid back into bed and kissed him.

"Your feet are cold."

The phone rang.

"God damn it." Rose picked up the receiver. "*What*. You, David.
It's Mel."

David took the phone. Mel's voice came through loud and
crisp.

"Where you been, partner?"

"At home, where the action is."

"Or isn't," Rose muttered.

David ignored her. "Somebody dropped by, night before last.
Killed the rabbit."

"Some kind of criminal cat in the neighborhood, huh? Probably
doesn't know you're the resident cop."

"Strangled."

"What?"

"You heard."

"Somebody strangled your rabbit? Jeez, no wonder Rose was
upset. How come she didn't tell me?"

"You pissed her off."

"That ain't difficult. Look, David, the Darnell woman . . .
uh, Millicent Darnell. She had a massive coronary day before
yesterday. She's at the hospital, fading in and out. Insists she
wants to talk to you. Della's over there right now, but says the
lady wants Detective Silver."

"I'm on my way."

David hated hospitals—one of the minor reasons being the
incredible slowness of their elevators. He knew his way around

Euclid Central, where they took the trauma patients. Most of his case victims wound up there. He'd never been to Southern Medical before, and he couldn't find their stairwell. Some detective.

The elevator came to an abrupt grinding stop and the door shushed open. David's steps were quiet on the thin blue carpet. He wrinkled his nose at the hospital smell of alcohol and dirty socks. He stopped at a central desk and looked over a grey counter. A woman sat behind a lit terminal. She didn't look up.

"Excuse me."

The woman stared at the small screen of the terminal.

"I'm Detective Silver, here to see Millicent Darnell." He flashed his badge.

The woman looked up reluctantly, her face shadowed with fatigue. "Sir, this is the coronary care unit. We won't have visitation until this afternoon."

He looked at her name tag. "Dr. Juddson? I didn't flash my ID there to impress you. I'm here on official business."

"Oh? Sorry. Been on duty too long." She looked up absently. "Harry?"

A nurse looked up from a switchboard. "One sec." He turned to the intercom. "I'll be down in a minute." He stood up and stretched. "What you need, Glenda?"

"Harry, this is Detective . . . gosh, I don't know. Whatever. Here to see somebody or other. Can you—"

"Thanks, Glenda, I'll take care of it." Harry came out from behind the partition. "You the one Darnell was asking for? Detective Silverman?"

"Silver."

"Come on, she's down here."

The nurse was a big guy, apish. He had a heavy head of dark hair and a full beard, and his body canted from side to side as he walked, like a captain on deck during heavy seas.

A knot of men and women in white jackets clustered around a tall, gliding Elaki. The Elaki had a white jacket too, and a stethoscope wound around its midsection. The men and women held clipboards and looked at the Elaki with absorbed reverence.

Several of them were talking, but a woman's voice rang above the others.

"But suppose the physical manifestations are psychosomatic in nature . . ."

David and Harry flattened themselves against the wall to avoid being trampled.

"The good doctor," Harry said mildly.

"How's she doing?" David asked.

"Darnell?" Harry shrugged. "You better ask her doctor."

"Would that be Juddson?"

"Juddson or Knapp."

"I'd rather ask you."

Harry shrugged again and started walking.

"Look, Harry, I'm not family. I'm a cop. Mrs. Darnell is a witness in a capital crime—she's important."

"Okay, then, she's dying. Needs a bypass and doesn't qualify. Her last attack was a bad one. She's in a lot of pain. She'll probably have another attack in the next twenty-four to forty-eight hours, and that will finish her off."

"There's nothing you can do for her?"

"Lots we can do for her, nothing we're budgeted for."

"So you stick her in a room, make her comfortable, and that's that."

"I wish we could do even that. But the fact is, she's *not* comfortable and she's in a *ward*."

They stopped in front of a large room divided by thin fiberboard partitions. A woman peered out from the third cubicle on the left.

"Della?"

"Here, David."

David turned to thank Harry, but the nurse was gone. Della met him in the hallway.

"How is she?" David asked.

"In and out," Della said. "She seems awful tired. Keeps asking me to open the window. I don' have the heart to tell her there isn't one."

"She talk any?"

"Not to me. She's had a few conversations with some dude named Earl. She's been holding out for you, Silver."

Della took a packet of crackers from her shirt pocket. The Southern Medical logo was stamped on the package.

"Really, Della. Have you no shame?"

"Honestly, Silver, guy named Harry gave these to me. Listen, I been working 'round the clock. My kids are gonna bark when I come in the door. I'm gone. Good luck with her."

"Sure."

David walked to the third partition, trying not to stare at the patients in the cubicles. Millicent Darnell's eyes were open and she watched him come around the corner.

"Finally," she said. He walked to the side of the bed. "You got that notebook, Detective?"

"I've got it. How are you, Mrs. Darnell?"

"Not so good."

She was right. Her color was bad, her lips bluish, eyeballs yellow and bloodshot. She seemed very, very tired.

"I'm going to die," she said conversationally.

"So I heard. I'm sorry." David pulled a chair close to the head of the bed.

"I'm sorry too," she said, sounding surprised. "He killed me, you know. Sure as you're sitting there. Courts won't recognize it, but you and I know better."

"Courts *will* recognize it."

She twisted a wad of sheet in her fist. "I keep thinking about him, in the house. What he did on the bed."

David dropped his pencil and it rolled under the bed. He bumped his head getting it back. The chair squeaked and scooted sideways when he sat back down.

He should never have taken her back to the house.

"You had something you wanted to tell me?"

"I saw him. That monster."

David sat forward. "You saw him?"

"Yeah. I was scared to tell you. I was afraid he'd come and get me. Asked my grandson what to do. He said the guy might come back."

"I wish you had asked me. I'd have protected you."

"It's bothered me, not telling you. But I was so scared, you see. I know what he done to them other people. I didn't want to get . . . cut up. And every time I thought to call you, I'd start thinking about him doing what he done on that bed, and doing it *after* he know'd I got away. He's got to figure I'm calling the cops. So, I say, this fella's got no sense. He's crazy. Them crazies are not to be fooled with."

"I understand. When did you see him?"

" 'Member I told you I heard him in the hall when I was in the living room?"

"Ah. Yes."

"I said I was too scared to turn and look, remember? Well, I was scared. But I still looked."

David folded his arms. "Tell me."

Millicent Darnell leaned back on her pillow and closed her eyes. "He was kind of plump. Brownish hair. Dirty-looking. He had a mustache, and red eyes."

"Red eyes?"

"More around the eyes. The skin under."

"Anything else?"

"He smelled bad. Like he was sweating. An animal smell."
Millicent Darnell winced and groaned. She looked very pale.

"Are you all right?" David asked. "Can I get you something?"
She shook her head.

"You said it was dark. How did you get such a clear look?"
Her eyes stayed closed but she smiled. "I told Dennis you were
tricky." Her smile faded. "The porch light was on. That's how I
saw him. I wish I hadn't. Can't seem to get his face out of my
head."

"Can I get a graphics unit in here? Make a sketch?"

Millicent Darnell opened her eyes. "You got all you're going
to get. I'll be dead soon. Right now I'm working on forgetting
that fella. I don't want to die with him in my mind."

The man in the next cubicle cried out and heaved loudly. The
sour smell of vomit rose in the air. David remembered Mrs. Darnell
crying softly when the paramedics took her away.

"You don't want to stay here," David said. "Can I take you
home?"

Mrs. Darnell smiled wanly. "My grandson's coming for me.
Going to take me home—his home. I'm going to lay down in
his den and look out his window, and if I'm lucky his big, fat
tom cat will sit in my lap and keep me company. And I'm going
to help myself to a big bowl of ice cream, too. If I know that cat,
he'll lick the bowl."

"What's your favorite ice cream?"

She grinned. "Chocolate chocolate chip." Her hands clutched
another fistful of sheet. "Here's what you *can* do for me. Talking
about you-know-who makes me nervous. I feel safe with you.
My grandson won't be here for a while. Sit with me while I fall
asleep."

He scooted his chair closer and held her hand.

She was asleep, snoring lightly, in minutes. David patted her
hand and tucked it under the sheet.

FOURTEEN

DAVID WASN'T SLEEPY. HE PROPPED UP ON HIS ELBOW AND watched Rose. She lay on her side, the cotton blanket pulled up under her chin. The top sheet was pale blue, and the hem was unraveling. The loose end fluttered with Rose's silent exhalations.

"Rose, I think Dyer's dead."

Rose's face stayed relaxed, sweet with the concentration of sleep.

"He was a good guy—good cop. I wish you'd seen him with the girls."

David closed his eyes, wondering if his words would lodge themselves in Rose's subconscious. They never had before, in any of the midnight talk sessions.

Confiding in Rose while she slept had begun accidentally. The girls had been babies—Mattie had yet to be born—and Rose was living in the fog of exhaustion inhabited by mothers of small children. For a long while it seemed that every time he cuddled close to her for a talk, or anything else, she fell instantly asleep. In fact, whenever she stopped moving, she fell instantly asleep.

At first he felt betrayed, even lonely. He missed the attention, the eye contact, the friendship of their conversations. Rose was bright, if opinionated, and he liked to bring things under the light of her intelligence. But after a while he began to appreciate the advantages of one-sided conversation. He could curl close to her warm soft back, trace the nape of her neck, and talk without interruption. There was none of the irritation that festered when she gave advice he didn't care to take—no quicksilver change of the subject when her grasshopper mind darted elsewhere, no losing his train of thought, and no tense stiffening of Rose's shoulders when his worries became her own.

"I think he's dead, but I keep hoping he's not." David scratched his stomach. "I wish I knew why the Elaki are so interested in Machete Man. And why Dyer was interested. There some kind of Dyer/Elaki connection? Or a vice/Elaki connection?" David rolled over on his back. "What was Dyer doing at that Elaki restaurant? He's going to stick out like crazy, place like the Ambassador, but the whole staff swears they didn't see him."

Rose sighed in her sleep.

"I know," David said. "I don't believe it either."

FIFTEEN

THERE WAS A FAIR TURNOUT AT MILLICENT DARNELL'S FUNER-
al. David and Mel stood a short distance from the graveside,
watchful, but not intrusive.

David checked his watch. Ten-fifteen and already hot. A breeze
would have been nice, something to stir the thick humid air. The
minister's voice droned like the buzz of an insect, and David
wished he could swat it away.

The presence of his mother's grave less than a hundred yards
away was a pressure against his back. Sweat rolled off his forehead,
trailed down his cheeks, and was sucked up by the stiff white collar
of his shirt. He badly wanted to loosen his tie.

He bent close to Mel. "Be right back."

Mel nodded, his eyes on the mourners.

The cemetery was lavishly landscaped. The grass was lush and
green, though there had been almost no rain in the last few weeks.
David spotted the grey heads of sprinklers, hidden in the grass. He
stepped over a border of heavy pink begonias and saw apples on
a row of crab apple trees.

A huge bouquet of white carnations marked an old, but tended
grave. The flowers were limp under the muggy blanket of air,
a brown discoloration edging the blossoms. David inhaled the
strong, sweet fragrance and thought of rotting fruit and women
who wore too much makeup. A swarm of gnats attacked his nose
and eyes, and he shooed them away, mopping his face with a
handkerchief.

He stopped at the edge of a man-made pond. The cement on the
sides had cracked; the water was dark green and scummy. Insects
dived at the surface. Fat black and orange koi opened their mouths
wide, looking up with avid stupidity. He moved away.

The hump of his mother's grave had settled a little. The tombstone, newly in place, was stark, simple, affordable. Exactly what
she would have wanted. There were no flowers. He had come
the day after the funeral to clear away the incredible clutter of
wreaths and arrangements sent by friends, coworkers, his father's
relatives.

Even Rose might not understand his compulsion to rid the grave of clutter. She would not see it for the courtesy it was.

Rose had never met the mother of his childhood, had never seen her explode in sudden rage when the disorder of their rooms began to press her. Newspapers on the floor made her sputter. She was infuriated by the magnificent fortresses he built—entire cities of boxes, blocks, army men, and toilet paper rolls. During calm, easy moments, she praised his ability to make do with materials at hand, calling it genius. But during the eruptions of anger, she would sweep his beloved cities to the floor, scream at him to throw them away, and retire to her bed, crying.

Once she had told him that she fantasized about living on the ceiling, where there was no furniture, no mess—just wide-open space. He learned to hang up his clothes, not leave them on the floor; make up his bed before answering the first call of nature; be unsentimental and throw things away.

But still the furies broke and his mother rampaged for reasons he could not fathom. What caused the rages? The depressions? Sometimes she yelled, sometimes she threw things. He would search her contorted, tear-streaked face, looking for the woman who could cook lasagna you would die for, who knew the answers to impossible math problems, who treated you like a prince when you were sick, who fended off teachers who didn't like little Jewish boys.

He had been afraid when they lived in Little Saigo—families were prey in Little Saigo. Lavinia had "wired" an alarm around their room, so the bad ones couldn't get in without an alert sounding in the police station. How often he had pictured the police cars, sirens blaring, coming to rescue them. He did not know that police cars rarely came to Little Saigo, and that protection came from payment to the tunnel rats, or allegiance to Maid Marion. And it was years later, when the tunnels were a bad, dark memory, that he realized that the "wired" alarm was a fake his mother devised to keep his sleep easy and his heart calm.

That woman was gone now. Lavinia Hicks Silver, born June second, 1986, had died by her own hand on July second, 2040.

She was not a Jew. He did not recite Kaddish for her, like he had for his father. He had been eight when his father disappeared—went out for doughnuts and never came back. Seven years later, when his father was declared legally dead, David said the Kaddish for him, every day for eleven months.

He was aware, suddenly, that Millicent Darnell's funeral was over, and people were drifting away. He turned and headed for the knot of mourners.

Mel had edged closer to the crowd.

"Which one's the grandson?" David asked. "What was his name?"

"Dennis Winston. One of those two guys over there. Blue suit or grey suit."

The two men talked to the minister, who put his hand on the shoulder of the man in the blue suit. Blue Suit was short, his hair dark and thinning. Grey Suit said something and the minister nodded. The funeral director joined them, speaking seriously to Blue Suit.

"That's got to be him," Mel said. "The one in blue."

Mel headed for Blue Suit and David followed. He noticed that Grey Suit had cat hair on his pant cuffs.

"Mr. Winston?" David asked.

"Yes?"

Mel, who had started to speak, closed his mouth.

"I'm Detective Silver, Homicide Task Force. Mind giving us a minute?"

Winston looked wary.

"Yeah, sure. Excuse us, Jeff."

Blue Suit watched them curiously.

Winston walked steadily to a large cottonwood tree, and turned his back to the trunk. He was an inch or two taller than David, his hair blond, fine, and falling into his eyes. His complexion was fair, tinged with pink at the moment. He had deep circles under his eyes, and his pants were loose and droopy under the belt. David wondered if Winston had been dieting.

"I'm sorry about your grandmother, Mr. Winston. She mentioned you several times. You were pretty close?"

"You're the detective that took her back through the house, Silver?"

David knew his face was red. "Yes."

"You sat with her at the hospital. Thanks."

David's heartbeat steadied. "I was glad to."

Winston adjusted his tie. He looked exhausted.

David thought of Millicent Darnell's ravaged bedroom. CATCH YOU LATER Machete Man had written on the wall—in lipstick, this time. Usually he used blood.

Mel cocked his head sideways. "Understand you told your grandmother not to give us an ID on this killer."

Winston backed against the tree, oblivious to the snags the bark made in his suit coat.

"I . . . she . . . was very frightened. She thought he might come back." Winston straightened up.

"Your grandmother told me that *you* suggested he might come back," David said. "What made you think so?"

Winston pulled a handkerchief from his coat pocket and wiped his forehead. "What about . . . what he wrote on the wall. 'See you around.' "

" 'Catch you later,' " Mel corrected.

"You don't know what's going on with somebody like that. I know you need to catch this bastard, but my grandmother was the important thing. I want . . . I wanted her to be safe. I never thought . . . I never suspected she'd be a target." Winston bit his lip. He wiped his face again and folded the handkerchief. He adjusted his tie.

"It's like lightning," Mel said. "Happens. Nothing you can do about it."

"You can stay out of the storm," Winston said bitterly.

"When did you put the new locks on her door?"

Winston paled. "Two . . . three months ago. I'm not sure." He rubbed his chin.

"A good thing you didn't get to the window," David said.

"The lock on it was fine," Winston said quickly. "It just squeaked. She'd been after me about it for . . . years, really. God, what if I had? She never would have . . ."

"Sure she would have," Mel said. "Earl would have seen to it."

Winston looked closely at Mel. "She told you that, huh? Listen, if anybody could come back and do that, it'd be my grandfather. He's buried over there." Winston waved an arm in the direction of the grave site. "She still died though. Didn't do any good."

"I agree with you, Mr. Winston," David said. "Machete Man is responsible for your grandmother's death."

"Seen it happen a hundred times," Mel said. "Vic—people survive the attack, but the stress of it, for the older ones, can kill them."

Winston's expression was wistful, and David quelled the urge to pat the man's shoulder. Winston was younger than he'd first thought—grief had added years.

"Look at it this way," David said. "She won. She got away. And her death was peaceful. You took her home, didn't you?"

"My place, yeah." Winston looked past David's shoulder.

"Did she get her ice cream?"

Winston's smile came, and died. "No. She didn't feel much like eating anything. She slept mostly. Looked out the window."

David wondered if the cat had kept her company. Silence settled over all of them. A bee buzzed by David's ear, liked what he saw, and flew back, circling. David swiped at it.

"Is there anything else? I have some things I need to do."

"Sure," said Mel. "That's all for now. We'll be in touch."

Winston had been moving away, but he stopped and looked at them. "In touch?"

"You want to know, don't you, when we catch this guy?" Mel said.

"Oh. Yeah. I sure do."

David watched him walk away.

"Something not right there," Mel said. "How come he didn't ask why we weren't out looking for Machete Man instead of bothering him? They all say that. It's getting to bother me when they don't."

"He doesn't think we'll catch Machete Man."

"Nervous too. Nervous as hell."

"He's afraid."

"Of what?"

"I got the feeling he was expecting trouble. He lets a squeaky window go for years, then he's suddenly over there installing locks."

Mel scratched his chin. "You think he read about Machete Man and got worried?"

"He's scared *now*, Mel. It's not like it's over for him."

"You trying to tell me he had something to do with it? Remember, she saw the guy."

"People who own cats don't chop up their grandmothers."

"Oh yeah, that's right. I remember reading that in the academy handbook."

"He did put the lock on the door."

"Could be to show what a concerned grandson he is. Maybe it was a copycat thing. He inherit?"

"We'll check."

"You know, David, it took her a while to tell us about seeing the guy. Her first instinct was not to say anything. Suppose she thought it was Winston. I mean, consider her description—dirty, animal smell, red eyes."

"I believe the smell, but the eyes are weird."

"The demon killer."

"Why give us a description at all?"

"Denial. It couldn't be *my* grandson. She convinced herself she saw something else."

They passed Millicent Darnell's coffin. It was decked with flowers and David sniffed, but could not catch a fragrance. He stopped in front of Earl Darnell's tombstone.

Mel looked at the inscription. "What is that, Hebrew?"

"Looks like."

"Can you read it? You must be reading something, you sure got a funny look on your face."

"It says . . . no, that can't be right. I'm not very good at this."

"What?"

"I think it says 'the Sox stink.' "

Mel laughed. "Jewish, huh? How come he's not buried over on Wharton?"

"Millicent Darnell wasn't Jewish. He was waiting for her."

"Earl and Millie."

David shrugged. "You can't help liking a guy who got up every morning and fixed his wife biscuits. And left in-jokes on his tombstone."

"You get up and fix Rose biscuits?"

"Rose doesn't like biscuits."

They opened the car doors and waited for the interior to cool.

"Tell you what, David. If you get whacked, I'll be sure and tell Rose you want a Hebrew joke on your tombstone."

"Thanks, Mel."

Mel stretched. "How'd you know which guy was Winston?"

"I'm a detective."

A light flashed on the control board. Mel slid into the front seat. David turned to scan the crowd. People were leaving. Winston was gone.

"David?"

He turned quickly. He knew that tone of voice. "What is it, Mel?"

"They found Dyer. Part of him, anyway."

SIXTEEN

"THIS CASE IS GETTING VERY WEIRD," MEL SAID.

David was quiet. He pictured Dyer giving candy to his girls, keeping food for the kids he ran across in vice. Mel looked at him, and David cleared his throat, hoping his voice sounded normal.

"They always do."

"What?"

"Our cases. They always get weird."

String was in the hallway outside the morgue, tottering on his fringe. Mel groaned. The Elaki was suddenly still.

"Please to say hello," String said. "I must apologize for the abrupt taking of leave on our last occasion."

"What brings you here?" Mel asked.

"I was informed by my superior. I am here to assist."

Mel smiled. "You ever been in a morgue, String?"

"No."

"Go ahead. Right through that door."

There were four bodies on tables—all of them covered with sheets. A man and a woman, both wearing blue smocks, sat at a lab table, eating lunch and playing cards.

"Spid!" The man grinned. "Got you."

The woman handed him a carrot stick. She took a sandwich from a brown bag and took a bite. "If you'd bring your own lunch, Bradston, you wouldn't have to work so hard to win mine."

Bradston crunched the carrot. "This way at least *one* of us loses weight. Want to go again?"

"What are you after this time?"

"I got my eye on that pickle."

The woman looked up. "Hi, David." She spotted the Elaki and stiffened. "Good afternoon, sir. May I help you?"

"I am to accompany these gentlemen."

"Say *hello*, Miriam," Mel said.

"*Hello*, Mel."

"You never did come back for your bathrobe."

"It wasn't mine, you shit." She stood up, still holding her sandwich. "Have this chair," she told String.

"They don't sit," Mel said.

"What?"

"Elaki don't sit, Miriam."

She blushed and motioned for them to follow her toward an examination table. "You guys here to see Dyer?"

"What there is of him," Bradston said. He reached toward Miriam's sack.

"Keep your hands off that pickle," she said.

"Eyes in back of her head."

Mel looked at Bradston. "What you playing?"

"Spid," Bradston said. "You never played?"

"Never heard of it."

"Elaki version of poker," Miriam said. "Probably over your head." She took a bite of sandwich and stopped beside a table. "Here he is."

The sheet was wet. David lifted the corner and pulled it back. Dyer's head and one of his legs had been fished out of Deer Lake, twenty miles northwest of Possum Head Lane.

Dyer's hair, still wet, was matted with dark mud and blood. His eyes were open, sleepy-looking, the face a pinched-looking bluish white. The head was severed just below the chin. The right leg, cut about six inches above the knee, was stretched on the table, also wet.

A sandal was strapped to the foot. Dyer's big toe was smashed and was swollen and blue. David looked at Miriam and pointed to the toe.

"Before death?"

She nodded. "Somebody stomped on it, somebody wearing boots of some kind. Leather heels. Probably couldn't resist that open shoe." She switched her sandwich to her left hand and pried Dyer's mouth open with her right. "See here?"

David walked around the edge of the table. Miriam peered into Dyer's mouth.

"Look at the tongue. Bitten, hard. The front tooth there is broken." She peeled back the lip. "And the tissue severely abraded."

The teeth had dark stains on the back.

"Blood?" David asked.

"Tobacco. But here." She pointed to a molar. "In the crown. *That'll* be blood."

"He was beaten then."

"Badly," Miriam said. "Bit his tongue almost clean through when the pain got bad."

String began to sway back and forth and David realized that the Elaki was losing his pinkness. The droop in String's left eye prong gave him a lop-eared look. There were two bald patches in his scales and the edges of his side flaps were slightly irregular—a far cry from the symmetrical elegance of Puzzle.

"Death bothers you?" David asked gently.

"It is not that. The corpse is, after all, not Elaki."

David frowned.

"It is . . . may I be honest? It is the smell of the corpse, and so many humans in a small room. And mixed with this chemical odor."

"Wait outside, then. I'll brief you later."

"No. Please. It must be more difficult for you—you knew the human. I will do what must for the job be handled. Could the window be raised?"

Bradston looked up. "Hell, no. We'd get a yellow code in our printout. Opening a window constitutes a security violation."

"I am not sure I follow."

"He means no," Mel said.

David looked back at Dyer. "Was he dead before they cut him up?"

Miriam stopped in front of the terminal next to the exam table. "Case number—" She looked at the ID stamp on Dyer's foot. "Two six three A four. Crime scene."

The computer beeped and flashed a drawing. David saw an empty chair in a ramshackle kitchen. Bloodstains fanned the wall behind the chair. He recognized the kitchen in the abandoned house on Possum Head Lane.

Miriam pointed to the arc of blood behind the chair. "Look at that. Now look at him." She took another bite of sandwich, smearing egg salad on the corner of her mouth. "I haven't programmed the data in, this is all prelim guessing. But I'll bet we'll find the guy was sat in this chair and beaten. He was tied up most likely—the wounds are close, he wasn't able to move much to protect himself. Then, somebody took his head off. Very little blood on the floor. You can see where it slid down the walls and went . . . nowhere. So there was plastic down, or something. Under the chair. They knew they were going to kill him. Whoever it was had a long blade, razor-sharp. Not your average pocketknife, folks."

"Machete?" Mel asked.

She nodded. "Easily. This may be our boy again. You okay, Silver?"

"Sure. When was the leg taken off?"

Miriam set her sandwich down on the terminal. "Dyer worked vice, didn't he? You know him?"

"Not well."

She peeled back the sliced edge of the pant leg, and David made himself look at the bone and muscle of the leg.

"He was cut up *afterward*, Silver. They tied him to the chair and beat the crap out of him. Then one of them chopped Dyer's head off, and it was over. They cut him up and dumped him in the lake." She lifted the cuff of the pant leg, her elbow resting on Dyer's big toe. "Look at the indentations on the shin here."

He folded his arms. "Tell me."

"Trunk latch, I'll bet you money."

"She'll bet you pickles," Bradston said.

"So cheer up, guys. He was stuffed in a trunk, which means there may be a car in the lake. Get me the car, and we'll find a million ways to nail your perp."

David touched Dyer's left ear. It was lacerated from the center to the edge of the lobe. Someone had ripped the unicorn earring out. Souvenir?

David looked up. "You said they, Miriam."

"Please?"

"You said they. More than one killer?"

"Oh. Yes, I think so. Unless the guy who worked him over had a powerhouse left *and* a powerhouse right. Most have one or the other. But I'm not sure."

Mel headed for the door. "Okay, David, let's split up. You go after vice. I want a talk with that Elaki shit in the museum." He crooked a finger at String. "Whyn't you come with me? We'll go and talk to your boss."

"You must promise no disrespect to this personage. Please, he is most eminent."

"You mean 'cause I called him a shit? Oh, String, *String*. No disrespect intended. It wasn't an insult or anything."

"No?"

"No, not in the idiomatic sense. Come on, I'll explain it on the way."

Bradston waved a pickle at them. "Don't be strangers."

SEVENTEEN

IT WAS COOL IN THE STAIRWELL, AND DARK AFTER THE HARSH afternoon sun. David hooked his ID to his belt. It had been a while since he'd been downtown to Avery Street and police headquarters. Two years, exactly, since Homicide Task Force had moved to Mitchell Avenue. David's footsteps echoed on the concrete stairs, and he stepped on a wad of dirty pink bubble gum. The gum was old and dried and did not string from his shoe, for which he was grateful. Stale cigarette smoke hung in the air, mingling with the familiar, musty odor he always associated with headquarters.

David went through orange double doors, down a hall, and through another set of doors that led to vice. There were eight desks, all but three empty. A man and a woman stared blearily at computer terminals, and another man talked on the phone. None of them looked up when David walked in.

At the back of the room was a glassed-in office. The name on the door was Lieutenant Coltrane. David knocked. The guy on the phone looked up.

"I help you?"

The man was fat and tired-looking. His black hair was combed back with something sticky, but his eyes were alert and friendly. The nameplate on his desk said Detective Harry Myer.

"I'm looking for Coltrane," David said.

"He's off taking a leak. Should be back soon, if that's his only business." Myer waved him to a chair. "Sit down, if you want. Coffee?"

"No thanks."

The woman looked up from her terminal. "He's not supposed to be in here," she said.

"Look at the ID," Myer said. "Purple code from upstairs. He's okay to be here."

"It gets us killed," the woman said grimly. "Let these guys in here, and surprise, surprise, we get fingered on the streets."

Myer shrugged and went back to the phone. "You still there, sir? Sorry to keep you waiting. Look, it's like I said. You want

78

a hooker, you call your *local* precinct. What? I ain't interested in what you want to do with *peanut* butter. You got to talk to the service about that." Myer looked at David and rolled his eyes. "No, I can't do referrals. I don't care what they do in Cleveland, buddy, here they got assigned areas. You got to go with the girls in your area. Or boys, yeah, whatever, I don't want to hear . . . they won't, huh? I don't think they *have* to do anything. Maybe if you was to bring your own? Tell me, since you brought it up, you use crunchy or smooth? I see. Maybe that's your problem. Ask 'em if they'll do crunchy." Myer hung up and shook his head. "Asshole." He looked over David's shoulder.

"Hey, Coltrane? Detective here to see you."

David stood up. Coltrane was young for a lieutenant. He was big, probably six-two, a couple hundred pounds. He had a hefty muscular build that was just turning to fat. His hair was brownish blond, very thick. His eyes were brown and bloodshot and his face was heavy-featured and coarse. He wore a white knit shirt and blue jeans. Sandals, too, like Dyer. David wondered if sandals were part of the vice uniform. His eyes strayed to Myer's feet. Myer wore traditional black lace-ups, polished. Myer saw his look and grinned.

Coltrane looked wary. "So, Detective . . ."

"Silver."

"Silver. Homicide?"

"I'm here about Dyer."

The room seemed suddenly quieter. David looked around, but no one would meet his eyes. Coltrane pointed to his office.

"Come on in. Should have let me know you were coming." He glanced at the detectives in the large workroom and winked. "Hate to keep homicide waiting."

David didn't like Coltrane. Was it justified? Was it the sandals? Dyer had worn sandals. He'd liked Dyer.

"Sit down, Silver."

David was tired of sitting. He wished he had the nerve to perch on the edge of Coltrane's desk. Mel would have. He sat on the edge of the chair and looked around the office. It was neat and dusty. He got the feeling Coltrane didn't spend a lot of time there. Which would be odd, for a lieutenant.

"Tell me about Dyer," Coltrane said.

"No." David folded his arms. "You tell me."

Coltrane looked irritated and David didn't blame him. He was scoring an all-time low on professional courtesy.

"What was Dyer working on?" David asked.

Coltrane shrugged. "Couple of things. This and that."

"Helpful," David said. "I'd like to see his case files."

Coltrane picked up the phone. "Myer, put together a list of Dyer's access codes. Silver will pick it up on his way out."

"Why was Dyer interested in Machete Man?"

Coltrane looked puzzled. "Far as I know, he wasn't. Maybe he thought you guys needed help." He grinned. "Not funny? Look, Dyer was working on some big dealers. Bringing in a new cocaine derivative called Black Diamond. You heard of it?"

He hadn't. "Vaguely."

"Potent stuff. Not the usual dealers, either. Far as I know, though, Dyer didn't have squat."

"When a vice cop gets hacked, he's got more than squat."

Coltrane leaned back in his chair and put his feet up on the desk. His feet were large and hairy on the top. His toenails were yellowish and needed trimming.

"You have to understand about Dyer." Coltrane bit the cuticle on his left thumb. "He was secretive, very closemouthed. Lots of vice guys work that way. They're out on the streets, they get paranoid. So long as they're getting results, I don't question it."

"Why wouldn't Dyer call you for backup?"

Coltrane flushed, a red haze spreading from the roots of his hair down his neck.

"He worked maverick. He liked it that way."

David sat back in his chair. The signs were there, he'd seen them before. Coltrane ran a crooked operation, and Dyer was straight. So Dyer worked as an outcast, trusted no one, and every case he handled would be a massive gnarl of workarounds that kept his own conscience clear, and took into account what could realistically be accomplished around bent cops. Coltrane was dirty. Vice was dirty. Dyer didn't trust Coltrane and neither did David.

"Who was Dyer's partner?"

"Ian Shavstik."

"He in?"

"No. But don't waste your time. They were partners on paper only. Didn't even work the same cases. Truth is, Dyer was a stick ass, and he didn't like Ian. Ian's a little slow, but he's okay."

David knew what okay meant. One of the guys.

He thought of Dyer climbing out of his smashed Datsun, looking up and down Possum Head Lane in the middle of the night. He was hurt, bleeding. A lonely man—a cop without backup. Dyer had no one to call, so he called David. Did it have anything to do with

Machete Man? He had met Dyer at the Darnell scene. The cases tied together.

"Silver?"

"What? I'm sorry?"

"I said, you sure you don't want some coffee?"

"I'm sure." David stood up. "Good-bye, Lieutenant Coltrane. Be seeing you."

"Drop in anytime."

He closed the door behind him. Myer stood up—a tall man, pear-shaped, heavy-jowled. He wore slacks, a white shirt, and a tie. Another vice outcast? Some of the most conservative-looking cops were dirty.

Myer handed him a stack of disks. "You'll need these. There's no access here outside the department. And here." He handed David a yellow sheet of note paper. "Dyer's access code. Come on, the coffee down the hall is better than what we got here."

David followed Myer down the hall and into the stairwell.

"Yeah, I know," Myer said. "You don't want a cup of coffee. You sure you're a cop?"

"Some days, not very."

Myer tapped the disks David held. "Those are nothing. Dyer kept his real stuff hidden."

"At home?"

"Probably not. He used to, but not anymore. He had a girl-friend—pretty steady. She might know something. Name of Judith. Rawley. R-A-W-L-E-Y."

David folded his arms. "What else do you know?"

Myer held up both hands. "Hey, I'm just a good ole boy, I don't know nothing. Except maybe that guys like Dyer always wind up in pieces somewhere, and I'm goddamn sick and tired of seeing it." Myer's eyes were sad. "That's all you get, Silver. Get to work."

Myer waved a hand and left. He walked slowly, with a slight limp, like a man whose shoes were too tight.

EIGHTEEN

THE PRECINCT ROOM WAS CROWDED AND NOISY. THE AIR-
conditioning was not working well and the temperature hovered
around eighty-six degrees. Saigo City Utilities was threatening
brownout.

David leaned back in his chair and rubbed his eyes. Dyer wrote
a dull report, which, as Myer had warned him, contained nothing
but surveillance notes. It was amazing how much Dyer could say
without giving out information. It was interesting, though, that
Dyer was doing a lot of surveillance work on Pitch Avenue and
Lombard Street—both of them bordered Little Saigo.

David frowned. Something about Little Saigo had clicked in
his mind, but he couldn't make the connection.

He picked up the phone and dialed. It rang once.

"Agent Weiler."

"Dawn? This is David Silver."

"You're psychic, David, I was just getting ready to call you."

"Yeah? Business or pleasure?"

"Business."

David felt mildly disappointed.

"Listen, I've got a bad case of the four o'clock munchies. You
hungry?"

He hadn't had lunch. He was very hungry.

"I have an incredible craving for an egg salad sandwich."

"Rose must be pregnant. Meet me at the Oriental taco stand on
Rand. You can just walk over, can't you?"

"Yeah, but it's out of your way."

"That's okay, I've got to pick something up in that area later.
See you in a half hour."

Mel came through the precinct doorway at top speed, String
gliding behind him. The cops behind their desks ignored the Elaki,
but suddenly there was an atmosphere. David wondered if Mel had
eaten. If God was good, he could leave Mel and String looking over
Dyer's case files, while he had tacos with Dawn.

"There's something funny going on," Mel said. His hair was
sweat-soaked and curling in the humidity.

"You find Puzzle Solver?"

"Yeah. He had an interesting lunch."

"He had a most terrible lunch," String muttered, gliding past them.

"At least he had lunch." Was it his imagination, David wondered, or was the Elaki actually sagging around the middle?

Mel scratched his ear. "Guess *where* he had lunch."

"The Ambassador?"

"Hey, David, you ever consider police work? Anyway, he's sitting—I mean standing—around the Ambassador eating with another Elaki hotshot, bellybrain they call Grammr. They finish and head back to the museum, and right when they get to the lobby this other Elaki, Grammr, falls down dead."

"Something he ate?"

Mel stuck his hands in his pockets. "You heard this one before."

David sat up. "No, I was kidding. *Was* he poisoned?"

"Yeah, but with prior knowledge. He was having that Japanese puffer fish."

"People die from eating that every year."

"Not Elaki," String said.

"Yeah," said Mel, "they love the stuff, but none of them ever died of it. Till recently. Evidently this guy's number two. *Both* after eating at the Ambassador. And that's not all.

"I had a talk with Bess Kellog, in statistical analysis. She knows a lot about Elaki. She says it would take concentrated quantities of the puffer fish to kill an Elaki—she researched it when the first one died."

"You think he was murdered? An *Elaki*?"

Mel sat on the edge of his desk. "Yeah, I know. Impossible. Their social structure is completely self-policing. The group mentality. No crime. An Elaki breaks the moral code and he is sanctioned. So unless this Elaki was up to something, this had to be an accident."

"Unless a human killed him."

"Difficult. Especially this way. But possible, I guess. Or hell, maybe he *was* up to something that got him sanctioned."

"How could we find out?"

"Bess says the whole thing's impossible. Elaki don't murder each other, sanctions don't happen so publicly, and Elaki don't die from eating puffer fish."

David checked his watch. "Look, Mel, I'm meeting Dawn for tacos. You hungry?"

"You go ahead. What you working on?"

"Dyer's case files. No, no, look at them later."

String edged closer. "Perhaps I could help?"

David shook his head. "These are critical."

"I can make the report. Be most happy to assist."

"I don't know. You sure you wouldn't rather come with us?"

"No, please. I stay here and do report."

Mel frowned. "David . . ."

"It's okay, Mel. He's part of the team. Okay, String. There's an open terminal. Over there. We'll bring you back a taco."

"You will? This is the authentic Earth taco?"

"Bring you two," Mel said.

String quivered. "Home boy food!"

"Got any questions, even little ones," Mel said, "you just go ask the captain. Don't knock or nothing. He don't stand on formality."

David and Mel left him hunched over a terminal.

"I feel like hanging around just to watch him type," Mel said. "Listen, you sure you want him looking through those disks? David?"

David frowned. "I was just thinking. You know those pictures we saw in Puzzle's office? The drug buys? I think they were all shot in and around Little Saigo."

"What a shock. Since half the drug deals in this city go down over there."

"True."

"Look, David, you sure about letting String go over Dyer's stuff?"

"I'm sure I don't want him along when I talk to Dawn. Nothing in those reports, anyway, I've seen them. Besides, I'm not sure the computer will come up for String's voice patterns."

Mel smiled. "Poor little sucker. Let's get him a beer to go with the tacos."

Dawn was sitting in a white metal chair under a tattered umbrella with fading aqua stripes. A knot of bobbing Elaki clustered around the food stand, inquiring about spices in the tacos. The owner nodded enthusiastically, assuring them of the meat's blandness. Flies and bees congregated at the dark, smelly mouth of a trash can. David wished Dawn had picked a place farther from the garbage.

"But authentic?" came a loud Elaki voice.

"Oh, yes, sir, ma'am . . ." The owner stared at the Elaki's belly slits. "The genuine article."

Dawn waved at David and tilted her head. "How come I had farther to go, and I got here first?"

David shrugged. "How many tacos, Dawn?"

"No, David, I'm buying."

She went to the stand and ordered tacos and two beers and a lime tea. David stuck his hands in his pockets. Just as well she was buying, he'd left the house without money. Mel walked up behind Dawn.

"Come on now, kitten, I'll get the beer and tea."

"Mel, I hate it when you call me kitten."

"Then don't drink tea when you're having tacos."

David sat down. He shooed a fly away from a sticky orange ring of grease. It was hot out, too hot for sidewalk dining.

He took a sip of the beer Mel handed him. Warm. He unwrapped a taco and took a large bite. Taco shell shattered and dropped pieces over the paper wrapper. The filling was bland and it left a sweet aftertaste. David chewed and wiped his mouth.

"*Jesus*," Mel said. "They put cinnamon in these."

Dawn grimaced. "The Elaki love cinnamon in everything."

David realized that the Elaki at the next table were watching them. He leaned forward, voice low.

"Dawn, I've got a problem with Machete Man."

She picked a shred of cheese off the top of her taco and nibbled it.

"Dawn, you eat like a mouse," Mel said.

"Mel, you eat like a pig."

"Don't leave me out," David said. "What do I eat like?"

Dawn cocked her head. "Like a man who missed lunch."

David felt excluded.

A small Elaki teetered back and forth on her fringe and watched them eat.

"What about Machete Man, David?"

He wiped his mouth with a napkin. "I get the feeling that I've heard it all before. Read it in a book somewhere, saw it on TV, I don't know. And I'll tell you what else. The range of victims makes no sense. I think we have a copycat, Dawn. There's more here than a psycho on the loose."

"More? What could be more than that?" Dawn asked. She gnawed at the edge of her taco and David got the feeling her mind was elsewhere.

"That Elaki kid's going to fall over," Mel muttered under his breath.

"You're the expert on serial whacks," David said. "And you said before things didn't feel right. Maybe we're not looking at a head case after all."

She shrugged. "Maybe."

"I also want to know about the Elaki, Puzzle Solver. What's his interest? How is he connected to String?"

"That's funny, David," Mel said. "Connected to String."

Dawn started eating quickly. She took a large bite of taco and, before it was chewed, crammed another into her mouth. She swallowed heavily.

"Why are you asking me?"

"Because his access code had an 08 digit at the end," Mel said. "That's FBI."

Dawn winced. "You guys trying to tell me the Elaki is an FBI agent? Don't make me laugh." She ate the rest of her taco in one bite. "I want another one. You guys want another one?"

David grabbed Dawn's wrist. "Dawn. Did you know Vernon Dyer?"

"No."

"He was a good cop. Now he's a dead cop. I am asking as a friend here. Officially, I am imposing on our friendship."

Dawn chewed her lip. "Heck-fire."

An Elaki turned a vid in their direction. Dawn glared at the Elaki, and it backed away.

Mel opened his mouth and David kicked him.

"Please," David said.

Dawn ran her finger up and down her paper cup, making lines in the cool water condensed on the side. "I don't know a lot," she said.

David didn't believe her.

"Three Elaki have died—unexpectedly. We don't interfere when Elaki carry out a sanction. But this time they *asked* for our help."

"Two of them were poisoned at the Ambassador restaurant," Mel said.

Dawn put her hands in her lap. "How did you know?"

"The other?" David said.

"Fell off the top of the museum."

"Not an accident?"

Dawn grimaced. "Elaki don't hang out on the top of buildings. They hate being up high. They can blow over the side if the wind is right. An Elaki on top of a building is about as likely as a human sleeping in the middle of the road."

"Anything else?"

"We're assisting, not running the investigation."

David smiled. "Thank you, Dawn."

"Don't leave," she said.

"Why?"

"David, what is Rose up to?"

"Rose? She's home. Probably in the garage fixing the grass machine, it's screwy again."

"Naw, she's sitting in the swing sulking," Mel said.

Dawn leaned back and folded her arms. "Of course, of course. Rose, the simple farmer. Has an unofficial repair business and"— she nodded at David—"pays taxes on the proceeds."

"You checked?"

"Not me," Dawn said. "But somebody's looking into things. Anything at all to do with Rose."

David leaned across the table. "Quit playing the line, Dawn. Who's checking up on Rose?"

Dawn held up her hands. "Remember, David, I told *you*. I don't know what's up. Company man named Ellwood. Somebody told him Rose and I worked together with DEA, years ago. He wanted to know what she was up to lately."

"*Company* man? Inquiring about my *sister*?" Mel laughed. "You can't mean charlie inza alpha."

"Use whatever euphemism you want, just so the A stands for asshole."

David chewed his thumb. "What does the CIA want with Rose?"

"No, David, that's *my* question."

"What did you tell Ellwood?" Mel said.

Dawn shrugged. "I gave him her recipe for Kelsey Lemon Cake and highly recommended her small engine repair service. He wanted to know if she hired out, and I said as far as I knew, she didn't take in laundry or look after anybody's kids but her own." Dawn sighed. "He wanted to know why she left the business."

David bit the cuticle on his left thumb. "And you said?"

Dawn stared at the table. "I said she was borderline manic depressive, and quick-tempered, and no longer suited for field work."

Mel folded his arms. "In other words, the truth."

The small Elaki teetered too far and fell over. It let out a squawky trumpet. Mel picked the Elaki up and dusted her off.

David felt his face getting warm.

"What's going on, David?" Dawn said. "What's Rose up to?"

"What exactly would Ellwood like to know?"

Two spots of red appeared on Dawn's smooth cheeks, like tiny perfect apples.

"Rose and I were friends long before you came along, David. You have no right to say that to me."

David stood up. "Rose can take care of herself. And she'll be a hell of a lot better off if the two of you butt out."

"Pardon me, David." Dawn stood up and gathered the trash. "I thought you might *appreciate* knowing the CIA was interested in your wife. I thought I was helping you out."

"If you want to help me," David said. "Do your job. Check out this Machete Man thing. Give me the Elaki case files so I've got a chance to figure what the hell is going on. And leave Rose the hell out of things." He glared down at Dawn and Mel. "And I'll tell both of you this. Nobody messes with my wife. I *pity* the operative that messes with my wife."

Mel folded his arms. "He's got a point. Rose is like eternal PMS."

Dawn shook her head. "I don't think that's what he meant."

NINETEEN

THE LINDALE BUILDING WAS AN OLD TOBACCO WAREHOUSE that had been converted. The bottom floor housed fruit and vegetable wholesalers, the second floor was a warehouse for the Bermuda Shoe Company, and the third floor a "penthouse" apartment for Judith Rawley.

The musky molasses smell of cut tobacco still hung in the air, along with the smell of overripe fruit and car exhaust. David sweated while he climbed the stairs. He was still angry at Mel and Dawn Weiler. And ashamed of losing his temper.

Damn Rose, anyway. What was going on? Hell, she didn't know, did she? Would she tell him? He pictured her at home, running down the gravel driveway in white cotton shorts, shaping up. He thought of Rose in her DEA fatigues, wielding an Uzi. He grinned. It was totally unfair to laugh at the notion. But Rose?

David realized that the door to Judith Rawley's apartment was open, and that a large woman was glaring at him from the inside. Had he knocked?

"What's so damn funny, buddy?"

The door swung shut and he stopped it with his elbow.

"I'm Detective Silver, Homicide Task Force." He flashed his ID. "I'm looking for Judith Rawley."

The woman quit shoving the door against his arm. "*You're* Silver?" She looked surprised. "I'm Judith Rawley."

She was large, maybe two hundred forty pounds. Her hair was brunette with reddish highlights—long, soft, and silky. David had the urge to touch it. Her eyes were green and intelligent. She wore faded jeans, a blue denim shirt with the sleeves rolled up, no shoes. Her toenails were painted frosty pink.

David tucked his ID back in his pocket. "Yeah, I'm Silver."

"Come in, please. You're here about Vern?"

"He listed you as his next of kin."

The apartment was huge, cavernous. Dark wood floors, polished and gleaming, creaked under his feet. The whole north wall was a bank of windows, and there was a skylight in the ceiling. Sunlight

flooded the room, but it was cool inside, and David felt the sweat
dry on his back. A winding staircase led to a loft bedroom. One
side of the great room held a drafting table, track lighting, a wood
file cabinet, and art supplies. A wooden chair sat in front of a
computer terminal. In the center of the room were two beige love
seats on a thick Indian rug, and a bar separated a small kitchen.
David felt at home.

"Have a seat," Judith Rawley said. "You look hot. How about
a glass of lemonade?"

"No thanks."

"I'm having one." Judith Rawley set two fresh lemons on the
counter. David wished he'd said yes.

"I'm making it fresh," she said. "Why don't you have some?"

"Okay."

David sat down. The couch was comfortable, and deep enough
so that he didn't feel like his butt was going to slide off the edge.
He was glad Dyer had been lucky enough to have Judith Rawley
to come home to.

"Ms. Rawley?"

"Judith."

"Judith. I'm very sorry about what happened to Vern."

She halved the lemons and placed them on the squeezer. "Thank
you, David Silver."

He studied the pictures on the wall. They were cartoons, some
of them framed. He got up and roamed the room, studying them.
The humor was gentle, with an undertone of sadness, the drawings
deceptively simple. Thurber, without the sting. The signature on
the bottom was a black scribble—J. Rawley.

"These are yours," David said.

"I know."

"But they're good!"

"Thank you for saying so."

David had the uneasy feeling he sounded foolish, but Judith
Rawley didn't seem to mind.

"Really now. Why haven't I seen your work? Why aren't you
in the T.W. Communications fold? Too much a maverick?"

Judith handed him a frosted glass of lemonade. He took a sip.
It was cold and tart. He sat down and Judith sat across from
him, cross-legged. The pads of her feet were callused. She went
barefoot a lot.

"I wish. T.W. Communications is a good old boy network. It's
hard as hell to break in. But believe me, I'd do almost anything
to get syndicated with them."

"You must be published somewhere."

"Here and there. Ain't nobody told me to quit my day job."

"Which is?"

"Traffic coordinator." She pointed to the computer. "Midnight to six A.M., six nights a week. I keep your car on track from Lombard to Elkin Street."

"Big area."

She shrugged. "Doesn't pay much, but it doesn't require much. Computer doesn't need my input all that often."

Judith quit talking, suddenly. She stared at the floor, but David had seen the sudden glint of tears before she turned away.

"Your apartment is very nice."

She looked up. "It's not usually this clean. I don't like the domestibot, so I do all the scut work."

"Yeah? We have an old bot, but it's schitzy. Two months ago it stripped the blankets and sheets off the beds and tried to stuff them in the trash recycler. Then it tried to cook the kids' pet monkey. We turned it off till my wife gets around to fixing it."

Judith smiled. "When my work is going bad, I clean. Vern could judge my productivity by walking in the door."

David glanced around involuntarily. The rooms were spotless.

"I know," she said. There were deep circles under her eyes. "Maybe I won't work anymore. Maybe it's gone."

She reminded him of Rose.

"You'll work again."

"Vern wanted to get married and have kids. I didn't want to. Nothing tangling my feet. I thought we had the perfect setup."

"Judith. Did Vern keep notes—unofficially?"

She nodded. "He didn't trust Coltrane, or anybody else. He'd been burned before. The job was getting to him, but he was hanging in. The plan was, he would stay in vice until my career took off. Then we'd get married and have a bunch of kids and he'd quit to look after them. Vern wanted a baby so bad. *My* baby, is what he said.

"I didn't want the mess and bother of kids and a family. So I said someday. Someday's easy." She pushed hair out of her eyes. "You go upstairs—you'll see neat closets and clean drawers. A place for everything, everything in its place."

"My mother would have loved you, Judith."

Her eyes filled. "It's *empty*, David Silver. Maybe that's what my work lacks. The muss and fuss."

"Did Vern talk to you about *his* work lately?"

She put her head in her hands. "I've been thinking about that. I'm afraid . . . it's been me doing the talking lately. I've had some disappointments." She stood up and ran a hand through the silk of her hair. "It's almost funny. The business end, God, it's been so bad. Just when I thought I was going somewhere, made a few small-time sales. I had a syndicate interested, requested my work. I can't tell you what it's like—to have someone *want* to see your work. But they turned me down. And they weren't too nice.

"But the work, it's going well, so damn well. I can't decide whether to throw a party or slit my wrists. So Vern's been doing a lot of listening while I've been doing a lot of talking."

"Did he seem worried?"

"Yes. But he did a lot. Worried. And worked incredible hours. And he said . . . not really said, but he was excited and tense. He gave me a key to a safe deposit box. His disks are in there, with all the work notes on them. He said give the key to anybody who shows up asking."

"Even Coltrane?"

"Especially Coltrane. I know, I know! He hated Coltrane. But see, Vern was always scared somebody might come after me through him. So he said just hand that key over and don't give anybody any trouble."

"Has anybody come for it?"

"Nope." She went to the drafting table. "Taped under here. Vern told me not to make it too easy." She peered under the table. "Here it is. From Arnon Financial Services on DeLing."

David took the key and put it in his pocket. "If anybody comes looking for it, tell them I've got it. Then call me."

"I will." She sat back down on the couch. "Vern mentioned you, before he died."

"He did?"

"He was taken with your little girls. He seemed . . . I think he was envious, a little. Of your family. He told me that you looked straight to him. That's a big compliment from Vern, let me tell you. And he kind of hinted that you two might be working together sometime, on a case."

David studied her face. "Are you sure now, Judith, that you don't know about any other disks Vern might have stashed?"

She looked away and her cheeks turned pink. "How did you know?"

He had almost gotten up to leave. David settled back down and folded his arms, right shoulder slightly higher than the left. "Tell me."

She picked a pillow up off the couch and tucked it into her lap. "You know and I know, that whatever's in that safe deposit box is no big deal. If Coltrane can have it, so could anyone. So I figured he had to have another hiding place. But one he wouldn't tell me about. I asked him and he said not. The only time I *know* he lied to me." She looked at David and smiled a little. "I can't stand it when people have secrets. So I . . . I followed him a couple times, when he'd made some notes using my system. And . . ." She got up and ripped a piece of drafting paper from her table. "Better draw you a map. It's in this parking lot on Fiori Avenue."

"Fiori?" Near Little Saigo, he thought.

She sketched quickly, deftly, and a few bold pencil lines turned into a detailed sketch of the parking lot, complete with landscaping.

David wondered what Judith Rawley had been like as a child. He pictured her at age eight. Long hair, of course, down to her waist. Eyes shy. Prone to reading and drawing, curled up in her room with a cat. He looked around. No sign of any cats.

"You have a cat?" David asked.

She looked at him strangely. "I'm allergic to cats. I used to have a dog, though. He played outfield for my T-ball team when I was a kid. He made tooth marks on the ball, and got slobber all over it. Drove the other kids nuts, but they left him alone or they'd deal with me. And I was their star hitter."

TWENTY

BY SEVEN O'CLOCK THE SUN WAS LOW IN THE SKY, AND THE heat of the day was draining. The Arrongi bar was two blocks down from The Ambassador. The outside facade was black marble with gold lettering. Nowhere did it say private club, but the place had the familiar feel of an Elaki-only establishment. All the nicer places were getting that way. David remembered when the Arrongi had been a restaurant, and a bar mitzvah there had been a big event.

Outside the Arrongi was a wood barrel full of healthy purple and white petunias. Two Elaki went through the door, swiveling once to stare at David. He heard a burst of music as the door opened and closed.

He checked his watch. Seven-fifteen. A man came out of the bar. He wore a black tuxedo that did not sit well on the bulge of his muscles. His hair was black, cut short, and his neck was short and thick. His face looked like somebody had hit it with a shovel.

"Sir?" The man's voice was a surprising tenor.

David folded his arms, one shoulder higher than the other.

"Sir? Can I help you?"

David cocked his head sideways. "Me? I'm waiting for somebody."

"Perhaps you would care to wait somewhere else."

"Perhaps you would care to explain why you're running Saigo citizens off the sidewalk." David flashed his badge.

The man smiled weakly and held up a hand. "Hey, no problem. Sorry, Detective, really."

"You the bouncer?"

"I'm employed by the Arrongi, yes."

"How long?"

"Three years."

"You look like a cop to me. What's your name?"

"Nimenz. *Ex*-cop."

"This kind of thing standard procedure for the club, Nimenz?"

94

Nimenz shrugged. "They don't like hot dogs."

David grimaced. "Maybe we should go in together. Have a talk with the management."

"It'll be my job, if you do."

David scratched his chin. "I'm coming in when my partner shows. I don't want any trouble, particularly not from you, Nimenz. You might find an errand to run, if you don't want to be caught in the middle."

Nimenz nodded. "Thanks. I'll do that."

"I hope the pay is worth it," David said to the man's disappearing back.

"What pay?"

Mel's voice was almost in his ear and David flinched.

"I hope you weren't too rushed," David said. "Getting here."

"I took String here out for a beer. Go with his tacos."

"Very good the authentic."

"We'd of been here sooner, but it took a while to pick the pieces of taco shell out of his belly scales." Mel pointed. "There, String, one we missed."

David jerked his head toward the Arrongi. "You sure Puzzle is in there?"

"Not *positive*, no. But String here was pretty sure he'd show up tonight. Guy's upset. Looking to get skunked, is my opinion."

David pushed the black-lacquered door and entered the Arrongi.

The interior was dark, and the lime scent of Elaki was strong. Polished wood bars lined the floor at six-foot intervals and Elaki huddled around them, talking, drinking, their bellies rippling. A human woman stood on a riser in the corner and played a flute. Men in tuxedos and white gloves carried drinks on silver trays.

The bar was cool, the carpet royal blue and thick. An Elaki in a khaki vest turned and looked at David.

"Hello, *hot dog*. You looking for some Eggs McMuffin?"

David felt the muscles tense in his stomach. He took a look at Mel and put a hand on his partner's arm.

"Easy, Mel."

"Easy, hell."

An Elaki scooted close to Mel.

"Hey, hot dog. How 'bout them Giants? What think you of that new quarterback?"

Mel glared silently.

"What's the matter, hot dog? The human *loves* football. Come, please, I buy the drink. I like talking sports with hot dogs—you people know the stuff, it is the fact of nature."

The bartender, a thin man with red hair and a pale complexion, leaned forward.

"This is a private club, sir." He looked at a waiter passing with a tray. "Get Nimenz. Hurry."

"What's the matter?" Mel said. "I look dangerous? Why don't you call the cops?" Mel pulled his badge and flipped it open. "Uh-oh! I *am* the cops."

The room grew silent. David drifted up and down the bars, hoping Mel was watching his back. The Elaki watched him, but went back to their drinks.

"It walk like the Elaki," came a voice from the back. "It talk like the Elaki. But it *smell* like a nose talker."

String swayed from side to side.

David remembered his Little Saigo days, when he'd stare at the passing cars. People locked their doors when they drove through his neighborhood.

Was that Puzzle at the far end of the last bar?

"Detective S-S-Silver. How 'bout them Giants?" Puzzle leered at him over the edge of a glass filled with bright yellow liquid. "Can I buy you a drink? One for your rough edge f-f-friend? Ah, Mr. String. We meet again."

"Is that Elaki beer or piss?" Mel said.

"Piss is precious," Puzzle said. "You may have beer. Aronald? Bring my friends a beer."

The waiter hesitated. Mel glared at him and he left.

"I am sorry for the remarks. Hot dog is not a term I care for." David shrugged.

"No," Puzzle said. "I like humans. I do. All I wanted to do was help. Help you, help us, yes, I admit it." Puzzle swayed and David realized he was very drunk. "Tell me, Mr. String. Why must these things become complicated, when there is so very much to do? Why?"

Mel edged close to him. "Don't you think it's time to come clean, Puzzle?"

Puzzle peered at String. "What do they mean by this?" He swiveled his eye stalk toward Mel. "You still think I am dirty, Detective Mel?"

"I think you got something on your mind, Puzzle."

"Puzz . . . puzz . . . Puzzle. My name is Sheesha. Use that, not the handle."

"Handle?"

Puzzle-Sheesha's belly rippled. "Have you not figured it out? You should have explained, String, or whoever you really are. We l-l-love the names. Smith for what was blacksmith. Tell me so, why not whitesmith? John's-son. At first we thought you were all named in the appropriate fashion, and we followed your lead. It began as a jokey way of accommodating you. Then it became . . . habit, I suppose. Insult. Ah, poor Liska. Who will be next? Me, no doubt. You are talking to one on the verge of eternal enlightenment."

David was aware that a number of Elaki were listening.

"Come on, Puzzle." He touched the Elaki's back, surprised at the cool velvet smoothness of the scales.

"Sheesha."

"Sheesha, then. Come on. Let's go grab a hot dog."

"Naw." Mel shook his head. "Let's go out for Eggs McMuffin."

Sheesha followed Mel and David brought up the rear.

String had taken the lead. "He might truly enjoy the genuine taco."

The black-lacquered door shut behind them.

"Mel, where's your car?" David asked.

"I sent it on. Where's your car?"

"The same, Mel, I thought you'd keep yours."

"I have a car," Sheesha said. "It is over there. And should be more comfortable for our interesting friend String." He headed for the street, pausing to look at the sky. "I enjoy very much the nighttime on this planet."

He sidled to the driver's side of the BMW. "Open," he said, then looked up. "Are you really going to take me out for the hot—"

Smoke and fire exploded from the driver's side of the car, and Puzzle flew backward into the street. David was thrown up on the sidewalk. His head slammed against the concrete.

TWENTY-ONE

DAVID HEARD A SIREN AND THE METALLIC GROAN OF A LARGE van braking. Red and blue lights flashed across his face.

"Come on, Quint. This Elaki's bad."

David felt someone lean over him and flash a light in his eyes.

"Go on," a voice said, close to his shoulder.

"Quint, we may need you. Somebody called Euclid Central. They're sending a team out."

"I'm not leaving this guy on the goddamn sidewalk, Franco. That Elaki hasn't got a chance, anyway."

David heard a bitten-off curse.

"Old lady Elmer's going to fry your butt. How about you, sir? Are you sure you won't let us take you in, have a doctor look you over?"

"No please. You must see to the human."

David recognized String's voice.

"Sorry, pal."

A heavy door slammed and a siren growled. The noise of the engine was startling, then it faded. David felt a hand on his shoulder.

"Listen," the voice said. "I need to get a look at your buddy over there. You'll be all right if you just lie still. Okay? You okay? My name is Quint. I'll be right back."

David sat up. His head hurt. He saw a knot of people standing to one side, staring. A fat woman in a blue dress smiled.

"You okay, honey?"

David's vision blurred, then focused. Chunks of twisted metal were strewn in every direction. Broken glass glittered across the sidewalk and pavement. David rubbed his eyes, remembering, suddenly, that Mel had been closer to the car.

He stood up quickly, grimacing at the ache in his head.

"Mel?"

David crouched beside String and Quint, laying two fingers by the side of Mel's neck.

"You mind?" Quint said mildly.

The pulse beat strong under David's fingertips. He sighed deeply.

"He's alive."

Quint rummaged through a red bag. "Yep. That's more than I can say for the Elaki. The other one."

"Dead?"

"Still jerking, but in way too many pieces. So long as the brain stem's in place they can do a lot, but unless they regenerate jelly, that guy is history."

David studied Mel's face. It was pale and smudged with black soot and blood. Quint wrapped a bandage around Mel's blood-soaked thigh.

"How bad is he?"

"Early to tell, but he's not missing any major pieces. What's his name?"

"Detective Mel," String said.

"Mel Burnett," said David.

"You hear me, Mel? You're going to be okay. Everything's all right." Quint glanced at David. "What happened here?"

"Elaki opened his car door and it blew."

"You knew this Elaki?"

"Sheesha," String said. "Puzzle."

David showed his badge. "I'm a cop. So's he. We were questioning him."

"I too am working the case," String said.

"Oh yeah? Elaki cops, now."

"What happened to the ambulance?" David asked.

"It took the Elaki to Bellmini."

"Why wouldn't they take my partner, here?"

Quint gave him a look. "I don't like it any more than you do, friend. It's an Elaki hospital, and they can't take people there."

"Can't or won't?"

A siren wailed, then stopped, and two uniformed patrol officers spilled out of their car, leaving the doors gaping open. David sighed and took charge of the scene.

The sky was dark and silent when David stepped out into the hospital parking lot. Mel was okay—hurt, but okay. He had a concussion, a hematoma on the side of his head, several contusions, and a laceration in his right thigh that had taken two ounces of skin glue to seal. It was early to tell, but internal views showed no major injuries, and like Quint had said, there hadn't been any parts missing.

He heard the scrape of belly scales on asphalt.

"Please?"

David turned around.

"Maybe best for me to accompany you to be safely home," String said. "It might be better for you the hospital, instead of alone."

"My wife will be home, String. I'll be okay."

"Ah, yes, you live together then?"

"Um-hmm. How about you? You be okay?"

String's right eye stalk was swollen, and he looked like he'd shed a few hundred scales.

"But yes. I am least injured. The best of the bunch, is that what you say?"

"Usually about bananas. You got somebody at home, waiting for you?"

"We do not marry, and we live separately."

"You be okay?"

"I be okay."

"We could share a car, but . . ."

"Most uncomfortable for one of us. I do not wish to ride sideways."

"And I don't feel like standing up."

"Good night then, Detective David."

"Good night, String. Watch yourself on rooftops."

David tucked a package of pain pills in his pants pocket, and stood beside his car, thinking. He'd gotten rid of String, now he needed to go to the parking lot and get Dyer's disks.

He wished he'd called Rose. His head ached, and he was so tired he swayed where he stood. If Rose were here, she would drive him home and tuck him in bed, hug him and fuss over him. Naturally he would protest. Insult her for babying him.

His head throbbed and he closed his eyes, shutting out the hospital lights. He couldn't face the parking lot tonight—not that near Little Saigo.

But he could drive if he had to. There would be grids to do the work most of the way home. He went back in the hospital to summon a car.

Twenty miles away from the farm, David was wondering if he'd made a mistake. Headlights from other cars stabbed into his eyes, making his vision blur and halo. An oncoming car honked and hugged the shoulder of the road. David realized he was off the grid and drifting toward the middle. He overcorrected, and the car swerved to the right.

David grimaced and cut his speed. He drove with exaggerated care, gritting his teeth against the tedium. Who had rigged the bomb on Puzzle-Sheesha's car? Was it an Elaki sanction? It didn't seem their style. Machete Man? Obviously not his style either, though it was too bad the lab couldn't look for come stains on the door handle.

When he turned, at last, into his own gravel drive, he was proud of himself for remembering to watch for the bullfrog. It wasn't there. The house was dark, except for one lamp burning in the living room. Rose was waiting up.

David stopped the car in front of the house and shut off the engine. He took a few deep breaths, and got out slowly.

"Open," he said.

The front door swung open. "Good evening, David Silver."

He nodded, wondering why he could never get out of the habit of nodding at a voice-activated door. His kids didn't, but they'd grown up with them.

He heard a bark and a whimper and Dead Meat ran to him and jumped on his legs, raking his pants with her toenails. She licked his hand with genuine joy.

"Hello, girl. Down, dog, down."

The living room was neat and empty. David looked for broken crayons, stuffed animals, books open and deserted on the floor. The room was quite clean. He wondered how his girls were doing. Asleep, now. Was Mattie homesick? Did she miss him at suppertime?

The house was quiet.

"Rose?"

A pile of chocolate-smeared candy wrappers were scattered on the floor near the side of the couch where Rose liked to curl up. Dead Meat nosed through the wrappers, picked one up between her teeth, and settled down to give it a good lick. David bent over and picked up the book that lay on the arm of the couch. He set it absently on the side table, then picked it up again. Rose had drawn large black nostrils and blackened the teeth of the man and woman on the cover.

"Rose?"

He headed for the bedroom. The bed was made, the room silent and cool. The clock on the bedside table said four-thirty.

"Rose?"

The girls' room still staggered under a load of toys, but the beds were made. David went in the kitchen and turned on the light. There was a note on the table.

David. I can't settle down worth a damn. Instead of shaping up, I'm eating the girls' candy and watching old movies. Did you know that Elliot Bernal was in *Mountain Gold*? He was so young then, I hardly recognized him!

Anyway, I'm going. If I sit around here I'll get fat and will have to subdue you know who by sitting on them. I *did* try to call you. Did you get any of my messages? Feed the dog, and get the girls on Monday, if I'm not back. And, honey, I'm going to hit savings. Sorry, you know I'm on my own this time. You're going to have to clear out your mom's place. We have to pay her rent this month and our finances are up shits creek.

What does that mean, shits creek?

Love, Rose—P.S. I can't get Mel, either. What are you two up to, anyway?

There was writing on the back of the note, and David flipped it over. Rose had scratched out a budget, divided into liabilities and assets. The assets side was short. The liability column ranged to the end of the page.

David took a pain pill with a glass of tepid tap water. He headed for the bedroom. Dead Meat followed him down the hall. The dog paused in front of the girls' room and whimpered.

David stripped to his briefs and crawled into bed. He reached for the phone and turned it off. The last thing he remembered was a thud at the end of the bed and the smell of dog hair. Then he was asleep.

TWENTY-TWO

A THICK WET TONGUE RASPED ACROSS THE BACK OF DAVID'S hand. He opened one eye. Dead Meat stood beside the bed and wagged her tail. She barked, bouncing upward, and licked his face.

"Want to go out?"

The dog whined.

David scratched his cheek, grimacing at the heavy growth of black beard. The sun was setting. He had slept all day—no wonder he was hungry. But he felt better—almost no headache and amazingly refreshed. He checked his watch. Seven-thirty. *Friday,* not Thursday. He'd been asleep thirty-six hours.

Dead Meat whimpered.

David jumped out of bed. "You bet."

It took him an hour to feed the dog, clean up the business she'd done in the corner of the hall, and get something to eat. There were leftover enchiladas in the refrigerator, and he ate quickly. His head ached faintly, so he bypassed the beer and drank Coke. He showered, shaved, and called the hospital. Mel answered the phone in his room.

"What?"

"Mel? It's David. How you feeling?"

"How am I feeling? How are *you* feeling? People been calling me all day, trying to get to you. Where the hell you been?"

"You don't sound too good."

"I feel like shit."

"Rest, then."

"Be *glad* to, but I've had people calling and dropping in, looking for you."

"Who?"

"A Sergeant Biller, for one. She sounds sexy."

"She thought you were pretty cute, too, lying like a hero on the stretcher."

"Oh, yeah?"

"She took charge of the scene," David said. "She got anything?"

103

"Puzzle's BMW was rigged with shytin 4."

"What's shytin 4?"

"Relieving you of your BMW."

"Huh?"

"Kind of stuff the drug lords use."

"So it wasn't an Elaki sanction?"

"Hardly. Oh, hell. Listen, David, somebody wants to haul me off for tests."

"I'll be in to see you tomorrow."

"I want out of here tomorrow."

"What's your doctor say?"

"Something like fat chance. Screw her. First thing in the morning, I'm out of here."

It was full dark by the time David made the outskirts of town. A large drop of rain smacked the windshield of the car. It took another twenty minutes to get to Fiori Avenue. The wind blew, rocking the car, but the rain did not come. David pulled over and studied the map Judith Rawley had drawn. The disks were hidden in a traffic control box on the third floor of the parking structure. David paid the auto box and drove to level C.

He pulled to the far right of the south side. Thunder echoed and rain splashed down. David got out of the car, hunching his shoulders against the splatter of droplets that blew in through the open sides of the structure. Runnels of water snaked across the concrete. He took a flashlight from his car and glanced over his shoulder. Level C was empty except for a Jeep parked at the far end. He walked along the south wall, shining the light.

Someone had been there ahead of him. The control box hung open—lock smashed, digitals hacked apart. And the only other person who knew about the box was Judith Rawley.

David ran back to the car. He jerked the door open and grabbed the radio. His hand shook.

"Lieutenant. It's Silver."

"Yeah, Silver. Where the hell you been?"

"I need a patrol car sent to the Lindale Building on Grant. It's an old tobacco warehouse." He got in the car, started the engine, and accelerated, going too quickly around the curve. He pushed the priority button. "No sirens . . . quiet approach. She lives on the third floor. Tell the officers to approach with extreme caution, we have a possible alpha bravo four. I'll be there in twenty minutes."

"Acknowledge, Silver. I'll get dispatch."

David bypassed the computer control and smashed the accelerator to the floor. The engine strained and the car spurted forward.

TWENTY-THREE

DAVID MADE GRANT BOULEVARD IN THIRTEEN MINUTES. THE rain was still coming down hard. His stomach sank when he saw the patrol car pulled up in front of the warehouse. The car's emergency lights made blue and red streaks on the shiny wet pavement.

Idiots.

He pulled his gun, gave the fingerprints time to register. The light on the barrel glowed green. The only time a cop got shot with his own weapon was when he did it himself. Which meant about ten officers shot themselves in the foot each year, and four or five stuck a barrel in their mouth.

There were lights on in Judith Rawley's apartment. With any luck, she'd be making lemonade for the uniforms.

David got out of his car, leaving the door ajar. Rain pelted him and ran in rivulets down his face and neck. He glanced once over his shoulder and scuttled across the sidewalk, trying to keep watch in all directions. He wished Mel were there to cover his back.

The bottom of the stairwell was tracked with muddy footprints. He heard a shot, and the sound of someone running. He backed into the corner of the landing, gun ready. Silence.

He looked for the smoke detector, spotting the telltale grid on the side of the wall. It would be good to know how many people were up there, and the detector should have kept track. What was that access code? Seven J something . . .

Someone shouted, a woman screamed, and gunfire echoed in the stairwell. David ran up the stairs. Two weapons, he decided. Maybe three. He heard a clatter and thump and stepped back.

A man rolled down the stairs, head first. He had curly black hair, a grimacing, beard-shadowed face, and a blood-spattered uniform. His left foot caught between the posts of the rail and he stopped falling. A runnel of dark blood dripped down to the next step.

David bent over him and saw the eyes glaze into a death stare. David went up quietly, stopping when he heard voices.

"You listen to *me*, bitch."

The door to Judith Rawley's apartment was ajar.

"We got no time no more. Your Silver is dead, he got blown up, and those disks weren't where you said."

David heard the sound of flesh hitting flesh, and a low animal wail. The skin on his back tightened and chilled.

Slow or fast?

"Nothing in the safe deposit box, and nothing on Fiori Avenue. So what? Vern move them again? Could be you hid them somewhere. Thought you might make a little money, babe? C'mon, sweetie." The man's voice was low, almost caressing. "I don't want to cut up your face."

David kicked the door open.

The couch had been slit—the foam cushions pulled out and slashed. The cabinets had been emptied, and the kitchen was strewn with broken dishes. The work station was a ruin of torn paper, splintered wood, pens, pencils, splattered paint. A uniformed cop, her blond braid dark with blood, lay tangled with another body.

Judith Rawley was tied to a chair.

A large man in slacks and a red sport shirt hunched over her. He straightened when he saw David, a slow smile spreading across his face.

"Police!" David steadied his aim. Point-blank range. Why was the guy smiling?

"Get away from her!" David kept moving, looking around. "Move it, *now*, away from her!"

Judith's eyes were dark and vacant, no flicker of recognition or relief. Her mouth was slack, and the jagged edge of a broken tooth trailed blood and saliva that dribbled down her chin.

"I said get away from her!"

David glanced around the apartment. Was it just the two men—the body on the floor, tangled with the cop, and the guy smiling at him? He resisted the incredible urge to look over his shoulder.

The man's hand was moving. David pulled the trigger.

It took a second for David to comprehend that the gun had *not* gone off, a hole had *not* opened in the man's chest, the man had *not* fallen over dead. He clicked the trigger three more times while the man smiled.

It was an engaging smile. The man was not bad-looking—blond-haired, blue-eyed. There were dark splatters on his shirt and pants—bloodstains. He had a straight razor in his right hand. He unfolded it slowly and stood behind Judith Rawley.

In his mind, David knew exactly what to do, how fast he would have to move. He lunged forward, knowing that the body did not respond with the speed of thought, but hoping he would be fast enough anyway.

Judith Rawley didn't flinch when the blond man tilted her head back and put the razor to her throat.

"No!"

The man's wrist snapped sideways and a red zigzag arced across the white flesh. Judith's eyes widened and she made a choking gurgle.

David rammed his fist and his gun at the killer's belly. The man arced and turned like a dancer, out of range before David could connect. He crouched, balancing on the balls of his feet, the bloodstained razor ready in his right hand.

David backed away, circling. The man made a tentative swipe. David jumped backward, feet crunching broken glass. He picked a chunk of foam cushion off the floor.

The comforting notes of a siren filled the air.

The man swiped again and David held the cushion up to deflect the blow. It was a feint. The man's hand whipped down and across, ripping through David's shirt and lightly grazing the skin. Blood beaded in a line across his belly.

Memories echoed in his mind, and suddenly he was crouched in the Little Saigo tunnels, with no place to run.

"Come on, Jewboy. You want some of this?"

David shook the memories away and took a step sideways. The killer was impatient, he would move first. He would feint and lunge, and David would be ready. He looked behind him for some kind of weapon, and saw a lamp turned on its side. He snatched it up off the floor, wrenching the cord out of the floor plug.

David swung the lamp and the man took a step backward, then rushed forward, slashing at David's hand. David grabbed the man's forearm and yanked, spinning him till his back was to David's face. David kicked the inside of the man's knee. The man grunted and sagged. David wrapped the lamp cord around his neck, crossed the ends, and yanked hard.

The man choked and flopped, bringing the knife up and jabbing at David's eyes. David jerked back, and the cord slipped out of his hands. The man fell to his knees.

Feet pounded the staircase and a uniformed policewoman crouched in the doorway. She aimed and fired. The gun did not go off.

The blond man ran for the doorway.

"Watch the razor!" David shouted.

The man flicked his wrist, fast and vicious.

The cop screamed and covered her eyes. She stumbled backward, blood dribbling through her fingertips. There were footsteps and shouts from the stairwell.

The blond man kept going and David ran after him.

String was halfway up the stairs, pistol at the ready in his left fin, a knot of cops in protective padding right behind him.

"No shoot," String yelled. *"No shoot,* is Silver!"

The blond man whipped back around, tennis shoes skidding on the polished wood floor.

"Down!" String shouted.

David hit the floor.

Guns blazed in the stairwell—the deep rap of police assault rifles and the resonant boom of a heavy caliber pistol. String fell backward, tucking himself into a ball like a frightened porcupine. The blond man somersaulted down the steps behind him, flowers of blood blossoming on his back and neck.

"Police officer!" David croaked. "I'm a cop!"

"Hold fire!"

A shot echoed.

"I said *hold fire.*"

The hallway smelled like a firing range. David took a deep shaky breath, the floorboards cool against his cheek. The officer behind him whimpered. David crawled toward her, and pulled her blood-soaked hands away from her eyes.

She jerked and squirmed away.

"It's Silver," he said. "I'm a cop. You saved my life, you know that? You saved my life."

He took a handkerchief from his pants pocket.

A deep slit ran from the left side of the woman's forehead, across her eyes, the bridge of her nose, and her right cheek. David wondered if he would vomit.

"I know," he said. "It hurts."

Blood soaked through the handkerchief and ran between his fingers. He grabbed a chunk of foam and pressed the edge to the wound.

"No, be still. Be still."

Someone stood at his elbow.

"Hold this," he said. "Not over her *nose.* There, like that. Press hard."

He stood up and went to Judith Rawley. Her head, nearly severed, lolled backward over the chair. A bib of blood made a half moon under the torn windpipe. David was vaguely aware of the people who filled the room, making an ungodly clatter and mess in their wet shoes and vests. Judith Rawley would have to clean for days, and her work would go to hell. Someone tried to talk to him and he waved them away.

He crouched in front of Judith Rawley, carefully easing her head forward, fitting it back to her neck. Her eyes were dull and uncaring.

"Hold on," he said. "Hold on. We'll have an ambulance here any minute."

Her hair hung limply over her shoulder, soaking up the blood on her neck. Beautiful silky hair. David gently pushed it back behind her ears.

TWENTY-FOUR

DAVID WATCHED THE RAIN SPLASH INTO HIS CUP AND TURN THE coffee grey. He shivered, clenching his teeth so they wouldn't chatter. Raindrops ran in streams down his face and into the collar of his shirt.

There were too many lights. They hurt his eyes.

Two men helped String toward an ambulance. The Elaki moved slowly, stiffly.

"Listen," one of them said. "We ought to get a stretcher."

"No, is not the necessity."

"He get hit?" David asked.

"Naw." The attendant was grinning. "Recoil of the gun knocked him down the stairs. Too much caliber for an Elaki."

David frowned. "Where'd you get the gun, String?"

"The Mel has recommended it."

"*Mel* told you to use it?"

The Elaki swayed. "The recommendation was to practice first, but there was not the time. Is good gun. Works the job."

"How'd you get here, String?"

"I was—"

"Just a coincidence, String? You show up at the restaurant, and Puzzle gets killed. You show up here, and Judith gets killed."

A shadow damped the lights and Halliday stood close to David.

"He was at the precinct, David, when your call came through. Doing reports he said you asked for."

"I have the trouble getting computer to accept the voiceprints, and I—"

"He rode with me," Halliday said. He looked at the medic. "He hurt bad?"

"A lot of soft tissue damage. Painful. He'll be stiff and sore a few days."

"Take care of him." Halliday took David's arm. "Detective Silver and I appreciate your assistance, Mr. String." He nodded and led David away, guiding him up under the eaves of the warehouse.

"David, are you all right?"

"Yeah." David pulled his arm free. "Fine, Roger."

Two ambulance attendants maneuvered a stretcher toward an emergency van. Judith Rawley's hand slipped out from under the sheet and flopped with the bounce of the wheels.

"For Christ's sake, Roger, they're getting her wet. Can't they even . . ."

Halliday took David's arm and walked him away from the warehouse.

"Come on, I'll drive you home."

"I don't want to go home! I want to know why our guns didn't work. *Theirs* did. Ours are the ones supposed to be field proof! And why—"

Halliday stopped and looked at him. David had a flash, suddenly, of hospitals, psychiatrists, departmental counseling. He remembered Millicent Darnell, crying softly while the EMTs hauled her away.

"Come on, David. Go on and get in the car. We can clean up the details later."

David got in.

"I'll take you home to Rose." Halliday slammed the car door. David felt like a child. Halliday got in on the other side, shaking drops of rainwater off his coat onto David's knees.

"Why don't you punch in the directions to your house. You live pretty far out, don't you?"

"Not my house." David put in the address of his mother's apartment. "Kellam Street. About a twenty-minute drive." He clenched his fists and stared at the floor.

Kellam Street was quiet, rain-sweet, and dark. The streetlight in front of Lavinia's building was out. Halliday watched David through the open window.

"You sure this is where you want to be?"

"Yeah." David glanced over his shoulder. "Too far to go home tonight. I'll crash here."

He headed up the sidewalk, knowing that Halliday watched him until he was inside the building.

Her initials were still on a brass plate next to the door. LHS— Lavinia Hicks Silver. David punched in the access codes.

He paused in the doorway. Rain shone on the windows, and a streetlight cast a glint of yellow into the room. He switched on a light, startled, as always, by the stark emptiness of his mother's home. The floors were wood, the walls white. There were no pictures, no curtains. The living room held one chair, a footstool, and a round wood table with a book on it.

David walked across the floor, footsteps echoing in the emptiness, and stood in the doorway of her bedroom. A large wardrobe stood against the wall. The bed was narrow, an antique iron bedstead, made up with a spotless white cotton bedspread. A white afghan was folded at the bottom.

There was nothing else in the room—no knickknacks, no pictures of grandchildren, no shoes under the bed.

David opened the wardrobe and inhaled the scent of his mother. It was not perfume he breathed, his mother could not bear such things. It was simply the smell of the sturdy wood dresser, the cotton sweaters, and the offbeat tang of despair.

David closed the wardrobe and went back into the living room. He ran a hand along the wall, looking for the scar where his mother had hammered a steel hook and anchored her rope.

The living-room light had been burned out the night he found her. He had walked through the doorway into the darkness, startled by the kneeling silhouette. A car had driven by, the headlights illuminating her bowed head, glinting on the soft white silver of her hair. A burst of loud music had come from the car's radio, then the headlights had snapped away, the music receding, leaving David alone in the dark.

And then, after a stone silent moment of paralysis, he had lifted her from the floor, and yanked the rope, ripping away a chunk of dry wall. Even as he had checked for heartbeat, pulse, and respiration, his mind had ticked coldly, noting the signs of advanced death, the small blood vessels in his mother's eyes that had bled when the rope compressed her neck.

He hadn't noticed the wound on her left wrist, a scalping of the delicate inner skin over the heavy blue veins. She had done it herself, just before she died, the razor blade left in the bathroom sink in a dried gob of flesh and brown blood.

The coroner had looked at the wound and turned a startled face to David, before the professional mask shuttered the man's emotions. He'd known David for years—they'd met over numerous corpses. He would not have connected David's mother to Little Saigo.

But the coroner had seen too many other wounds like it—some self-inflicted, some not—not to recognize the implication.

Lavinia had not wanted to die bearing a toogim, the stamp of Little Saigo, that had grown so deeply into her skin that she'd severed a nerve to get it out. Wearing a toogim fashioned to match her body chemistry had been a matter of survival in Little Saigo, identifying her as made, a do-not-touch sign, putting her under the protection of Maid Marion. One had a toogim from Marion, or a tattoo from the tunnel rats, or the chances of being robbed, beaten, and murdered went up exponentially.

Even children wore them, though David hadn't. Lavinia had been adamant that he would never be marked, convinced that such a stamp would keep him from rising above Little Saigo into Saigo proper.

He had argued that *not* having one made his life dangerous. She told him to restrict his movements, and said there were worse things than death.

David had been shocked by his mother's suicide, but not surprised. He had seen it hit her before. One moment, placid, accepting; the next, overwhelmed with depression so heavy she would sink in a chair and not move for hours.

He had gone over the apartment carefully, but he hadn't been able to find the discarded talisman. Even now, she would see he didn't have one.

Packing her things would not take long. It was time to let the apartment go.

David went into the kitchen. He opened the cabinet over the sink and took out a white metal box—white, white, always white. In the box were all the papers his mother kept—recipes, a will, bank numbers, keepsakes. There were three letters his father had written her, a picture he had drawn of a horse, and a thick bundle of handwritten recipes.

David thumbed through the box, finding a banded packet of checks. There were a lot of them, two thick inches of them, all dating from the Little Saigo years. Lavinia Hicks Silver from Ruth Silver, six thousand dollars. Lavinia Hicks Silver from Ruth Silver, seven hundred dollars.

David blinked, unsure that what he was seeing was real.

All those years she had told him they were abandoned—his father's people didn't want them, she had none of her own. And all the while his grandmother had sent checks—as much, it seemed, as she could spare. Why had his mother never cashed them? Why all the years in Little Saigo, working and sweating, doing piecework for the factory pimp—sewing pockets onto jeans, scraping to get back out? Was it *pride*? Had the family made demands she could not meet? They had gone *hungry*. What incredible hurdle had his mother not been able to see her way around, what had made her put him to bed, hungry and cold and afraid, with help right there for the taking?

What kind of anger was this?

David jammed the checks back in the box, and a scrap of paper fell to the floor. It was an old piece of notebook paper, the kind he'd used in school. He picked it up. One one side was a recipe for chili; on the other an old budget. It reminded him of the note that Rose had left him. The figures were smaller, but they told the same story—more outgo than income.

He thought of Rose, juggling figures late at night. His mother had done the same, there in Little Saigo, probably as he slept. He wiped a tear away, but more came, and more, till he sat on the floor and let them come.

In his mind he saw Judith Rawley, and her long, long hair, and he knew she had a budget somewhere just like this one. He thought of his daughters, grown up, with daughters of their own, and he knew that they, too, would sweat figures into the night.

The floorboard, uneven in the groove, shifted under his thigh. David got his pocketknife out and pried a corner loose. It moved, but would not come up. He ran his fingertip around the edges. Recently glued. He ran the blade of the knife all around the edges of the loose board, slid the thin blade beneath the wood. The wood creaked, then popped up, snapping the knife blade in half.

A bloodstained dish towel had been jammed into the grey grit of dirt beneath the board. David unwrapped the cloth.

The toogim was circular, and about the size of a belly button. It was streaked with dried blood. David unbuttoned the cuff of his shirt sleeve, and pressed the toogim to his wrist. The talisman burrowed into his flesh. David held his breath, wondering if his body chemistry was a close enough match to his mother's.

Why, he wondered, did she kill herself now? She didn't need to worry about money anymore. Why did she give up now? He would never know. But he missed her; yes, he missed her very much.

And yes, he was his mother's son. The toogim began to glow— not the vibrant emerald green he had seen on his mother's wrist, but a dark, dreary, black-streaked shade of green.

It could only help. Like it or not, it was time to go back. Home to Little Saigo. Common wisdom said you could never go home. The thought comforted him.

TWENTY-FIVE

LITTLE SAIGO WAS A CARNIVAL IN THE SUMMER. DAVID HAD forgotten the color, the noise, the throb of life. The sidewalks radiated heat, and the air was full of dry, gritty dust. People spilled out of the tunnels, like flies at the moist mouth of a garbage can. Women and men wore red and purple and yellow. They yelled, laughed, cursed—all at the top of their lungs.

He shoved his hands in his pockets, wondering if the looks he got were too long, too knowing. He hadn't showered, shaved, or changed his clothes. The worse he looked, the more likely he'd blend in.

Three men played guitars next to the steps that led down to the main tunnel entrance. David leaned against a streetlight and listened. He was surprised by the surge of *good* memories. He and Gregorio Alonso had spent hours out front here, listening to the music, looking at the girls. God knows, some of them had been worth looking at.

He tried to remember the name of the girl who refused to tie her shoes. Maybelle? Yeah, Maybelle. How could he forget? She had let him put it all the way in before she got interested in that boy from Arlin Street. He had come afterward about a million times just thinking about it.

A little boy wandered up and stared at David. The child was dirty, his knees were covered with scabs, and he wore nothing but a sagging soiled diaper. He was a beautiful child, in spite of the dirt, and David smiled at him. The child cocked his head to one side, then toddled away. David felt dismissed.

Little Saigo had been excavated in the late 1990s during the hysterical skin cancer years, when sunscreens and sunblocks were found to be carcinogenic, as well as the cause of some nasty allergies. Little Saigo was intended to be an underground city for the elite, a grand scheme that called for elegant apartments clustered around a spiraling skylight that reached down five levels. There would be stores, restaurants, and apartments grouped near the light, and offices, artificially lit, in the farther recesses. Everything would be connected by a mag lev tram system, and nothing would show at ground level except a large glass bubble, and the various entrances to and from. But construction costs escalated, people settled to the simple, time-honored solution of protective clothing and intelligent exposure, and one by one the backers balked.

The original contractor persevered. Official AMA policy still held that no sunshine was the best sunshine. There would be people to buy. The telling complication came when hammering through the rock proved to be three times as expensive as estimated. The contractor disappeared halfway through construction, one step ahead of a posse of debt.

Little Saigo had been abandoned, though not for long. Soon it was infiltrated by the down and out, the people with their backs to the wall. Like David and his mother had been, after his father disappeared.

David studied all three entrances to Little Saigo. He could use the main one, of course, where the men played their guitars. Might as well throw money in the air, he'd get about as much attention. The east entrance looked like the new teen hangout. That left the south tunnel—and the hummers.

There were, of course, countless small ways in and out, some of them secret ones leading into buildings miles away. But the odds of meeting somebody you didn't want to meet were higher there, and it would be easy to get lost. It would have to be the hummers.

The streetlight over his head lit up, though it wasn't dark yet. David edged past the sidewalk, into the weedy dirt field that would take him to the south tunnel. A scrawny tiger-striped cat approached him. David stopped and held out his hand. The cat veered left and ran away.

David, his hand still out, crouched and listened. He could already hear the slow, heavy murmurs.

It was dark in the tunnel, and he had to duck to get in. The bare flesh of his arms puckered with chill bumps. He had forgotten how cool it was inside, the temperature a steady fifty-three degrees.

The humming was soft but intense, and though David could see little in the thick darkness, he could feel the press of people crouched close, lining both sides of the arched rock walls. They could not be unaware of him, in the middle of the tunnel, temporarily blind and very out of place; but there was no ripple of that knowledge in their song.

He had worked with the hummers only once, knowing his mother would make him sorry if she found out. Once had been enough—back-straining, mind-numbing labor. Huge piggyback freight trucks pulled up at the south entrance, and merchandise was passed down the line of hummers to the armed-to-the-teeth tunnel rats.

Sometimes there were mysterious shipments from unmarked trucks manned by heavily armed drivers. Other times there were donations from the city, or the Salvation Army, or food from the community kitchen. Businesses often sent their surplus, and took an inflated donation off on their tax returns.

And after the merchandise was delivered down to the rats, each hummer got their packet of choice. Yammers, a hard, down-pulling pill; dolpins, endorphins of happiness in a syringe; Jackie, a box of Jack Daniel's; or the grub bag, which was food, and David's packet of choice.

One of the hummers had opened a box, the night that David worked the wall. David had held his breath, terrified a tunnel rat would see and shoot them all. The man had not seemed disappointed to find a gross of lavender hair nets. He had put one on his head, stuffed a handful in his shirt, then passed the box on down. Three other hummers had furtively helped themselves.

Working as a hummer was step one into the province of the tunnel rats—dangerous, when he and his mother had already cast their lot with the Maid. The work was mindless and the pay a pittance. Tunnel rats were volatile, some of them hard-core sociopaths, capable of killing on a whim.

But the main reason he hadn't gone back was the smell.

David put his handkerchief over his nose.

The humming swelled and rose around him. His vision adjusted to the blue-purple darkness, and he could see the hopeless eyes and twisted mouths of the people who lined the walls. Some of them, he knew, never left their place on the wall, afraid to miss a shipment, and a chance at their packet of choice.

A breeze wafted through the tunnel, carrying the hot oily smell of exhaust mingled with the human muskiness of sweat and urine. David got a light from his pocket and focused it to a thin point of reddish illumination.

He walked.

The hummers lined the tunnel for almost half a mile. No sunlight for these tired faces—the wind would suck them dry. Their music rolled over him in loose easy waves. It was a spiritual, a chant, a litany. His blood pulsed with each wail of music and he thought of a beehive. Did the humming join the people on the wall into one central intelligence? Did it share pain, spread pain, relieve pain?

David turned a corner and edged into a blessedly silent section of tunnel. The turns were familiar—he could get where he was going if he didn't think too much, and trusted to the worn grooves of memory and instinct. The tunnel got narrow, and he had to stoop. The passages had not seemed so tight before, but he had been a child, then, and smaller. The path ought to intersect with a main tunnel very soon.

He was afraid, here in the darkness, he could not be anything else. He had seen things, in the tight, twisted passageways. Though he had been a child, watching with an imperfect understanding, there had been a sure sense of menace, wrongness, vulnerability.

He had been stalked in these tunnels. He had run, sobbing, up and down the passageways, and been ashamed of the flight. Would his father have run away? Was he dead because he had *not* run away?

Awash as he was in memories of flight, it was no surprise to hear the sliding scuffle of a footstep. David paused, and heard it again—no memory this. The way ahead was clear, and David saw himself running, shrinking smaller and smaller, until he became, again, the frightened child.

David stopped, and the footsteps stopped. He turned around and pointed the red tip of his light into the tunnel behind him.

Suiters. They stalked their prey outside the tunnels and in, and had forged an uneasy alliance with the Maid.

Their dress was modeled after one they called First Victim. Funny, he'd thought, the first time he had seen them. They wore identical black slacks, vests but no shirts, and suit coats with the sleeves neatly removed. Their hair was long and banded back, and their shoes were shiny black lace-ups. They rouged their lips and powdered their faces, and there were three of them there in the darkness, watching.

He would not run, though his knees trembled, and his stomach was tight, and he smelled his own sweat and fear. He could not, would not, be the frightened child again.

One of them smiled, the one in the middle, his red lips a parody of friendliness. His white-powdered face was luminous in the darkness and moving slowly closer. David braced himself, legs apart. Marion tolerated the suiters, but just barely, and such things could always change. David lifted his left arm, showing the glowing toogim on his wrist. Sweat welled on his face and neck.

The suiter stopped. David laid a hand on his gun. He waited and the suiters watched him, making no move to come closer. David backed away finally, deeper into the dark tunnel. He turned a corner, and passed out of sight. His heart was pounding, his hands slippery. He drew his gun and leaned against the wall, listening. No one followed. He wiped sweat off his forehead with the back of his hand, then turned the penlight to the face of his watch.

He was going to be late. He hoped Maid Marion would wait.

TWENTY-SIX

DAVID CREPT OUT OF THE BACK TUNNEL INTO A MAIN BRANCH.
Violet light glowed in a tube along the wall. Maid Marion was
waiting for him.

She was an old woman—had been old when he was a child.
Her skin had faded from black to grey, and her hair was white and
wooly. Her eyes were brown, the whites yellowed and bloodshot.
Her striped cotton dress hung loosely from her shoulders, and
David realized she'd lost weight. She turned her head in his
direction, though he crept up quietly enough, and her sightless
eyes stared past his left shoulder.

"Do I know you?" Her voice sent memories shivering up and
down his spine. "It's David Silver, isn't it? Boy, it's been a long
time. Hello, David Silver."

"Good to see you, Marion."

"Now *hear* your voice, son, *hear your voice*. I can see you're
grown and been places. Come here, let me touch you."

Her bony hand stretched toward him and he ducked closer. Her
fingertips, dry and cool, swept over his head like a summer breeze,
flowing to the contours of his cheeks, lips, and eyes.

"You growing a beard, boy?"

"No ma'am."

She sank to the cool stone floor. "Tell me, David. 'Bout yourself."

He glanced over his shoulder.

"We're safe, hon. Nobody bother Marion."

That, at least, was true.

"Be comfortable, David Silver. Sit down now."

He sat beside her, cross-legged. She sat with her knees up,
covering them over with the loose skirt of her dress. The stone
floor was cool. He thought of the tons of dirt pressing over their
heads. The walls were damp. He could hear a trickle, somewhere
down in the tunnel, where water wore its way down.

He talked about Rose, and his girls, and the hurt animals they
raised. She liked hearing about the farm, so he closed his eyes

and told her how the grass smelled in the heat, how cool the barn was when a breeze flowed through the cracks, and how his children used a pile of field stone for a fort. And as he talked, he could see his girls, sitting under the ash tree with a canteen and a sack lunch. In his mind he hugged them close, and smelled the hay smell of their fine baby hair.

Marion listened closely, and he knew what he said would be woven into her stories. Marion snagged everything and everyone who came her way, feeding on their lives, weaving them into her master work. She recorded her tales on tape at night, leaving her door open for those who would gather close and listen.

Marion tapped his arm.

"What about *her*? You haven't mentioned your mama. She still got that limp? I always feel bad on that. I set that ankle best I could, but it was broke worse than anything I seen."

"Doesn't matter. She's dead now."

"What happened?"

"She hung herself."

Marion patted David's hand. "Bless your heart, son. Bless your heart."

"She left her soul down here, Marion."

"Naw, David. Your mama's troubles come before Little Saigo."

"This place didn't help."

"That I grant you. How was she livin' when she died?"

"How?"

"Where she live? What she working on?"

David scratched the stubble of beard on his chin. "She was peaceful enough, after she left the bank. She had money. But she lived in empty rooms. Not even curtains on the windows."

"You gone have to quit being mad at her, David. She couldn't help what she was."

David rubbed his thumb on the stone floor.

"I can pay for information, Marion," he said at last. "It's in the police budget."

"So you're a cop, now, are you, boy? Offer this old woman money?"

"I—"

"But that's not how it work, David. You're not supposed to pay, till you hear what I say. No cash from the man, till you show him your hand."

David put his head in his hands and closed his eyes. "The offer was poorly worded, but honestly meant."

"Ain't nothing you got, tempt Marion. What you need, son?"

"Something's going on down here."

Marion laughed, and laughed hard. "Something going on here? You think so?"

"Something new, I mean. There are people watching this place, different people, deals going down, cops disappearing . . ."

"Funny you should say that."

"What?"

"Cops disappearing. There's folks gone missing, David. More than a few. And talk about midnight abduction."

"You're sure?"

"Down here, David, folk don't need to make things up."

"Give me details."

She leaned her head back against the wall. "People don't show up, who should be showing up, made people, under the right protection. And we all looking over our shoulders." She cocked her head sideways. "Money. It be cropping up in places it shouldn't."

"Drug deals?"

"You said new. That's not."

"Anybody see anything?"

"Girl I know."

"Can I see her?"

"Not likely. Real hard to reach. Some of what she says is true, the rest in her head. She comes to listen when I work at night, even though she hangs out with the rats. Moves back and forth. An odd one. She asked for my help, while back. Said folks was getting into her mind and stealing her thoughts."

"Schizo?"

"Surely is. I told her I'd make her a magic box—something to protect her thoughts. She the one told me what happen to Paxon."

"Who's he?"

"A guy. Hangs around, pimping a little and such. This girl, she says that folks came into the tunnel and took Paxon. She saw it. And it may be true. He ain't been seen."

"*Folks*, Marion? Where did it happen?"

"She didn't say."

"How many? Men? Women?"

"I didn't ask."

"But how—"

"I don't know."

"You know everything else."

"That's gratitude."

"I need to see this girl."

"Luck with that."

"You know where she lives?"

"I got an idea."

"Where?"

"It'll cost you."

"Name it."

"Not money, hon. You got to deliver that box. Think you can do that for me?"

"My pleasure."

TWENTY-SEVEN

THE MAGIC BOX WAS MADE OF PINE AND SANDED TO A SOFT fine sheen. David tucked it under his arm and walked deeper into the tunnels. He headed toward the southeast section—the oldest part of Little Saigo, and the most dangerous. He would slip in from the back.

There were mag levs running through the southeast section. He remembered the publicity about them—"the future of transportation." England, with help from Germany, had one of the first major mag lev railways, and had ditched them after the tragic maiden voyage of the British Charleton Lines, much the same way hydrogen aircraft had been abandoned after the Hindenburg disaster. Mag levs became a byword for untrustworthy technology.

The speeds had been incredible.

The Little Saigo contractor had planned a network of mag lev cars throughout his underground city, and had already installed roadbeds in the southeast area. They still worked, in sections, though there were parts of the roadbed that no longer functioned. What did function was controlled by the tunnel rats, who considered southeast Little Saigo, as well as a piece of every organized racket in the city, a particular piece of their turf.

Naomi Chessfield was a tunnel rat.

David smelled cigarette smoke. A metallic voice echoed through the tunnel, sounding austerely hostile.

"The part you have installed is not the proper fitting. You need part number—"

"Look, stupid, it's a rubber belt, that's all, it doesn't have to be part number X47 series 12. It fits, it works, it's safe!"

"Overrule."

"Why?"

"Replacement with any part other than the designated part is a safety violation."

"I got to go for a ride. I *got* to feel the wind, and I'm going to—"

David heard the clank of metal just as he turned a corner in the passage. A woman was hunched over a mag lev car, the side panel exposed for repair. A shower of sparks spewed from the panel.

The woman jumped back.

"Son of a *bitch*. You do that again and you're scrap."

She sat on the edge of the mag lev car and lit a cigarette.

He had expected someone older—some ragged unkempt hag. Naomi Chessfield was dressed in skintight black jeans and green leather boots. She wore a brown leather vest, with no shirt, and her skin gleamed whitely. Her hair was short, brown, and feathered like the plume of a bird. The grim visage of a rat was tattooed on her left shoulder. David tried not to stare at the swell of her breasts over the top button of the vest.

She squinted, took a drag of the cigarette, and kicked her left leg up and down, hitting the metal car with her heels. She put her face in her right hand, the left hand hanging loose, cigarette clamped between long, supple fingers. She sobbed once, laughed bitterly, and sobbed again.

David approached softly. She looked up suddenly, muscles tense.

"Hi." David spread his arms and held out the box. "I have something for you."

She cocked her head, watching him.

"This is from Marion. Maid Marion. It's your . . . magic box."

The cigarette burned between her fingers. David waited.

"May I hand it to you?"

She nodded jerkily.

He took a few steps toward her, but she held up a hand when he was two feet away. He stopped. She reached for the box. Her hands shook.

David put the box in her left hand, and took her right hand gently, placing it over the top of the box. His thumb came too close to the cigarette and he jerked it back.

"Sorry," she said. She took a final drag, her cheeks going hollow. Greyish-blue smoke drifted in front of her face. She stubbed the cigarette out against the wall, adding to a score of other black burn marks. She put the rest of the cigarette in her pocket.

"How's it work?" she asked.

David opened his mouth, then shut it.

"Well, it's . . . it's magic."

"Yeah?"

He thought for a moment. "Are there any directions?"

She looked on the sides of the box, and along the bottom. "Don't think so." She opened the lid about an inch. The hinge squeaked and she peered inside. "Nope."

"I'm sorry," David said. "Marion just asked me to deliver it."

"I can ask her. Later on."

The silence settled around them.

"You want a cigarette?" she asked.

"No. Thank you." What would Mel do with this one, he wondered.

She smiled and patted the side of the mag lev car. "Wish I could give you a ride. You'd like that, wouldn't you?"

He nodded.

"This one doesn't work. This stretch of track bed's gone wrong. That's the difference between high tech and low tech, right?" She swung her legs. "Low tech, things start to go bad, it just doesn't work as well. But high tech?" She patted the hood of the car. "This was made during the age of didactic machinery. It goes glitchy, and that's it. The whole thing comes to a stop."

He stepped away from her and sat down, his back against the wall. "Marion was telling me about people disappearing."

She nodded her head vigorously. "You know about that?"

"I'm interested." He shrugged. "Maybe these people just wandered off."

"That's a comfortable thought." She jumped off the car and paced in front of him. "But I saw them get somebody. Old Paxon. Nobody special, but he was harmless enough."

"Who, Naomi? Who came for him?"

"How'd you know my name?"

"Marion told me. I'm David Silver."

"A pleasure." She leaned down and shook his hand. "God, Silver, all this temptation and you look at my face?"

He grinned. "Tell me what happened to Paxon."

"Why do you care?"

"I'm a cop."

"A *cop*? From up there?" She waved a hand toward the surface. "What do you care what happens down here?"

"I come from down here."

"But you left."

"I missed the sunshine."

"It's crazy up there."

"You feel safer down here?"

"Things that can get you down here, I can handle. But when the others come after me—that's dangerous. They haven't found me down here. You're right though, I do miss the sunshine. The heat. The rain. Can't get a good taco down here, either."

"That's beginning to be true up there, too. You never leave?"

"Not too often. It's dangerous. Sometimes . . . I don't know, it doesn't seem worth it anymore, and I want to go back to the surface. But I can't do that, can I? You can't give up. You have to hang in, hope for better times. Someday, maybe I can go back, live like everybody else."

"You think that's what happened to Paxon? You think he went back to the surface?"

"Paxon went to the surface all the time. He was a pimp. Worked the non-union girls and boys for Johns who like it with Little Saigo mole rats. You'd be surprised how many do."

"Not really."

"You don't like pimps?"

"No."

"I think some of them are hooked on the illegal part. And with naked mole rats, it's anonymous." She frowned. "Oh, hell, you being a cop, I probably shouldn't tell you this. But it can't hurt Paxon now."

"What exactly happened to him?"

"It looked like a meet. Set up beforehand."

"With a man or woman?"

"You know, I couldn't tell? Usually you can get it from the walk. Anyway, they talked, then Paxon slumped down. I heard a whistle, and two guys came out of nowhere, and hauled him off. I heard one of them say . . . um, 'last one tonight.' " She sat down beside him. "What you think is going on? 'Cause Paxon, he was with the rats. And he was protected."

David shrugged. "You get much of a look at anybody?"

"Not much. They were ratty-looking. Dirty. Like they were dressed down especially for Little Saigo. Clothes didn't go with the walk."

David was suddenly aware that she smelled clean and scrubbed, and he was in need of a shower. He handed her a card. "This is my name and number." He took a pen and wrote his home phone number on the back. "You see anything else, or remember something, give me a call, okay?"

"Sure, David."

"Here." He handed her a few bills. "You need this?"

Her hand hesitated over the bills. "I can't. You already brought me my box."

"Take it." He got up. "Take care of yourself."

"I will."

He remembered the wistful sob, the bitter laugh. "Look, why don't you come out with me? I know somebody who can help with your problem."

"I got people after me up there." She stood up and dusted off the back of her pants. "You're nice, okay, but you got no idea how powerful they are."

"Try me."

She shook her head. "You're like a baby who kicks his foot, sees the curtain move, and thinks he caused it. Believe me, you don't know these people. I do."

"You aren't what I expected," he said sadly.

She cocked her head sideways, her eyes large and serious.

"If you change your mind," David said. "If you need anything. Call me, okay?"

"Okay."

He glanced back, once, over his shoulder. She clutched his card and waved it at him.

TWENTY-EIGHT

DAVID HUNCHED FORWARD IN THE SEAT OF THE CAR, HIS WRIST resting loosely on the steering wheel. The windows were down and warm air swirled through his hair. He couldn't get Naomi Chessfield out of his mind.

A light flashed on the dash.

"Direction, David Silver."

"Leave me alone."

"Random pattern. Will query again in fifteen minutes."

If he didn't want to think about Naomi, there was always Judith Rawley.

He didn't want to go home; the house was empty without the girls. Maybe he should go to the office. He didn't like working at night, didn't like the way his desk lamp threw shadows over the dark and silent precinct. But tonight he craved the familiarity of his desk, his files. Peace, quiet, and no interruptions.

He started to turn the car around, then didn't. There was no guarantee that he would be alone. Lieutenant Halliday was frequently there, working late. He would go home.

The bullfrog was in the driveway, waiting like a malevolent Buddha. He drove around it without stopping to argue. There were lights on all over the house, and the girls' night-light glowed behind the curtains. Haas's Jeep was on the side of the drive. David put his car in the barn, and avoided looking at the empty rabbit cage.

The back porch light flicked on. The door was unlocked. Rose was in the kitchen, making coffee. The smell of it warmed him.

"David?"

She had her back to him. Her hair was braided, and loose strands curled around her ears and the nape of her neck. He put his arms around her and rested his chin on her shoulder.

"David?"

"No. Haas."

"You shrank then."

He bumped his hips into her back. "Not where it counts."

"Be *careful*, the coffee's hot."

129

She put the pot down and squirmed around to face him. He kissed her hard, pressing her back into the sink.

"God, I missed you, too. David, stop. No, listen. *David.*"

He stepped back. "What?"

"I found . . . is that *blood* on your shirt?"

David had a flash, suddenly, of Judith Rawley slumped in a chair.

"You look awful." Rose ran her knuckles across his cheek. "Are you growing a beard?"

"Maybe."

She put a hand behind his head and pulled him down for a kiss. "I hope you're all right. I forgot to worry about you."

"Ouch." He took her hand away.

"What is ouch?" Haas walked into the kitchen. His khaki pants were mud-stained at the knees and along one thigh. His shirt was torn, and his cheek bruised and scraped raw.

David's jaw tightened. "Rose, are you all right?"

"*She* is fine," Haas said. He sat at the table and put his chin in his hand. He winced, and moved the hand away.

David wrapped ice cubes in a dish towel, ran it under water, and handed it to Haas. Haas took it wordlessly and held it to the right side of his jaw. Rose put a cup of coffee in front of him.

David shook his head. He took the coffee mug and tipped it into the sink, watching the dark liquid steam, pool, and run down the drain. He poured a heavy slosh of Wild Turkey into the cup and handed it to Haas, along with two aspirin he rummaged out of the cabinet over the stove.

"*Thank* you." Haas sighed deeply.

"What *is* ouch?" Rose touched David's head again.

"Long story. Let me kiss the girls, and I'll—"

She took a gulp of coffee. "Ooo, *shit*, that's hot. David, listen." She grabbed his arm. "I was right. They're using animals, but Jesus, that's not all . . . how did you get a lump on the back of your head?"

"Let me see the kids—"

"Sit. The girls are asleep, anyway, look at them later."

David sat at the round wood table. "Mel and I were in an explosion."

"You have concussion?" Haas asked. "I can see from the eyes."

"Mel?" Rose said. "I should have known he'd have something to do with this. Is he all right? Why didn't you call me? Oh, hell, you couldn't call me. I should go and see—"

David grabbed her wrist. "Rose. He's okay. Still in the hospital, but probably out tomorrow."

"But what happened?" Rose asked.

"Remember the Elaki I told you about? Puzzle?"

"Elaki?" Rose hopped up and put more coffee in her almost full cup. "Listen, David, the lab we got into was definitely an Elaki operation. We've got documentation, but not courtroom stuff. They're doing some kind of drug experimentation. God, it's infuriating, why anyone . . . David, you look really bad. When was this explosion?"

"A few days ago."

"That shirt looks like you washed it in a sink."

"I did."

Haas sighed deeply. "This conversation is most difficult to follow."

"Perhaps if my wife would let me finish a sentence—"

Rose leaned back and folded her arms. "You know, David, you're not the only one who's had a rough week. I almost got my butt fried, Haas and I are getting no backup—as a matter of fact, our people have pulled back entirely! You know how long I've been working for these—these idiots?" Rose shoved hair out of her eyes. "What I've risked?"

"We, Rose," Haas said. "What *we've* risked."

"What do you *mean*, you almost got fried?" David asked.

"*I* am the one who is fried," Haas said.

"David, you know you're not supposed to ask me stuff like that. Besides, you haven't told me about your explosion."

David spoke quickly, before she could go off again. "Puzzle's car was wired, and Mel and I—String too—we got caught when it went off. Mel's pretty banged up, bad laceration on his leg, some internal stuff they wanted to watch."

"And the Elaki?"

"Smeared across the sidewalk."

"String's dead?"

"No, Puzzle. String is fine. Too fine."

"Another dead Elaki," Rose said thoughtfully. She looked at Haas.

"Tell him," Haas said.

"Tell me what?"

"There isn't any connection with our Elaki and his Elaki," Rose said.

"Tell him anyway. He deals with them."

David sat back and folded his arms. Rose frowned.

"Talk, Rose." Haas's accent was thicker than usual. "And do not hop from point to point. I am very tired."

Rose took a gulp of coffee and curled her feet under her in the chair.

"The labs are Elaki connected, no doubt there. And they're not just using animals. They're using people."

David leaned forward. "People? What do you mean using?"

Rose threw up her hands. "What do you *think*?"

"In the labs," Haas said. "Experiment subjects."

David chewed his lip.

"You take it coolly enough," Rose said.

"You got any evidence? Hard evidence?"

"I am *sharing* information with you, David, against my better judgment, and I—"

"We screw it up," Haas said. "Got caught before we were finished. But is Elaki operation. There were high desks, no chairs. Elaki accommodation, if you will."

"Did you see any people there?"

"No. But we know they were there. Were signs unmistakable. We went through research results—saw them. Some kind of drug experimentation. We have tracked telespondence and linked to name Horizon."

"Project Horizon?"

"This means something to you, then?"

"How could it?" Rose said. "He's tracking a serial killer. Machete Man has nothing to do with this."

"What are you going to do?" David asked.

"I have a news connection."

"The press?"

"Best way to go. Nobody gets to drag their ass that way. They'll have to move quick."

"Look, Rose. There's a link here—with *my* Elaki. It looks like a drug connection. Dyer was in it somehow, and Dyer was vice."

"What are you saying, David?"

"I'm saying I don't want the whole world in on this till I figure what's up."

"I don't *believe* what I'm hearing. You accuse me time and again of worrying about animals more than people. It wasn't very nice, David, up at that lab. You want details, you want—"

"Blow it open now, and they'll just go underground, move the location, deny it all. You know how these things work, Rose."

"Oh, I *know*, David, I know. I did it for the DEA, year after bloody year, circling around and building a case and going after the people in charge. Meanwhile the victims get screwed right and left—that's why I left the business, David. I don't care about cases, prosecution, snagging the big perp. I go straight for *results*."

"She is upset," Haas said.

David bit back the reply that came to his mind.

"I told you we run into trouble. From the looks of things, maybe old enemy involved here. Not sure."

"I'm sure," Rose said.

"Is Santana, we think." Haas looked worried.

David was quiet a long while. He noticed a hole in the flooring. He would have to get a kit and grow it back together.

"Perspective, Rose," he said finally. "Give me some time. I'm asking you to trust me."

"No."

"Just no?"

"Okay, how about *fuck* no."

David slammed his coffee cup on the table. "You must have been fun to work with, in your DEA days."

Haas put his head in his hands. "Am going home." He stood up slowly and touched Rose's shoulder.

"Best to wait, you know this. Give him time." He headed for the back door, nodded at David, and went.

Rose didn't meet his eyes.

"There are people at stake this time, David. Don't drag your ass."

David leaned back in his chair. He should be grateful, he supposed, that Rose listened to somebody.

TWENTY-NINE

THE DOG WAS BARKING. DAVID ROLLED OVER AND GROANED. Dead Meat snarled—frantic, fearful. David opened his eyes. A light flashed across the bedroom window, then was gone.

"Rose?" he whispered.

He put out a hand in the darkness. No one was there.

The dog barked and whimpered. From the sound of it she was in the hall, outside the girls' room. David heard footsteps. No time to load the gun. He reached for the baseball bat under the bed.

The dog snarled and yelped, and David heard the high-pitched screams of his little girls. He ran, saw the flash of blade just as he reached the doorway, and dropped and hit the floor. He felt a swoosh of air and the blade sliced the space over his head.

The man was medium height, chubby—the details hard to make out in the gloom of the dark hallway. But David recognized him— he had seen his actions simulated time and time again, on the screen of his computer. Machete Man.

Why here? It made no sense. But he knew the man's next move.

The machete arced, and David rolled. His chest was bare and vulnerable, and sweat gathered under his arms. The blade chunked into the floor. Something soft hit his head, and a rain of stuffed animals came like scattershot from the girls' room. David looked up to the nightmare comedy of his daughters, clad in short nighties and T-shirts, throwing stuffed animals at Machete Man.

The dog snapped at Machete Man's ankles. A vicious kick sent her up against the wall. She yelped and snarled weakly. David grabbed the baseball bat and hit Machete Man below the knees. He went down, sliding on a pile of Legos that had spilled from a bin. But he was up again, quickly, and David realized he should have hit him on the shins. The man lifted the machete and swung.

The bedroom window shattered and Rose burst through the glass. Like magic, red streaks of blood blossomed across her arms, but she kept coming, and Machete Man whirled toward her, arcing the blade.

She twisted sideways and kicked, shattering Machete Man's elbow. He howled and the machete dropped and clanged on the floor. Rose reached for him, but her foot slipped on an open book, and she landed hard on one knee.

Machete Man ran. Rose was on her feet in an instant, but she was limping.

"*God* damn it."

David grabbed the baseball bat and went after them.

He heard the front door slam into the wall, and the pounding of footsteps. The security lights were up now, and the front lawn was bathed in brightness. Machete Man was moving, holding his shattered elbow with his good hand, breaking stride only once to look back over his shoulder.

Barefooted, unarmed, wearing a cotton T-shirt and a pair of grey sweats, Rose was oddly formidable. She wasn't limping now. Her legs, lean and sure, cycled with the kind of fierce grace and energy David had only seen in ball players running bases.

And she was gaining.

David ran hard. The grass was cool, and rocks pierced the calluses on the soles of his feet. A giant moth swooped in front of him, fluttering thin black wings. He waved it away. He tasted sweat on his upper lip. A cramp grabbed his side, but it was a small one and he kept going. They had to get the bastard before he slipped out of the light, into the darkness and the woods.

David saw Rose lunge, and he ran faster. She would need help holding him, but by heaven the monster was caught. Machete Man was a pawn. If they cracked him—and he *knew* he could do it—they would get their connections.

Rose slammed into Machete Man and brought him down. He landed hard on the broken elbow and his cry echoed with a peculiar animal intensity. Rose's movements were fast, practiced, graceful. She rolled Machete Man to his back, lifted his shoulders, took his left ear in her right hand, and jerked his head, hard, to the right. David heard the neck snap, saw the wide fearful eyes of the dead man. Rose sat back on her haunches, panting, Machete Man's head lying at an awkward angle in her lap.

David stared at her. The cramp in his side tightened and ached. Rose stared back, chest heaving, sweat shining on her face. The girls were crying, and their wails rode the air like the cry of small birds. David turned his back on Rose and went to the house.

THIRTY

THE KITCHEN WAS FULL OF BRIGHT LIGHT, RADIO TRANSMISsions, and people David didn't know. The floor was dirty, and getting dirtier. He saw lab people walk by, toting plastic bags full of Legos, stuffed animals, torn books. The air was acrid with the smell of the nano machines that had been unleashed in the girls' room. They had grown and picked up every molecule of evidence, and then been dispersed. No expense was being spared on this one.

The smell of the nanos mingled with the scent of rewarmed coffee and the lingering dinnertime aroma of garlic and tomatoes.

They would be forever, getting things cleaned up.

In spite of the racket, the girls were asleep, snug in his arms. His butt was numb; he was sitting at an angle. He shifted position carefully. Someone had thrown a big wool blanket over the lot of them, which mostly hid the fact that he was still in pajama bottoms.

David studied the round, smooth faces of his daughters. Their eyes were tightly shut, lashes long and dark and beautiful. Anything could happen to a child, and often did. He could understand Rose's cold fury, and envy her the satisfaction of breaking the killer's neck. But it was an indulgence they could not afford. There was more to this than Machete Man—much, much more.

What did the attack mean? Was it connected to the work Rose was doing, or had he just come after the cop on his heels? And, more importantly, would there be another?

He had lost the direct route to the answers when Rose had snapped the man's neck. He would lay awake at night, now, listening. When he tried to concentrate on the work, he would be jolted by visions of his daughters at the hands of killers wielding sharp blades with honed gleaming edges.

He avoided Rose's eyes, watching, instead, the paramedic swab the blood off her arms.

"That *hurts*."

"Don't wake the girls," David said coldly.

The medic gave him a quick, puzzled look. "Going to need to glue this one."

"Please don't use that stuff on me," Rose said. "It *itches*. Ouch."

"Sorry. Listen, it wasn't that long ago, they used to sew stitches in people."

"Tell me another one."

Mel walked into the kitchen, followed by Captain Halliday. Halliday studied Rose glumly. She looked small, perched on the edge of the chair, the men towering over her. Her eyes were wide and innocent.

"I'll be putting it down as self-defense," he said. He glanced at David, and David kept his expression bland.

Rose nodded. "Any questions now?"

She looked too young, David thought. Did killing leave no mark on her?

None visible.

Then he realized there *was* something different about her. It was an air of distraction, an intense preoccupation. The smiles were slow and forced, the eyes bland, emotionless.

So it was there, if you knew to look for it. And it bothered him, knowing he had seen that look about her before.

David shifted in his seat. Halliday was suspicious, but he was keeping it to himself. Machete Man's execution had been swift and professional. Halliday wasn't stupid.

"No questions right now." Halliday put a friendly hand on Rose's shoulder. "You've had enough for one night."

He was giving them time to get their stories straight, David decided. Unnecessary. They'd done that before the cops got within a mile.

Mel laughed. "Listen, Captain, anybody messing with Rose is the one going to be sorry."

Shut up, David thought.

"Hell, it's a wonder I survived growing up with her."

The wind chimes hanging outside the kitchen window tinged in the small breeze. The red pulse of an emergency flasher battered the window at regular intervals. The red swatch of light hit Lisa's face, and David eased her sideways in his lap, so that she would not be disturbed.

David was tired. Machete Man was dead, the case would be closed, and they hadn't scratched the surface. God damn Rose. She hadn't had to kill him. He wished everybody would leave. There was a lot he wanted to say to her.

A tall, slender man walked into the kitchen and Rose looked up.

"Haas!"

"You are all right?" Haas looked at David. "The children?"

"Bad scare, but not hurt."

Haas took a deep breath. He had cleaned the blood off his face, but the bruise was livid. He looked exhausted.

Halliday came into the room from the hall. He studied the bruise on Haas's face. "Who the hell is this?"

"I called him," Rose said. She turned her back on all of them, leaving Halliday openmouthed, and the medic dripping skin glue on the table.

"Look here, friend, this is a crime scene," Halliday began.

"He's here to see to the dog," Rose said. She took Haas's arm and pulled him out of the room.

Halliday stared after them. "Silver, maybe you better explain what *crime scene* means to your wife."

"Explain it yourself," David said. He stood up, staggering under the weight of his daughters. Mel took Kendra from him and followed him down the hall.

"Don't get pissed, David," Mel said. "Roger's trying to help you, in case you ain't figured it out. And he don't know Rose like you and me."

"Lucky Roger."

Mel's look was sharp and speculative.

"Put them in our bed," David said.

Haas and Rose were in the hallway, bending over the dog. Dead Meat whimpered and licked Haas's hand.

David nodded curtly, edging around them. His home looked so much the same, so intimately familiar, that the out-of-place things struck him all the harder—glass scattered over the girls' bedroom, coworkers going through the familiar routines in familiar surroundings, a surreal combination of work and home. No escaping this one.

Machete Man had crept down the hallway, stalking his daughters. David's shoulders jerked.

He laid Mattie and Lisa on the bed. Then he peered around the corner of the bedroom and watched. Haas was gentle and expert, but the dog whined weakly.

The blankets and sheets rustled as Mel tucked Kendra in beside her sisters.

"Listen, David, you better—"

"Shhh."

Mel crept quietly behind him and looked over his shoulder.

" . . . please, Haas." Rose was pulling on his jacket.

"We talk later. The dog I take home. I need to make the tests, but I think she will heal. And please, we call her Hildegarde. This 'Dead Meat' is not name for brave little dog."

"Thanks, Haas."

"Of course. Rosy, if you are right . . . if this is *Santana*—"

"I'm not sure. I'm not making sense of all this."

"And you're not going to," David muttered. "Now you killed my boy."

"What are you mumbling?" Mel asked.

"Shhh."

"You will need help," Haas was saying.

"Not on this one."

"*My* help, Rosy." Haas touched her cheek. "I . . ." He looked up and saw David and Mel peering around the corner. He grinned and touched Rose's shoulder.

David would have given a lot not to be wearing pajamas.

Haas smiled at him. "I will take Hildegarde here, and see to her for you. I am good vet for animals."

"She answers to Dead Meat."

"Hilde is much better name, David, do you not think?" The dog licked his hand. "Yes, she thinks so. Could I have a towel, please, to wrap her in?"

"Sure. Rose, where . . ."

"Rose," Haas said. "Go finish in the kitchen. You are bleeding on this dog. Surely David can get me what I need."

Rose headed for the kitchen, obedient twice on the same night. David went to the linen closet for an old towel. The baseball bat, unfortunately, was being tagged as evidence.

THIRTY-ONE

HAAS WAS GONE, AS WERE THE UNIFORMS, THE AMBULANCE, the medic, the ME, Machete Man's body. Della Martinas was browsing through the refrigerator. The sun was coming up, taking away the dark edge of the night and the nightmare. The kitchen window glowed with pink light. The wind chimes were still now. The house seemed quiet, empty. David wondered where Rose was.

Della unwrapped a foil package. "Umm," she said. She closed the refrigerator and picked up a pork chop, biting a hunk of meat off the side. "We got us a connection, Silver. Between Machete Man's victims."

David clenched and unclenched his right fist. "No good. Halliday will close the case."

"Don't think so," Della said. She took another bite of meat. "Hey, these are good. You grill these?"

"Yeah."

"Where's the beer?"

"Bottom right. Get me one."

She handed him a can, got one for herself, and rustled in the foil package for another pork chop. "We never have leftovers at my house."

"You got to cook it first."

Della wiped her fingers on a dish towel. "Don't you want to know what the connection is?"

Mel walked into the kitchen and helped himself to a beer. "What connection?" He took a large swallow and belched discreetly into the top of his fist. "What you eating, Della?"

She handed him a pork chop.

He bit into the edge and looked thoughtful. "These are good. You grill these, David?"

"What connection?" David said.

Della smiled. "Health care."

"Same doctor?"

"No. Nothing that direct. Some of them—about sixty-five percent—have the same insurance carrier."

"It's got to be one of three anyway," Mel said.

"S'why we didn't pick up on it right away. Taking under consideration the trends of this city, Americana Health should have about forty-seven percent of them. It has sixty-five. Did a little thinking, and the thing is, Americana does a lot of government business. And they give price breaks to your family. Immediate and otherwise. And guess what I found out."

"What?"

"A lot of the victims have a relative on a government project. A cousin, nephew—something like that. None of them immediate, all of them secondary."

"Any particular project?"

"Project Horizon."

David looked at Mel.

"Boys, I see that pulls your chain." Della opened the refrigerator, leaving greasy fingerprints on the door. David got up and wiped them away with the dish towel. Mel crowded close to Della and they both stared into the refrigerator. David wasn't about to tell them where the girls kept their stash of candy bars.

Della shook her head. "You eat too healthy, Silver." She swung the refrigerator door, and Mel jerked his head out of the way. "Got to go home to my boys." She paused in the doorway. "I want to know, Silver. When your wife hears a noise in the middle of the night. She ask you to go see?"

"No."

"No. I guess she don't."

David curled his lip and Mel handed him a beer. It had been at the back of the refrigerator and it was ice-cold. David took a large swallow.

Mel sat beside him at the table.

"How's your leg?" David asked.

"It's bitchy. Too close to my crotch for comfort."

David swallowed beer. "You been in the hospital too long, Mel."

"Yeah. What you thinking, there, David? You got a mean look."

"Women."

"Oh yeah. Them."

"Why are women so *violent*, Mel?"

"Just Rose."

"No. It's all of them. You should have seen my girls, pelting this pervert with stuffed animals." David laughed suddenly, sputtering beer on the wall. "You know Rose believes in reinstating the death penalty?"

"Lots of people do, David."

"Even my mother."

"She believe in the death penalty?"

"No. But look at how she kills herself. Hammers in a hook, strings up a rope . . . I mean, she probably went down to a hardware store, bought all this stuff, and then went right home and hung herself. No second thoughts. No agonizing. So goddamn direct. One minute, baking in the kitchen. The next, hanging from a rope. I just don't understand the mind-set."

"A shame about Machete Man, David, but we'll get it figured. It's connected somehow—Machete Man and this Project Horizon. Halliday won't shut us off."

"I don't care what he does, I'm not letting go of this."

"Me neither. Not after what they did to Dyer. Not to mention here."

"Damn straight."

Mel got up and found two more cans of beer. "So, David. Tell me."

"Huh?"

"What about Machete Man, really? Was it self-defense, or did Rose just off this guy?"

David belched.

"I knew it," Mel said.

THIRTY-TWO

DAVID'S BLADDER WOKE HIM. HIS NECK WAS STIFF AND SORE from sleeping hunched over in the easy chair. Mel was asleep on the couch, a beer can clutched in his hand. David stood up and stretched. He ran a hand over his face. Almost a beard. Maybe he wouldn't shave.

He showered and put on clean jeans and a T-shirt, moving quietly around the room to get his clothes. The girls, looking like a pile of exhausted kittens, were asleep in the middle of the bed.

He heard the crackle of gravel in the drive and he went out front.

Rose was asleep on the porch swing, nestled so deep in a blanket he could barely see the top of her head. They ought to have talked. He wiggled his toes. The sun was high; it was late. The warmth of the plank porch felt good on his bare feet.

The car stopped a hundred feet from the house. It was a maroon and silver Audi, and it had the Elaki adaptation. David shaded his eyes. The car door swung up and an Elaki flowed out into the yard. It was a handsome Elaki, one he'd never seen. The color was vivid—the trim coal-black, and the front deep pink. The side pouches were loose and pronounced, so the Elaki was a female who'd borne children. She was taller than average and her eye prongs curved gracefully at the top. Reflections glanced off her scales, like sunlight on water.

David waited for her to come to the porch. The Elaki did not move.

He headed across the drive, rocks and tufts of dirt hurting the soles of his feet. Unlike Rose, he rarely went barefoot. The Elaki acknowledged him with a ripple spreading from fringe to waist. David stopped in front of the car, feeling the warmth of the engine radiating through the hood.

"You are the David Silver?"

"Yes."

"I come to you from the Solver of Puzzles."

"Sheesha?"

The Elaki jerked.

"How is he?" David asked.

"He is . . . here." The Elaki held up a small leather case.

For a short moment David was sure that the case contained Puzzle's ashes. Ridiculous. Cremation was a human burial custom.

"You have a message?" David asked. An ant crawled over his big toe and he bent down to scratch.

"A message? Yes, it is that." The Elaki handed him the case. "Have you received a probe before?"

David looked blank.

"My apology. Question stupid. Please accept me to advise. It can only use once, then it is gone. So very important, the lasting impression."

David scratched the back of his head. "Who are you?"

"One Sheesha trusted. It is most frowned for, this probe. Like your suicide."

"What are you talking about? Look, maybe I better talk to Puzzle."

"You *cannot* do that. He is here. This is all. You must understand this."

David leaned against the car. He had a bad feeling and he kept his hands off the leather case.

"Please, *take*." The Elaki touched his arm.

"*What* is it?"

"You must not refuse." The Elaki began to sway from side to side. "The sacrifice is most extreme, David Silver."

"Look, take it easy, friend. Friend of Puzzle."

"Yes. *Trusted* friend. I cannot fail the final request."

"Puzzle's dying, isn't he?"

"Sheesha dead, now dead." The Elaki swayed again, back and forth, and David reached out a hand and steadied her. "Understand, David Silver. The existence of mind only was not to satisfy Sheesha. That was all to be left after explosion."

"I knew he was bad. But he—"

"Nothing but mental left for Sheesha. You were in it, the explosion?"

"Yes."

"They put you together most well. I salute."

"Is Puzzle dead?"

"But *yes*."

"He . . . killed himself?"

"He had . . . things for you to know. And he knew he did not have your trust. He felt you thought there was . . . there was . . . dirt on him?"

"Dirty."

"He was not. But he felt no hope, so he sends you the rhythm of his life." The Elaki rippled, and handed David the leather case.

"I don't understand this." David took the case and folded his arms. "Tell me."

"We have done much of the brain analysis. Each cell is mapped. To do this, it is necessary to remove the cell after mapping. In order to get to the next one. Very crude, I know this."

David leaned back against the car, feeling the skin on his back tighten and twitch. "He didn't do it."

"Oh yes. Very much he did."

"And his *brains* are in this bag!"

"No, please. A recording of his thoughts—his beliefs, experience. His rhythm."

"My God."

"Yes. It is understood that you have that here." The Elaki unzipped the bag, and held it under David's nose. David sniffed, smelling leather and lime.

"No, not smell. *See*. Look."

David saw two small black cylinders, connected by wire to a metal plate.

"The microchips are on the plate. Too small to see. Turn please." The touch on the back of David's head was soft, tickly. "Put probe here, and here."

The sun was harsh in David's eyes, and he turned back to face the Elaki.

"There are small needles. They will grow into your head. There is no pain. Pinprick, no more. It will be like a dream. Like a video story—a format chosen by Puzzle for most understanding by the human. You must not be interrupted, David Silver. It will play only once, then it is lost, except for what you remember."

"I have a good memory."

"Yes, but you are human, which will be problems."

"A stupid hot dog?"

"No, you misinterpret. The human mind has different reference points than the Elaki mind. Your brain will interpret the data immediately, according to what you already know. It will slant the viewpoint. So you will get Sheesha's rhythm, but mixed with some of your own."

"And you . . . you're sure he's dead?"

"Oh, most yes." The Elaki swayed again. "The analysis stripped the cells and destroyed them. Sheesha is gone. Sheesha will always be gone."

"A message from the dead."

The Elaki was still for a long moment. "Wear it well, David Silver."

THIRTY-THREE

THE GARDEN WAS A MESS. THE TOMATOES HAD GROWN OUT and around their cages, snarling across the bed in evident pursuit of the squash. The paths between the beds had disappeared under a tangle of vines and weeds. The leaves on the vines were dry and full of holes—too many insects, too little water.

David had gone back to the house for his running shoes. Everyone had still been asleep, except Rose, who had pretended to be.

David followed the track across the field. They were getting the occasional cool day now, but this wasn't one of them. The grass was coarse and knee high. Pale yellow butterflies swooped and dipped in front of him, trembling near his fingertips, then drifting away. The ground rose and slanted to the left. He passed under a tree, savoring the shade, but did not slow his pace.

An old barn sagged at the edge of the tree line, marking the end of his property. The barn was grey and weathered. A clump of dead trees loomed over the side.

David pulled the double door open. The hinges creaked, and sunlight spilled into the blackness. The window near the roof gaped open, and dust jittered in the light that filtered through the cracks in the wood.

David shivered. It was cool inside, almost cold. The smell of dried tobacco was still strong, though the barn was almost empty, and he felt a rush of despair he did not understand. An ancient piece of harness hung in one corner. David rubbed his finger across the old leather. He walked across the hard-packed dirt, kicking the clumps of desiccated straw.

He went to the back of the barn and sat, leaning against the rough wood planks. His fingers shook as he unzipped the leather pouch. He studied the probes that were supposed to "grow" into his head. Was he crazy to go along with this?

Crazy or not, he would take the probe, or anything else that was necessary, to get into the mind of a key player.

Three short, slender needles were clumped at the end of each probe. David took a deep breath and positioned the ends on the back of his head, where he remembered the light spidery touch of the Elaki. His skin popped where the needles went in, feeling like the tines of a TB test.

Warmth coursed through the back of his head and suddenly there was sound, light, an explosion of sensation. He knew he was breathing too hard, too fast, and he wanted to open his eyes. He felt tinier, and tinier—big, then small; big, then small.

His head jerked from side to side, and he felt the itchy roughness of straw on his cheek.

"Please," he heard a voice. His voice. "Please."

His heartbeat steadied and his breath slowed. All right, he thought. I'm okay. He closed his eyes, feeling peaceful.

ONCE UPON A TIME.

I, Sheesha, came of small litter—only three pouchmates, two taken early in the Gleen epidemic.

Mother-One was small, determined—phenomenally intelligent. Secretly delighted with the unconventional, probing, questioning of self, Sheesha. She did not penalize because I found distasteful the retreat into self. Benevolent she was, wary of trouble.

And there was trouble.

Elders were ever fascinating, full of strange full wisdoms that did not then ring true to me. But I loved their opinions, and their persons. They were flattered by the interest, but also frustrated by my viewpoints, and my inability and disinclination to withdraw into the mental states that give true perspective.

I was, by the elder ones, encouraged to become laiku.

Mother-One put an end to such suggestions, telling me that such a vocation is achieved solely by decision of self. But she did not hide her opinion that my self-satisfaction—and intense frustration—would lie in that direction.

I lived on the knife edge of sanction. Not cho, of course. But I was often fined and many times required to perform social caretaking services. I took such sanctions as a gift, using the opportunities to observe other Elaki. This pleased the sanction committee, who tailored my sanctions carefully, and felt the pleasure of events coming full circle.

Catal, an elder herself, did not like me, or the care the other elders used in issuing my sanctions. She found my curiosity impertinent, and my distaste for submerging in self foreboding. She predicted a troubled adolescence, when such inclinations would become intense.

And indeed, when I reached the changing, these tendencies were strong.

I felt left out by my inability to connect to self. It created in me a need for companionship not shared by other Elaki, a need they did not understand.

Mother-One often explained that the mental connections, the synapses required to connect with self, were lacking in me. She apologized for this, but did not accept the explanation as excuse for trouble.

And trouble came.

For I could not believe that this hunger of mine, this loneliness, was so very idiosyncratic. This need made the elders too uncomfortable for it not to exist in others.

So I investigated, interviewing pouchmates and peers, challenging the solace of self. And of course, chronicling the actions of elders. It was this that caused the trouble—violating the privacy of elders. This, coupled with my conclusions and interferences, provoked the elders to new levels of anger.

Which meant to me that I had something valid to pursue.

Led by Catal, the sanction committee decided to exile me from my home. I was sent to contemplate. Instead, I sought Mother-One.

I found her in the bog, deep in meditation. She went there often for self-argument, myself the problem more often than not.

Her internal arguments, I later learned, raged heatedly.

Had she given me too many liberties and thus not the discipline necessary to connect with self? Or, perhaps, had the upbringing been too rigid? With less squelching of natural instincts, might I find my own, albeit unique, way to connect with self? Was the problem too strong (or weak?) a connection to the pouchling, crippling him with too much (too little?) care?

I stood nearby, afraid to disturb. She had been there for many hours, poised on the soft pudding dirt, careful not to sink into the abyss. She had been deep in thought when the sky had swelled with final brightness, drifting from grey to black. She had ignored the clammy humidity, and the chill quiet before dawn.

But she noticed me—the only Elaki who would interrupt her obvious need for privacy, and the only Elaki likely to be in enough trouble to warrant the intrusion.

It was difficult for me to begin the explanation. She waited with patience, discreetly rippling in vain attempt to excise the stiffness beneath her scales.

She knew already of my trouble.

But for her the night had served. Faults in nurturing were unavoidable; looking backward useless. And so she advised me.

She knew also that the sanction was tempered with the requirement that I spend the exile at university—an exception made for early study, for a promising if uncomfortable student. She helped me see past the panic to the joy of semiprotected and broadening environment of university.

I did not then know of her fears of an environment that would provide no restraints on my dangerous antisociety tendencies. Or of her fear to let me go, heightened by the conviction that without her influence, I would not learn crucial restraint.

I did not know how often she thought back to me as an uninhibited pouchling, stomach rippling at interesting thoughts and sounds, an abandoned shining child. And how she remembered pleasure and pain from knowing the shine could not last.

Or that she looked at me, there in the bog, committing as a measure of course the socially unthinkable, and knew that I was that rare creature, a lonely Elaki. But I remember that a sudden sharp wind ruffled our scales, and chilled us.

How strange it is that the *humans* taught me the necessity of the code. The code was all that kept society from unraveling into bloody, crazy mess. Like human society. From birth, one must be taught the code—where you step and where you do not.

At once I had great pity for humans, their stick shapes, their jerky, speedy, uncomfortable movements. No good system for keeping themselves in line—undisciplined children running rampant on their planet.

And yet. They are not without their charm. So often do I see flashes of Mother-One in the way they deal with their young!

They are intelligent enough, these nose talkers, intelligent enough to have the problem. Escape, chemical, the bane of every promising species. How to fill the lonely voids? It would seem that the mind expanding to certain capacities must find relief.

Study them, solve our problem.

They have an expression here—the end justifies the means. So perfect, so true, and eventually . . . such trouble.

I have been working with them too long. They fit the stereotype—violent, undisciplined, unsteady. But knowing them on a personal level . . . one becomes fond.

Ironic that the cure applies to them, but not my own. *Because* of their undisciplined socializing and patterns of social dependency! Things we so often joke about!

The substance is dangerous for Elaki. For the human, the drug can be engineered not to be habit forming—it can be tailored so that it will cause minimal desire, in the totally balanced human. The catch, of course, for them will be "totally balanced." But the blood groupings, the family unit, properly supported, can provide that balance, as long as the danger of the dysfunctional family unit is well understood. That will be the battle—curing the dysfunctional unit. But at least they have a chance.

The drug will not work to limit addiction for the Elaki. The Elaki physiology must always find a way around the chemical barriers.

Still, it is progress. We are close to announce. The first batch of Black Diamond, *non*-addictive this time, ready for test.

And the trouble now out of hand.

And always, that String, watching. Official Izicho representative, authorized to carry out cho—the death sanction. Always the sanction, hanging!

And if String knew how bad things were out of hand . . . if he knew I, Puzzle, have lost *control* of Horizon. Would he sanction? Would he show mercy?

One does not expect mercy from the Izicho. At home, in one's own community . . . but I am a long way from home.

And I will not see home again, or stand on the trembling bogs.

I hate String. String the Izicho, the watcher, the genuine hot dog lover. Value a hot dog on the same level as Elaki! To sacrifice humans for Elaki is morally reprehensible to a purist like String, though their own government turns a blind eye.

And yet, for all his morality, if String stops Horizon he will damage humans more than help them. Why can he not see that to sacrifice a few lost ones from the warren called Little Saigo will benefit them all?

The work has to stay, the project go a little longer or there will be untold damage. This must be understood.

And I cannot do that. I can only leave it behind.

So hard to disengage, to sail the darkness. Mother-One was correct.

I am dying. Is it not possible that there is trouble in the darkness? More sanctions to come?

And what else?

THIRTY-FOUR

DAVID WOULD HAVE BEEN HAPPIER WITH MEL DRIVING, BUT he didn't like to admit it. It was difficult now, keeping his thoughts from wandering. Awake, he could keep the patchwork bits of memories—Puzzle's memories—under control. Sleep was another matter. He would drift off, then jerk awake, Puzzle's thoughts like a loud noise in his mind.

Mel cracked his knuckles. "I was thinking the Inman Hotel."

David shrugged. "How many stories?"

"Twelve. Whoa. Slow down, there he is."

"How can you tell?"

"He's the one looks like he been chewed by a dog. Hey there . . . *String*." Mel whistled. "Over here."

String rippled across the sidewalk. Streetlights glinted off his scales. A woman in an evening dress and an Elaki at a hot dog stand stopped and watched String get into the car with two humans. String folded himself across the back seat.

"I am very excited, Detective Mel. And think much of this invitation."

"You sure you want to do Mexican?"

"*Authentic* Mexican, yes. Earth flavoring, nothing adapted up to Elaki standard."

"You liked the tacos, huh?"

"But yes."

"Good, String. Good."

David glanced in the rearview mirror. String was twisted sideways, left prong drooping.

David accelerated over a rough patch in the road, bumping the car hard. String smacked into the back of the seat. Mel looked at David. David slowed and drove more carefully.

He almost missed the hotel.

He braked sharply, swinging into the circle of pavement in front of the Inman. A concrete tub was full of weeds. The lobby had the musty odor of an ill-kept, indoor pool.

There was no one behind the desk. An old man in brown slacks and a sport shirt was slumped on a battered couch. His head jerked up as they passed. His eyes opened to slits, then closed.

String looked around, then got into the elevator with David and Mel.

"This is most interesting. This guy relationship. It is like a reunion of pouchmates."

"That like brothers and sisters?" Mel leaned against the right side of the elevator and scratched his thigh.

"Yes, very like. I remember one time . . ."

The elevator dinged and opened.

"Food smell," String said. Someone was playing a guitar. String sidled forward.

"Not our floor," Mel said.

"Oh. But I was going to tell you—"

Behind String's back, Mel looked at David and stuck a finger up his nose.

"I had a pouchmate, female, who traveled to Kinsan—Kinsan, it is a famous gathering place—and did not come back for a too long space. Other female pouchmate and I went to this Kinsan to look for Ceech. Ceech is the . . . the name of the female pouchmate who went to Kinsan. To find Ceech we . . ."

The elevator door opened.

"After you," Mel said.

" . . . decided, in order not to interfere with—" String stepped out onto the roof and looked around. "Where is the Mexican food, Detective Mel?"

The elevator closed. String turned and faced them. The breeze was a small one, but String swayed sideways.

"We need to talk to you, String," Mel said. "We thought this might be the best place. So we can be private."

The signs of distress were obvious, now that David knew what to look for. The greenish sheen of the scales. The stiffness of the eye prongs. Almost, he felt sorry for String. Almost.

"The rooftop is most dangerous for Elaki. Did you not know that, Detectives?"

Mel stuck his hands in his pockets. "Yeah, actually, we did."

String moved back, closer to the edge.

"Talk to me about the Izicho," David said. "And what you do."

String teetered from side to side. "What is Izicho, please?"

"Puzzle sent me a brain probe," David said.

String stilled. "Ah."

"We know all about you," Mel said.

"Sheesha suspected then? He was aware?"

"He was scared to death of you," David said.

"Yes."

"You did the sanction. You killed him."

"But no."

Mel made a rude noise. "Don't tell me you don't do sanctions."

"I do, yes. Even cho, the death sanction. But not Sheesha, though it might, yes, have come to that point."

"It did come to that point. You blew him up, and caught me and David at the same time. Should have used more explosive, you'd have gotten us all."

"You forget, Detective Mel, that I was also caught in—"

"You weren't hurt," David said.

"If I had for the intention you and Mel to be killed, you would be dead. No joke, sirs."

"Aw, now he's *bragging*," Mel said. "I *hate* it when they start bragging."

"Izicho is very like human police. More centered on the will of the masses, perhaps, but our jobs very alike."

"So now we're all cops together. Buddies. But see, String, we aren't killers."

"That is relief. Please to let me pass, then, back to people chute."

"*Elevator.* What I meant to say is, we aren't *usually* killers. It's not a regular part of our job."

String held out a gun, pointing it between Mel and David.

"*Jesus*, you going to threaten me with the gun I got you? Where you been hiding that, anyway?"

"Please, let me pass to peop . . . elevator."

"Is it loaded?" Mel asked.

String raised the muzzle of the gun. "But yes."

"I'd be careful, then, about sticking it down in your shorts there."

"Pouch."

"Whatever. And put it away. You fire that, and you'll go over the edge of the roof."

"I will not have to fire. I have seen videos of human behavior. Discharge is dangerous, and rarely required. It is necessary only to point the weapon to make a human do your will. Are those not the rules?"

Mel grinned. "You know, David, it's awful hard to stay mad at him."

David folded his arms. "Mother-One to Puzzle might not agree."

String's voice was gentle. "Mother-One to Puzzle is long deceased, David Silver."

David frowned. He should have realized . . . He closed his eyes. Mother-One had died years ago, when Sheesha was at the university. She had sent him a partial brain probe. That was how Sheesha had learned the skills to merge with self—from her memories.

David took a deep breath and rubbed his face in his hands. A vein of lightning lit the sky. String swayed from side to side.

"Please."

Mel smiled reassuringly. "Just heat lightning, Gumby."

"We could be most useful together. You share your information, and I can share mine. Fairly. We work the same problem, different approach. It is time for cooperation."

Mel looked at David. "What you think?"

"We have to get him off the roof anyway."

"Unload that gun before you put it away, String." Mel pointed to the elevator. "Then down the hatch."

The guitar player was still there, strumming for an unappreciative group of four. String stood at the bar and David and Mel sat on either side of him. The guitar player sang like a sad and sorry hound dog. The music had a definite country twang, and David could tell that Mel liked it and String didn't. He was with String.

"You want a drink," Mel was saying, "just push this—"

"Detective Mel, I am alien, not stupid. And you have made a mistake. When you cut the sequence, the machine thinks you have had amounts deducted from account, when in truth you have not."

The robocart rolled toward them.

"At home," String said sadly, "it is not looked upon with such suspicion to use actual cash."

"On Earth," David said, "it means you're a drug dealer."

The robocart served String first.

Mel peered in the glass. "What's that you drinking?"

"Elaki beer and Tennessee whiskey."

"Together?"

David took a sip of beer and turned his stool so he could look at String. "I thought you were working for Puzzle. You weren't. You were watching him."

"This beer is warm," Mel said. "I like it the way it was when I was a kid. I miss crumpling the cans."

String drained his glass, then punched for another.

"I was watching him, yes."

"Why? Mel, be careful how you hold that."

"I'm not going to spill it."

"Two reasons," String said. "One—his methodology was suspect. He is allowed a certain level of harm. Not to exceed."

"What level?" Mel said. "Aw, hell."

"I told you it would spill."

"It's an ugly carpet anyway."

String peered at the floor. "What color do you call that?"

"Looks like peanut brittle," Mel said. "A little beer would improve it."

String sloshed beer onto the floor.

David grabbed the Elaki's fin. It was velvet soft, and slipped out of his grasp.

"What's the other reason, String?"

"Other reason? Elaki murders. Three."

"So they *weren't* sanctions?"

"But no. At least two, and likely three, were victims of the Machete Human."

"Machete *Man*," Mel said.

David frowned. "Then who killed Puzzle?"

"I do not know. It could not have been the Machete Human."

"Man," said Mel.

"And now you, David Silver. You have experienced the mind probe. You have learned what is to be invaluable."

David put his beer down and rubbed his temples. "It's not that easy to sort. Sometimes . . . something comes to me, and it's like I always knew it. And others, I get bits and pieces. Nothing to make a coherent whole."

"You know, did you not? That Puzzle feared the sanction?"

"Yeah."

String faced David. "What was it he was guilty about?"

"He . . . he didn't like you. He was . . . contemptuous. Because you were a hot dog lover."

"Yes. Puzzle was bigot."

"No." David frowned. "Yeah. He was a bigot." David sighed and leaned back on his stool. "He was up to something that had to do with the project. He was close to a cure, but it wouldn't work for Elaki."

"Ah."

"But somehow . . . don't ask me how, I'm not sure. Somehow things were out of hand. He was afraid. Something he'd started and couldn't back down from. Something to do with the deaths."

"So, String," Mel said. "How long you been doing these sanctions?" He punched up another drink.

"It is not an easy topic of discussion, Detective Mel. Yes, thank you, I will have another."

David shredded the wet napkin under his beer. "I just remembered."

The robocart rolled over and served String.

"Tell me, Gumby, why's it always serve *yours* first?"

"Mel," David said. "Pay attention. You remember those pictures in Puzzle's office?"

"Yeah. Looked like they were studying the dealers. Small-time."

"But *all* of them were shot in and around Little Saigo."

"So?"

David shrugged.

"I remember well the first sanction of cho." String slipped a few inches to the left. "Most distressing. Final bequests are, of course, recognized by law, and this particular . . ."

Mel ordered another drink and David stared at him.

Mel shrugged. "Another won't hurt. Get me through the story, and it looks like a long one."

"*You* got him started. Make him stop."

" . . . being had a certain amount of property, but not enough—"

"Hey, *String*, don't it depress you?"

"Don't what depress me?"

"The sanctions. Carrying them out."

String slipped farther sideways. "At first, yes. But later, no."

"Got used to it, huh?" Mel straightened String up.

"No. It is a strange thing. So much bad to see. Bad this, bad that, some sickening. All waste and cruelty."

Mel nodded solemnly.

David set his glass down. "I think . . . I think I'm beginning to figure this out, Mel."

"But then," String said, "after so much bad goes by . . ."

"Goes down the hatch," Mel said, swallowing hugely.

"Then when a goodness, a kindness comes. When there are things decent. Then it seems such a miracle. Not matter how much swirl of badness . . . the good cannot be stomped out."

"Stamped out," Mel said.

"Think about it." David turned sideways and faced them. "Project Horizon is going to cure drug addiction. And suddenly there's a psychopath on the loose. No connection, except all the victims have some association with Horizon. Human victims. Elaki victims. An Elaki/Human project."

"Work together," Mel said, "get killed together."

"The brotherhood of the races," said String.

"Because something has gone wrong," David herded the pieces of wet napkin into a ball. "Something is out of hand and that something draws a vice cop, in search of a new street candy. Black Diamond."

"To Black Diamond!" Mel held his glass in the air.

David's head was hurting, but everything made sense. What he needed was a good long talk with Dennis Winston. Tomorrow, when he was sober.

"To Black Diamond! I am empty, Detective Mel. We must all order another."

THIRTY-FIVE

THE RAINBOW TOWNHOMES WERE CHEAPLY BUILT UNDER A facade of elegance, the rent ridiculous for the minuscule square footage.

"Elaki beer," Mel muttered. "And Tennessee whiskey."

"Could they not make car for Elaki and human compatible?" The voice from the back was small and pained.

"Poor Gumby," Mel said. "You should see the back seat, David. This sucker's shed a lot of scales."

David parked the car by the curb. Mel smiled knowingly.

" 'Member when this place opened up—five years ago? Friend of mine came out here. Said the parking structure had been peppered with BMWs, Jags, and Myshenas—leased from the dealer. And the pool and grounds were full of girls and guys. Models, rented for the day. Place filled up in no time." Mel shook his head. "Got busted too, couple years ago. Discriminating against children. Charged an extra hundred a month for each kid."

"Special rates for goldfish?"

"Probably an extra twenty."

String rustled in the back seat. "You say this Winston has the tie-in to Machete Human?"

"Man. Yeah, guy tried to chop up his grandmother."

"Grandmother. A family relation?"

"Mother-One to Mother-One."

"Winston works on Project Horizon," David said.

"And you also feel this project makes illegal use of human subject?"

"I think so, yeah. And something's gone wrong with a cure they call Black Diamond."

"Which probably means it's the new drug on the streets. That the way you read it, David?"

He nodded. "That's where Dyer came in."

"How does the Machete Human relate?"

"Don't know," Mel said. "That's why we need to see Mr. Winston. And, Gumby?" Mel turned around in his seat. "Just watch, okay? Let me and Detective David do the talking."

"As you say."

There was a Jeep in Winston's driveway. The small patch of ground by the sidewalk was covered in ivy, and two birch trees twined together in the small space.

Mel squinted in the sunlight, and there was sweat on his forehead, though the heat of the day was cooling. David heard a thump and a moan and turned to see String scuttling sideways from the car to the grass.

Mel gave him time to get to his fringe, then rang the bell.

"Good evening. This is the Winston residence. State your name and business."

David leaned against the jamb. "David Silver, Homicide Task Force."

They waited. David thought he saw movement, though it was hard to tell, the blinds were shut. Someone peered at them through a peephole, then started undoing locks. There were clicks and twists, then a buzzer.

Mel looked at David. "Heavy security."

"Yeah. One good kick would splinter the bottom panel of that door."

"He'd know you were coming."

The door swung open.

If anything, Winston looked thinner, in sagging grey sweats and a white T-shirt. He had dirty tennis shoes on, and an oversize fork in his left hand. David smelled fish. String made a small noise.

"Excuse the interruption, Mr. Winston," he said. "You remember me, don't you? Detective Silver."

"Of . . . of course. Beard's new, isn't it?" He eyed the Elaki. "I read about how you caught that guy. Saw it in the paper. Good work."

"May we come in? We have a few details we want to discuss."

"Don't worry," Mel said. "Gumby's house broke."

"Come on in." Winston stepped back and Mel went in first.

The entranceway was oak parquet, polished. A dark hall led straight to a bright white kitchen. David heard the pop of sizzling oil. Winston led them into the living room. It was dim, unlit. The couch and chair were shabby, but comfortable-looking, and one side of the room was taken up with exercise equipment.

"We don't mind talking in the kitchen," Mel said. "So you can cook your dinner."

The corners of Winston's mouth turned down. "Okay."

The kitchen was small, but streaming with light. The tile floor was white, the cabinets imitation cherry. Accent lights were set in the woodwork, illuminating dust balls and crumbs.

A huge cat sat in the center of the glass table. He was white with patches of grey tiger stripe, and he probably weighed sixteen pounds. His belly was enormous, lying in folds on the table, and his face was small and triangular. His eyes were slightly crossed. He purred loudly and beamed contentedly at David. He lifted his head slightly and sniffed. He was on his feet, suddenly, back arched and fur swelled. He glared at String and hissed.

Winston turned the fish. Grease popped with vigor and hostility.

"Actually," he said. "It's not my dinner. This is for Alex."

"Alex?" Mel asked.

"The cat," Winston said. "It's not good for him—settle *down*, Alex—but he loves fried food."

"I believe it," Mel said.

String backed away. "The *animal*—"

"S'okay, String," Mel said. "Just a little kitty."

"It does not like me."

"Highly evolved intelligence."

David ran a hand down the cat's back. Alex settled on the table, but kept an eye on String.

"Can't believe you caught that guy. So quickly, I mean." Dennis glanced at them over his shoulder. "Can I get you guys something to drink?"

"No thanks," David said.

Mel straddled a chair. "So, how are things with Project Horizon?"

Winston glanced warily at String. "Project what?" He turned the burner off, and placed the fish on a napkin to drain. The napkin grew sodden, and grease pooled out from under it.

"Any more threats?" Mel asked.

Winston grabbed a dish towel. He turned and faced them, wiping his hands nervously. "What do you mean?"

String edged around the room, steering clear of the cat. Alex's ears went back.

"I understand," String said, easing back into a corner, "that you have unusual knowledge of Machete Human?"

"What's he talking about?"

David smiled gently and pulled out a chair. "Why don't you sit down. We have a lot to talk about."

Winston sat. The cat stood up and stretched, then jumped off the table. He hit the floor with a loud thud, and stood under the counter sniffing. He miaowed and looked at Winston.

"Too hot, Alex. In a minute."

David rummaged through the cabinets and selected a plate. Winston watched out of the corner of his eye.

"This one okay?" David said.

"What? Sure."

David put the fish on the plate.

"You have to cut it up," Winston said.

David picked up the fork. "Machete Man went after your grandmother, and he went after Mishi Toyobi's cousin, and Edna Yarby's aunt. And you, and Toyobi, and Yarby, all work on Project Horizon."

"I been doing some checking," Mel said. " 'Bout you guys. Little Saigo—"

Winston jerked in his seat.

" . . . Black Diamond."

Winston looked at the floor.

"It's time to talk to us, Winston," David said. "Past time."

The cat yowled and David set the plate next to a ceramic water bowl that said ALEX. No one spoke. Alex purred, tonguing delicate morsels of fish into his mouth.

Mel shook his head. "Cat eats better than you do, Dennis."

"I don't . . . I'm not so hungry, these days."

David sat down and leaned across the table. "Tell me."

Winston sat back in his chair. His chin jutted forward and there were lines around his mouth. "I don't know why this killer went after these people. Why would it concern Horizon? If it was connected with us, why didn't they go closer? Think about it. Edna has kids. Toyobi's newly married."

"And hell, you got Alex." Mel stood up and wandered around to the back of Winston's chair. "But you said 'they,' Dennis. Not him. And you're right, it is a they. Is that what *they* told you? Nobody will know, 'cause the first time we don't get that close. First time is a warning."

"You don't make sense."

"I think I make perfect sense. What's next, Dennis? You got a girlfriend? Think they'll come after *you*?"

"No."

"Why? Did Edna cooperate? Her records show a miscarriage two months ago."

"They couldn't have done *that*!"

"Why not?"

"Because they wouldn't."

"Wouldn't they? What do you do, on this project?"

"I'm a chemist."

"So you know it's possible. Was Edna cooperating? Are you cooperating?"

"I . . ."

Mel leaned over him. "What did they threaten you with, Winston? What did they say? Maybe they offered to pay you."

"I didn't have a *choice*, Detective. You saw what happened to my grandmother, in spite of all my precautions. They said they'd go back for her. So I went along, long enough to let her die in peace."

"To hurt a grandmother is lacking in moral integrity."

"You tell 'em, Gumby." Mel sighed. "So what now, Dennis? You going to let them get away with it?"

Sweat slipped down the taut pale face. "They haven't asked me anything in a while."

"What kind of things do they want you to do?"

Winston licked his lips.

"Sit down, Mel," David said. "I think Mr. Winston has had a pretty bad time of it. I think you stood up to them pretty well, Dennis. Machete Man is dead, but there are more where he came from. I understand that." He leaned closer. "But, Dennis, you don't want this hanging over you. I'll bet you're good at what you do. I'll bet you'd just like to work in peace, go on with your life."

"The project was supposed to help people."

Mel snorted. "By using them as lab rats?"

David looked at Mel, then back to Dennis. "What went wrong?"

Winston leaned back in his chair and closed his eyes.

David folded his arms. "Tell me."

Alex miaowed and put a paw on Winston's leg. Winston pulled him into his lap and stroked the cat's wide white belly. Alex purred and shut his eyes, dangling his left hind leg over Winston's knee.

"We were working with the Elaki."

String muttered something.

"They were trying to understand drug addiction, and were running into some walls. So they set up what they said would be a controlled study. They—we—came up with something called Black Diamond." Winston stared into space. "It stimulates endorphins. Gives a quick, incredible rush. Better than runner's high, more intense than sex. It's like what a baby gets at birth, going through the birth canal. Happy hormones. Babies come out wide-eyed and alert, then zonk for days. It's a very interesting substance, chemically. Unlimited potential. It can be refined so that it . . . let's just say eventually it will be harmless. Right now, it's addictive as hell." Winston scratched his ear. "And bloody cheap to make. The Elaki were interested in all aspects of addictive behavior. Not just the chemistry, but the, I don't know, the sociology. The forces in society that pressure the individual to . . . partake. So they set up a dealer, and sat back to watch."

"And you didn't object?" Mel said.

"The stuff they were selling was dilute—very. And it brought funds into the project. They just sold it to people who'd use something else anyway."

"Little Saigo throwaways," David said.

"I—"

"Nice little circle." Mel shook his head. "What went wrong?"

"Working with the Elaki . . ." He glanced at String. "It's like being a grad student all over again. You get told what to do, and no one lets you know everything that's going on. But I got suspicious. They were too good, these Elaki. Their predictions were too close to the mark. They didn't make enough mistakes. I decided they were using the stuff full force under controlled conditions. I'm talking about people used like you said, like lab rats—caged, the whole nine yards."

"What did you do?"

"About the time I started questioning their methods, I got my first threat." His hands curled into fists. "I didn't want to just quit or walk away. I'd been a part of it. I wanted it stopped. I was friends with this Elaki. Grammr. He and I . . . he admitted to me about them taking people."

"From where?"

"Little Saigo. But he said things were out of hand, and that their own police—I can't remember what he—"

"Izicho," String said.

"Yeah, that's what he called them. And he was scared of somebody named Cho."

"Izicho had nothing to do with death of Elaki on Horizon Project."

"Grammr said they did. And Grammr's dead."

"Is not from Izicho. That is for I am here. To understand Elaki death."

Winston looked at David. "Grammr said the drug network they'd set up was functioning on its own—it was a nightmare, way out of their hands. Like you say"—he looked at String—"even Elaki started dying. Black Diamond was hitting the streets, and Puzzle was going to shut us down, but the network people said no. We were the source. We were to go on with the research, and supply them with Black Diamond. And the Elaki were divided. Some wanted to keep on, some didn't. Puzzle decided to quit production. Then Puzzle died."

"Names," Mel said. "I need names."

"I don't know any!"

"Come on. You must know some."

"They talk about S. And they're funny too. Not he, not she. Just S. Or sometimes . . . it."

"You want protection?" Mel asked.

"Last cop who asked me that, he turned up in pieces."

"Why don't you take a vacation, Dennis." David stood up. "You and Alex, go off somewhere. And give me a number. I'll call you when it's over."

"He can't do that, he can't leave town," Mel said.

"I didn't tell him to stick around. Did you, Mel?"

"But—"

"He won't do us any good dead. Just be sure I get that number, Dennis."

"Look," Winston said. "I can't disappear right now. We did some good work, and I'm keeping on with it. The Black Diamond can be formulated . . . look, trust me on this. It can solve more problems than it causes."

"They'll come after you, Dennis."

"No, listen. Why do you think I haven't talked before now? I'm not kidding about the Diamond. The Elaki have done it! I may not agree with their methods, but they've made incredible progress. They should announce a cure anytime. Think of that. A cure *not just* for drug addicts, but for addictive behavior, across the board. Societal cure."

David sat back down. "Suppose, for reasons I won't go into, suppose I believe you're right. Why don't they announce now?"

"Look, this isn't what you may expect. We're not talking about a magic pill here. It's a whole concept of a balanced mental state and a balanced life. They have to go through the proper channels, have to maintain credibility. That's why I haven't blown the lid on this. I could have gone to the press any day I wanted, torn the whole thing wide open. Can you imagine—Elaki using humans as lab subjects? They won't even let us have mice these days and hey"—he held up a hand—"I'm all for simulation models. But you tell John Q. Public they got people in cages and that's it. People will want to kick butt. Nobody will listen, and nobody will care."

"We'll do what we can," David said.

"Just think on it. Think what *your* job will be like—no addicts, no drugs."

"First they take away traffic, then they cure the schizos, now you say the addicts will be gone." Mel stood up and stretched. "What the fuck am I going to *do* all day?"

THIRTY-SIX

DAVID SAT BESIDE MEL AND TRIED TO PRETEND THAT HIS CO-workers weren't taking surreptitious looks at him. He could thank Rose for this.

Captain Halliday sat at the end of the table, his head back on the edge of the chair, fingers making a tent. His eyes were closed. String stood quietly in a corner. Someone had put a podium in front of him, so he could stack his notes.

Pete Ridel was handing everyone a piece of paper.

"This the stuff on Machete Man?" Mel asked.

"Naw, that's not up yet. This here's the list of what everyone's bringing to the department picnic. Labor Day, remember? Hey, everybody, captain's springing for the meat this year. Thanks, Roger."

"Yeah, Roger."

"Thanks, man."

Captain Halliday waved a hand, his expression glum.

"Mel, you going to be able play in the game this year? Your leg okay?"

"Yeah, I'll just hobble from base to base. You'll have to make allowances."

"We always do."

"David, you bringing Rose and the girls? I swear, Rose pitches like a son of a bitch."

"We're not pitching this year. Gonna use a tee so the kids can play."

"Aw, shit, whose idea was this?"

"Yours. Last year, remember? So nobody has to sit on the sidelines and watch."

"Bring the Elaki. He can be the tee."

"Yeah, String—why don't you come?"

"Della's boys will knock us out of the ball field."

"Just make sure the beer's *cold* this time. Man, this is going to be pitiful."

"Dawn, you bringing that Mannelli guy this year? He's a hell of a hitter. What's he do, anyway?"

167

"He's a gangster."

"So long as he don't pack a machete."

The room grew silent. Halliday looked at his watch. "I have to be at a departmental meeting in twenty minutes." He cleared his throat. "The results are back from the lab. The suspect apprehended by Rose Silver was our boy. Machete Man. What we don't understand is what motivated him to show up at David's place."

It wasn't a question and David said nothing. Halliday had accepted his story quietly, with unusual seriousness. There was a wedge of discomfort between them.

Dawn Weiler cleared her throat. She sat between Pete Ridel and Della Martinas, and she looked through some notes.

"There's an old case file, some of you may have read it, on one Rory Hardin."

David frowned. The name was vaguely familiar.

"Rory Hardin spent a little time in Austin, Texas, and parts of Mexico. Used a machete."

"Same M.O.?" David asked.

"No. Just the machete. But there's another one, a Clifton Webber. Sexual sadist, very fond of a butcher knife. He took hands, feet, placed them over the victim's abdomen, et cetera, et cetera."

"Jacked off," Mel said.

"Yes, Mel. Jacked off, shot his wad, got his rocks off."

Somebody laughed.

"Is this in the realm of normal sexual behavior?"

Dawn gritted her teeth.

"Not for people, String," Mel said slowly. "I can't account for Elaki."

Halliday's tone was cutting. "Both perps dead?"

"Executed," Dawn said. "One by electrocution, that was Webber. Hardin's was lethal injection."

Ridel grimaced. "DNA doesn't match, I reckon."

"Information unavailable. But what it looks like, to me, is someone read up on these cases, maybe a few others, and came up with a deliberate M.O. that combined the habits of Webber and Hardin." She looked at David. "That would keep us busy, looking for a sociopath. Everything would ring right for the shrinks. Everything except the selection of victims. But it kept us looking for random psychopaths—crazies work alone, so we're out hunting one little nut, not extortionists, or drug dealers going for enforcement."

"Why?" Ridel said. "Dealers off people every day, think nothing of it. Why get so elaborate?"

David leaned forward. "Project Horizon had to be kept going—no interference. At least until they got the Diamond in production, and their people in place."

"So now what?" Della said.

Halliday looked at Silver.

David sat back in his chair. "You've read the report. Maybe Project Horizon found a cure for addicts, maybe not. One thing we're sure of. They've started a distribution network for this new drug. Vice is only just starting to see it on the streets, but if it's as cheap and effective as they say it is, we may find ourselves back in the 1980s."

"Where do we go from here?"

"According to Dennis Winston, the project is still ongoing, still researching. There's lots more work to do, duplicating results, so the research can be published through legitimate channels, with no taint of sloppiness or unprofessionalism. These things take time."

"So they still need guinea pigs," Mel said. "Little Saigo, then."

"Right," said David. "We go to Little Saigo, set up someone as bait. Follow through to the lab. That way we'll get our evidence, and things hold up in court."

Pete looked at String. "Excuse me, Captain. But what's to stop this Elaki here from blowing it all to his friends at Horizon?"

"Project Horizon is in violation of Elaki law. As member of Izicho—"

"Pete." David's voice was quiet, but everyone grew silent. "String is okay."

"But what if they have the cure?" Della said. "We could blow that wide open."

"We'll be careful. We'll be quiet. We'll be discreet." David rubbed a hand across his jaw. "But we go after these dealers. *They're* endangering the project, if that makes your conscience easier. No telling what will happen when they get everything they want."

Ridel looked up. "Vice in on this, Captain?"

Halliday looked at all of them. "No."

No one said anything for a long moment.

"Who's the bait?" Dawn asked.

"Please explain term of bait."

"The hook, the lure, the tease, the—"

"Ah," String said. "Like the hormone."

Mel frowned. "I don't think so."

"I grew up there, Dawn, in Little Saigo," David said. "I'm bait."

THIRTY-SEVEN

IT WAS GOOD TO KNOW HE COULD STILL HAVE FUN, GOOD TO know he could throw off Machete Man, and Little Saigo, and feel that lift of the heart that turned his mind to nothing more taxing than hitting a ball and running a base.

And somehow the hot smell of asphalt and dusty grass filled his mind with a vision, of himself as Elaki, standing in a mound of churned-up dirt, miles and miles of emptiness in every direction. A warm breeze blew around and through him, and the aloneness made him sad.

David shook his head. *Elaki memory*.

He felt the sun on his back, and wondered if his neck would burn. He wiped sweat from his eyes, adjusted the ball cap that shaded his head, scratched the new beard.

Rose stared at him from the pitcher's mound. The women were two runs ahead. David concentrated.

The ball sailed close to his shoulder. He swung and missed.

String stood behind him in full catcher's regalia. Mel had been teaching him a song while they were waiting around for the game to start. David could still hear the Elaki monotone.

" 'Take me out to the ball game . . . ' "

Was String unusual or were all Elaki unable to carry a tune?

" 'Buy me some peanuts and Cracker Jacks' . . . who, Detective Mel, is this Jack Cracker?"

Something about the song was sticking in David's mind. He shook his head, realizing that the Elaki had signaled Rose. She nodded, rubbed her right shoulder, and threw again.

The ball came fast, and David pulled back. He felt the crack of the bat as it connected and sent the ball between second and third. He ran to first, the loose red dirt of the playing field clouding his feet.

There were lots of kids in the outfield, including his daughters, and he had to restrain himself from running to second. Candy Ridel screamed for Lisa to get the ball that had rolled an inch from her foot. It was a different game this year, with the kids and an Elaki involved. David enjoyed their pleasure and the camaraderie they brought out, but another part of him wanted them safely tucked in the stands, so he could do some down and dirty playing.

Lisa picked up the ball and threw it to Rose. The ball fell short, but the aim was good. She had the moves, Lisa did, if she'd pay attention. He needed to get out with her, and pitch a ball around.

Mel was in the lineup behind him. He hit the ball between first and second, limping his way slowly to the base. Della was on second and, damn, Rose had the ball already. Della's mitt was out, waiting to catch it.

David ran hard, barely aware of the heat and humidity, his stomach tight. Della was straining backward, her tongue stuck out like it did when she was concentrating. He was going to have to slide.

He was down, now, skidding on his right thigh, dirt swirling, leg hurting, hip aching where he'd twisted sideways. The ball smacked into Della's glove as the tip of his shoe slammed into the white square base. He stayed where he was, heart slamming in his chest. He wiped the grime from his face with the bottom of his T-shirt.

Captain Halliday's arms swung out.

"Safe!" he yelled.

David grinned, felt grit between his teeth, and spit. He got up slowly, under Della's hot glare, knowing he was going to pay for the slide in the morning. Rose raised her arms to the heavens, then turned her hard cold gaze to the next hitter.

She didn't throw the ball right away. Something in the stands surprised her, and David knew from the lines of tension in her shoulders, and the sour set of her face, she'd caught sight of something she didn't like.

The next guy she struck out.

David wondered about it later, while they ate. The sun was going down, and it was cooler. His plate was piled with potato salad, baked beans, and three hot dogs running over with ketchup, mustard, onions, and sauerkraut. His stomach yearned toward the food, but he patiently cut up a hot dog for Mattie, and poured ketchup in a large red pool beside it. She swung her legs and ate an empty bun.

"Just a few beans," he said.

She shook her head. He put them on her plate anyway, scoring points for parents. Rose had seen to Lisa and Kendra; it was legal to eat now.

No, not quite.

String stood near the grill, smoke from the charcoal blowing across his eye stalks. He held a plate in one fin, and a beer in the other. David waved at him.

"Come on over. Share the table."

String came toward them.

"Rest your plate here," Rose said, "and you can eat."

"Not necessary." Another section of fin extruded and picked up a bean.

"His hand split!" Mattie said.

"Useful," David said.

"These are the baby humans of your pouch?" String asked.

"He's the father," Rose said. "But they come from *my* pouch."

"Most honored, the Mother-One."

"Call me Rose."

David took a bite of hot dog. The meat had been cooked just a shade too long and tasted slightly of charcoal, reminding him of other summers, ball games, and picnics. He watched Kendra hold a can of Coke with both hands—sipping, sipping, ignoring her food. He took a large swallow of cold beer, and realized he had nothing to eat his potato salad and beans with.

Rose absently handed him a fork. "See those two guys over there?" She nodded toward two men joylessly tossing a football back and forth. "CIA."

"What?"

"Central Intelligence Agency," String said.

"I *know* that, but what makes you think, Rose, that—"

"Central Intelligence Agency," Mattie chanted. Kendra and Lisa picked it up. "Central Intelligence—"

"*Hush*," David said. "Rose, are you sure?"

"Look at them. Tall, sunglasses, hair cut an inch away from their ears. The main thing is the skin. Pink and waxy and fresh-scrubbed. Got to be."

"Maybe they're on a break or something. Taking the day off."

"Nah." Rose gave him a crooked half smile. "I'm under surveillance."

That night he leaned against the kitchen counter and rubbed lotion into the sunburn on the back of his neck. He was dirty and tired, his muscles stiff, his breath rich with beer and onions.

Rose was putting away food and picnic supplies, and he felt guilty for not helping her. The girls had fallen asleep in the car on the long drive home, and he had put them in bed, grimy and sun-drenched.

The kitchen lights were bright, lighting the peculiar deep darkness of a sky so far from the city. He wanted to sit on the porch swing with Rose, and look at the stars.

Rose looked at him while she slid the beans into the refrigerator. She looked at him, but did not see him. David thought about the picnic, and the way Halliday had watched Rose. It was a look he was beginning to recognize.

He leaned against the counter and folded his arms. "Tell me, Rose."

She looked at him over her shoulder. "Tell you what?"

"What did you *do* for the DEA? Assassin?"

"David, I'm tired. We had a good day. Let's don't go into this."

"No? The mother of my children kills without a second thought, and you say you don't go into it? It's ones like you that scare cops, Rose."

"Fuck cops. Fuck you."

"That's redundant, Rose."

"Fuck redundant."

"Look at you." He touched her cheek, the pale white cheek, cold despite the heat. She pulled away. He backed her into the sink and reached for her hand.

"Look at the delicate bones," he said. "The long, sensitive fingers. What *hands* you have, Rose. All the things you do with these hands. It makes me think, Rose."

Rose smiled. "Think what?"

"Your reputation in my department is unparalleled. Detective Silver's wife is famous."

"You're jealous, David."

"Jealous of what?"

"I killed him, so you couldn't."

"I *wouldn't* have killed him. He was valuable, Rose. He could have broken the case."

"You're a cold man, David. He could have murdered our girls."

"I'm not cold, Rose, my love, I'm a cop."

"Same thing. I can't do that. Run hot and then cold. I've never been able to do that." She hugged him, suddenly, and her voice was muffled against his chest. "Did you know that I'm lonely, David?" Her voice was thick now, and he thought she might cry. "You're right, you know. I don't know where I fit in. I blew it with the DEA, but I can't stay out of things. I don't know how to have conversations with normal people. I have weird laundry problems. Who wants to chat about getting death smells out of clothes?"

David held her tightly, picturing her bursting through the window in the girls' room, then twisting Machete Man's neck.

"I don't think you're lonely, Rose. I think you're afraid."

"Santana," she said, and shuddered.

He remembered Winston talking about "S." He would have to research this Santana. Tomorrow, he'd do it, first thing.

He put a hand under Rose's shirt. Her breasts were cooler than the rest of her, and he unsnapped the front of her bra. Her hand went to the inside of his leg, and up. He shivered, and kissed her, and forgot about the swing.

Her knees buckled. He held her and eased her to the floor, resisting the impulse to question her deviation from locked doors and privacy, heated by her capitulation to the fantasies that distracted him on restless afternoons.

They helped each other out of their clothes like polite strangers. He tucked his shirt beneath the small of her back, and cushioned her head with his hands. She arched her back and kissed him, and he sighed, and closed his eyes, and grabbed handfuls of her silky, tangled hair.

So soft, she was, belly warm against his.

"Closer," she whispered. "Cover me up."

He pulled her tighter, and buried himself inside her, giving her all of the closeness that he could.

THIRTY-EIGHT

DAVID STOOD IN FRONT OF THE DIAGRAM OF LITTLE SAIGO.
He pictured Rose as he had left her that morning—sitting on
the porch swing, one leg hooked over the side. He had cleared
the breakfast dishes, made the beds, programmed the laundry to
begin. He knew he would return home to dishes on the table, food
in the sink, puzzle pieces and plastic animals strewn from one end
of the house to the other. It worried him that she was content to
sit in the swing, when Santana was somewhere out there.

Would he come home one day and find her hanging from the
end of a rope?

"Anything else, David?" Captain Halliday was watching him.

David looked through the glass partition and saw Dawn Weiler.
A computer printout hung from her briefcase, and she clutched a
thick file in her left hand.

"No." He looked at their faces—Pete, Della, Mel. String's visage was looking more and more like a face. "Study your map of
Little Saigo," he said. "Memorize it and be ready."

"You really think this Winston will work with us?" Della asked.

"It's all we've got," Halliday said. "So do your homework and
when the call comes we'll be ready. We can't afford any sloppy
backup."

Dawn hesitated outside the door, and Mel opened it for her.

"You're late, kitten."

She smiled nervously and sat down.

"So what you got on this guy?"

Dawn pulled out a stack of papers and passed them around.
"Not a guy, exactly."

"Got to be one or the other," Mel said. "Want I should show
you the difference?"

She handed David a mug shot. "This is Santana. Your hunch
was right, he did time with Vernon Ray Clinton."

"Machete Man," Della said.

"The same."

David studied the picture. Santana looked sleepy. He had thin
sideburns and long black hair pulled into a ponytail. The skin of

175

the face looked silky and smooth, even in a bad photo under harsh light. David concentrated on the eyes—brown, dark underneath, bedroom eyes. He noted the smirk at the edges of the drooping bottom lip.

Dawn leaned back in her chair, tapping a pencil softly on the table. Small chips of graphite fell off the end of the pencil and gathered, like ashes, next to her briefcase. She smoothed her collar.

"Santana is what you would term a hermaphrodite."

"Not what I would call it," Mel said.

David passed the picture to Della.

"Please explain terminology."

"He has the sexual organs of a man and a woman."

"This guy's done time?"

"Probably voted most popular in his cell block."

Dawn shook her head. "According to the records, Santana was suspected of several assaults and two deaths, and this was in the first three months of incarceration. Nobody talked about it—nobody in the can ever sees anything, and they couldn't pin anything on him. But unofficially, Santana was a major power base the eighteen months he was there."

"Don't look the type," Mel said.

"The man is walking death. And he's connected. He's a free-lance dirty chore man. Worked for the O'Banions—"

"Irish mob?" Ridel asked.

"Yes. And Mickey Sifuente, among others." She glanced at David. "The DEA has been after this boy for a long time. Interpol wants him, the Sûreté. He's killed a lot of good people."

David stared at his hands. "Background. Where was he born?"

"New Orleans. Left on the doorstep of a birthing center."

"I wonder why?" Mel said. "I mean, mother's got to want a boy or girl. Either way, Santana's got it covered."

"This does seem sensible, Detective Mel. But mothers are known to abandon pouchlings. Possibly, she knew he was mind-diseased."

"Elaki mothers abandon their babies?" Mel asked.

"But yes, when they are incorrectly formed or they come at difficult moments."

"But—"

"What about Clinton?" David asked.

Dawn passed him a sheet of paper. "Assault. Armed robbery. Assault again. Manslaughter. PFO."

David scratched his chin under the beard. "He and Santana met in prison?"

Dawn nodded. "One of those synergy things. Guys like this get together . . ."

David nodded.

"Santana is a sexual sadist," Dawn said. "As is, obviously, Machete Man."

"Ain't that nice," Mel said. "They shared a hobby."

"I've got Clinton's juvie record."

"That's sealed," Halliday said.

"You want it or not?"

David spoke softly. "Arson, first-degree cruelty to animals, assault."

Dawn nodded. "You know your sociopath."

Mel leaned back and put his feet on the desk. "So how you figure it, David? The Elaki get hold of Santana. Bankroll him to distribute this Diamond, pick up victims for study, and put the pressure on anybody on Project Horizon who don't like the way things go."

David laid his hands flat on the table and looked at Halliday. "We can get him a lot of ways. Dealing, kidnapping, conspiracy to commit murder."

"Or all of the above," Halliday said. "See what you can get out of Winston. Maybe the worm will turn." He tapped the desk absently. "We need to connect him with Machete Man. Ridel, you and Della work on Clinton's apartment. And see if you can get somewhere with one of the victims on the project. Maybe somebody saw them together."

Mel scratched under his arm. "Hey, Dawn, you heard the sociopath theme song? Sung to the tune of 'Home On De-Range.' Goes like . . ."

Dawn walked out and Mel followed her.

David waited until the room was clear, the door closed. Halliday stared at him.

"I want Myer," David said.

"Myer's another issue. I'm giving it to IAD."

"Roger, Coltrane's been in business a long time, and IAD hasn't come close. People are covering. If they cover Coltrane, they'll cover Myer."

Roger eyed him coldly. "You are awfully sure."

"Nobody knew about Judith Rawley but me and Myer. He suggested I go to her."

"What did he need you for? Why not go himself? Or send his people?"

"Why? When the easiest thing would be to let me do the legwork and lead them to it. Then I got caught in the explosion, so they had to do it the hard way."

"I'd like to know what happened to Dyer's notes."

David leaned across the table. "Two cops got killed. Judith Rawley was beaten, *tortured*, and her throat was cut. You *saw* her, Captain."

Halliday turned his face away. "It's not our case."

"It *is* our case. If you want it done right, it's our case."

"What do you have in mind?"

"We find Dyer's disks."

"They could be anywhere. Even Judith Rawley didn't know, and she died for it."

"Maybe Dyer moved them."

"Della and Pete have been over and over his stuff. Nothing."

"All we have to do is convince Myer I've got them. Judith got killed for them, they've got to hurt. We'll set him up to buy them back."

"He's an old hand. He'd never go for it."

"Not if *I* offer them. But he might go for Winston."

"What makes you think Winston will work with us?"

"Blackmail. If he won't go along, I'll blow his Elaki project to the press—make accusations that'll have the animal rights people all over them. They'll lose credibility. The project might even get pulled. Hell, they're *using people*, Roger. The public will tear them apart."

"You can't prove that."

"Reporters don't have to. They imply."

"He care that much about it?"

"I think he does."

"Will he believe you? That you'd do it?"

"Not *me*," David said. "Mel."

THIRTY-NINE

DAVID GUIDED THE FORD INTO A PARKING GRID ACROSS FROM Winston's townhouse.

"I can't believe I'm missing Gumby."

"String? Where is he?"

"Don't know. Said he'd be out of town. He's a sneaky little sucker, I'd like to know . . . head's up, there he is."

Winston was on the porch, locking the front door.

"Jesus," Mel said. "Taking his cat for a walk."

"At least he's home."

"Come *on*, Alex." Winston tugged the leash. The cat lowered his head and tried to work the leather over his ear.

Mel stepped up on the curb. "Dennis, you got that cat registered with the local kennel club?"

Winston stroked Alex's head. "Walking is good exercise and he needs to lose weight. He won't do anything, you know, but sleep and eat. Lick on a catnip mouse. And he hates those health pebbles they sell at the vet."

David put his hands in his pockets. "How've you been, Winston?"

Winston's grip tightened on Alex's leash. "It doesn't help me much for you guys to keep showing up here."

"We were wondering if you'd had any more trouble," Mel said. "I take it you're still cooperating?"

"Nobody's bothering me."

He did look better, David thought. Like he was sleeping again. His jeans were black, clean, snug-fitting. The white shirt was coated with cat hair, but otherwise pristine.

"Look, thanks for stopping by. Everything's okay, now." Winston tugged the leash. "*Alex*. Come on, boy."

Alex collapsed on his side and purred. Winston nudged the cat's rump with his toe. Alex lolled backward, exposing the soft white fur on his belly.

"That cat ain't going nowhere," Mel said. "Come on, Dennis. Let's go in. We got to talk."

"I really don't think we have anything else to cover."

"Maybe we'll just tag along with you."

The wind blew a dry leaf behind a bush. Alex sprang forward and disappeared.

"Alex!" Winston dragged the cat from behind the bushes and tucked him under his arm. Alex purred, striped tail twitching.

"Thing is," Mel said. "We need your help."

"My help? Oh, please."

"Just information, Winston. You know a guy named Santana?"

"Who?"

"Come on, Dennis. Santana."

"Don't know him."

"I think you do know him. Now we can do this one of two ways. We can check around quietly, use our contacts—that's *you*, Dennis—and sort this out without causing any ripples. Or we can swear out search warrants, take people down to the precinct, and show mug shots on the evening news. But me and David, we don't like all the fuss and bother."

"Which means you don't *have* anything."

"We got you, Dennis."

"I don't know Santana."

"Look, Winston." Mel's face was serious. "It comes down to this. If my partner and I got to go about this the hard way, it's going to be noisy. We get the press in on this, no telling what could happen. The animal rights people have had it slack, lately, and they could use a target. You guys might face some pretty strict inquiries."

"You won't do that."

"Really?" Mel cocked his head sideways. "Why won't I?"

"If you do, you'll risk having Horizon shut down or discredited. You don't want that any more than I do. We're going to see the end of *addiction*—the beginning of a whole new era. And you care about that as much as I do. Maybe more. It will make your cop life a whole lot easier."

Mel stopped walking. "I'm interested in two things, Winston. Santana, and a dirty cop I won't name just now. I think you can help me get them, but if you won't, believe me I don't give a rat's ass about your project. I'll come right down in the middle, and your academic credibility can go to hell."

Winston took a deep breath. "You guys are way out of line. I can't help you."

"You mean you won't."

"No chance. You'll get me killed."

"We can protect you," David said.

"No."

"Let's go." Mel stretched and yawned. "Nice idea, David, but I told you it wouldn't work. Let's do it my way." He turned to Winston and slapped him on the back. "Better be looking, pal. You'll be out of work before long."

"We're going to close it down," David said sadly. "You understand that? We'll go public with the information that the Elaki set up a drug cartel to study addictive behavior. That they're using human beings as test subjects."

"Don't forget the animals," Mel said. "All those poor sick bunnies. Going to look bad, but, hey, I don't blame you, Dennis. Some days, you know, no matter what you do, life just sucks. Let's go, David."

Winston put a hand on David's arm. "Please. Can't you stop him? We're so *close*. Give me a month. Just a little more time."

"I'm sorry." David peeled Winston's hand off his forearm. "I'd like to work something out, Dennis. But Mel's right. We can't let these people get away with what they're doing. Nothing is worth that. And you're part of it, Winston. We'll come after you, too."

Winston squeezed Alex too hard and the cat miaowed. "Okay, listen. What if I help you? Will you protect me?"

"You bet."

"I want to keep working."

"Risky."

"Look, I know this Elaki. She and Grammr were pouchlings together, and she was close to Puzzle. Did you know Puzzle?"

"Yes."

"So she and I . . . I think maybe we can give you what you need. We can try it, anyway, can't we?"

"Depends on what we get," Mel said. "Why don't we go inside, Dennis. Talk it over."

FORTY

THE SKY LOOKED PURPLE AND BRUISED, DUSK EDGING THE SUN away. The air was heavy. David rolled the car window down and hit the weather button on the dash. Possibility of showers, eighty percent. He knew tornado weather when he felt it. He was glad to be going home.

The bullfrog wasn't in the driveway, and Rose wasn't out on the swing. Everybody taking refuge, he thought.

David put the car in the barn. He heard a dog bark. Dead Meat bounded out the door, joyously twining in and out of his legs, showing off the bandages on her side. David scratched her ears. She smelled different—doggie, still, overlaid with medicine. Her tail wagged, thumping rhythmically against his leg.

The kitchen window was bright with yellow light. David wiped his shoes on the mat before he went inside.

Something smelled good. He looked in the skillet on the stove. Rose had made fajitas. The table was set for six. He heard laughter.

"David?" Rose walked in the kitchen. "There you are. I knew I heard the car. That Elaki called you. Mr. String."

"What did he want?"

"Said he needed to talk. I told him you'd call." She hugged him, but did not meet his eyes. "Haas brought Dead Meat back."

"*Hilde.*" Haas paused in the doorway. "Hello, David."

David opened the refrigerator. "Beer?"

"Please."

David tossed him a can, feeling mildly disappointed when he caught it. "Want one, Rose?"

She left the kitchen without answering. David took a sip of beer and leaned against the counter.

Haas winked at him. "You are not missing someone? Perhaps, three someones?"

David went into the living room. Mattie's foot stuck out from behind his chair.

"Where's my daughters?" David said loudly. "Didn't we use to have kids, Rose?"

"What kids?"

The phone rang.

"No girls on the roof, are there?" David opened the front door and peeped out. The wind was picking up, and dust swirled in the air. A good night to be inside.

"Mattie? Lisa? Kendra? Anybody up there?" He heard giggles coming from behind the couch. He closed the door and smoothed his hair back into place. "Nope. Nobody on the roof."

"David." Rose held out the phone. "Sounds like a crank. Definitely for you."

He took the phone. "Silver."

"David Silver?"

"Yes." He knew that voice. "Who is this?"

"You said I could call you. If I needed something. And they . . . they came back."

"Who is they? Listen, relax, I'm right here. Tell me where you are."

"You *know* where I am. It's me. It's Naomi."

The girl who needed a magic box. David felt his mouth go dry.

"They came back," she said. "They're going to get me this time. I was going to get directions on my box, and I saw them take her. *Marion.* I can't believe they took *Marion.* Look, there's a storm coming. I got to get back down." She whimpered.

Real trouble, he wondered, or imagined?

"Naomi?"

"Oh God."

"Naomi! Honey, don't go back in the tunnels."

No one answered.

Rose was staring at him.

"Got to go," he said. "Call Mel. Tell him to meet me in Little Saigo."

"David, what—"

"Do it."

He heard one of the girls crying as he ran out the kitchen door.

FORTY-ONE

THE WIND WAS BLOWING HARD AND THE CAR ROCKED BACK and forth in the grid. David kept both hands on the steering wheel. Dirt blew across the beam of his headlights.

They're back. They'll get me. They've got her.

David's spine was stiff and twitchy. How much of what Naomi saw was truth—how much delusion?

She had been right before.

David clenched the steering wheel. Should he call Halliday? Send some uniforms? He pictured patrol officers clomping through Little Saigo. They'd arrive in a large group—cops hated the tunnels. And they'd be decked out in riot gear. Hell, they might take an armored bot with them.

No.

A vein of lightning lit the black smudged sky. David was moving at priority speed and the car bucked staying in the track. Mel didn't have as far to go. He'd be there ahead of him. David hoped he'd wait before he went in.

David parked two blocks away. He tucked his gun in a shoulder holster and took a raincoat from the trunk. He was hot in the coat, but it would be cool in the tunnels. His jeans fit snugly—no room in the pockets. He put quick loads in the side pockets of the raincoat, and sent the car on. He glanced up and down the street. No sign of Mel.

The streetlights were on. The raincoat whipped loosely around his legs, the lapels blowing across his neck. The streets were barren. He could not remember seeing them empty before.

There were no phones in Little Saigo, so Naomi had been up on the surface. Where would she go from there?

The closest phone junction was by the side alley on Ashton. David walked into the wind, hair plastered backward, eyes watering. His coat flapped out behind him, exposing the gun under his arm.

The phone terminal was empty. David smelled urine and rotting garbage. An empty box of Jack Daniel's was crumpled in a corner.

A phone receiver hung from the box. The wind snatched it up, smashing it against the wall of the terminal. David caught it and hung it back on the hook.

Had Naomi Chessfield called from here?

A flash of movement caught his eye. A man ran out of the main tunnel entrance. The wind blew his fine blond hair and made his T-shirt billow.

"Winston?"

David ran carefully across the broken, buckled sidewalk.

Winston was a good runner, or he was scared. David put on a burst of speed, gaining slowly. He reached out, grazing the man's shoulder with his fingertips.

"Winston!"

Winston faltered and looked over his shoulder.

"Silver?"

David grabbed him. Winston pulled away and David tightened his grip.

"What's up?" David said. "What are you doing down here?"

"Nothing's going on. Let me go!"

"You're not here to walk the cat, Dennis."

"Look, there's no time. Tester's down there. I got—"

"Tester? An Elaki? You left him down in the tunnels alone?"

"Her. Yes, alone. I have to get a car. Feel the wind, *stupid.* An Elaki would blow to pieces. Now let me go!"

A siren wailed, and Dennis looked over his shoulder.

"That your backup, Silver? Let me go, please."

"That's the warning system, idiot." David looked up and saw black clouds. "Tornado or genetic warheads. Come on."

They headed for the tunnels, running with the wind this time. David let go of Winston's arm and let the man sprint ahead.

A group of teenagers watched the storm from the main tunnel entrance. Winston raced past them. David thought about warning the kids to move inside. A tornado could suck them out of the tunnel and sweep them away.

"Tester?" Winston stopped a hundred feet into the tunnel. "Tester?"

An Elaki slid away from the wall. "Here. I am here."

Winston put a hand to his heart. "Thank God. Are you all right?"

The Elaki rippled. "All right. Yes for me. The car you have?"

"No," Winston said. "Storm coming. The siren's blowing; they've spotted tornadoes."

The Elaki swayed from side to side. "This tornado is a live thing?"

"Dangerous wind," Winston said.

"*Wind?* Bad wind?"

"You'll be safe farther in," David said. "Come on. This way."

The Elaki slid along behind them.

David saw a side tunnel, and motioned both of them into the darkness. "Should be okay back here." He shoved his hands into the pockets of his raincoat. "Okay, you two, what's up?"

Winston and the Elaki looked at each other.

"This is who?" Tester asked.

"Silver," Winston said. "The detective I told you about."

"The one that pushes with words."

"That's my partner." David folded his arms. "Tell me what you're doing down here."

The Elaki's belly rippled, then she turned slightly, looking from David to Winston.

"The Santana is here."

David glared at Winston. "You knew he was coming?"

"We just found out about it," Winston said. "We were going to call you."

"After we check," Tester said.

"Check?" David glanced over his shoulder. Where the hell was Mel? Taking refuge in a ditch somewhere? He hoped the girls were okay.

"We need to see. Is the job the victim snatch—or the drug going up?"

Winston rubbed his chin. "What she means . . ."

"What she means is you weren't going to call me." David looked from the Elaki to Winston. "So it must be a snatch. I thought we had a deal, Winston. I thought you wanted to keep your project going."

"But yes!" The Elaki began to sway again. "You take the Santana for snatching the experimental human, then so bad the community feeling! Take him for the drug going up—that will be okay."

David was breathing hard. "You're still sitting back and letting them . . ."

"No," Winston said. "That part of the research is done. Santana's not supposed to be *doing* this. There's no point now. That phase of the operation is *over*."

"Over, huh? Wishful thinking, Winston. What's Santana doing here, then? Why did you have to 'check' before you called me?"

"It not over," the Elaki said.

"But they said . . ."

"They always say. Is not to believe, Winston. I have told you."

"Oh God."

"Where are they?" David said.

"Back," Winston said. "Way back. Where all the apartments are. The families."

"Family units," Tester said.

"Okay." David took a deep breath. "How many?"

"Santana. Two that stay with Santana. And more—three from my memory—who hunt."

David swallowed. "Stay here. If you see my partner, tell him what you told me. Keep to the walls, and stay out of the main tunnel."

Winston grabbed his arm. "Look, Detective. Your partner isn't coming, not with tornadoes blowing across the city. Let this one go. I'll help you get him the next time."

"There won't *be* a next time."

"You can't go in there by yourself."

"Mel will be here. So *you* be around to tell him what's up."

Winston stepped back, shoulders sagging. "Whatever."

"Just stay put until Burnett gets here."

Partway down the tunnel, David looked back over his shoulder. The two of them watched him, heads stretched into the corridor. David sighed but kept moving, hoping they would have the sense to pull back, hug the walls, and stay quiet.

FORTY-TWO

THEY'D CALLED THEM THE PUSSY TUNNELS WHEN HE WAS A kid, because they were tight and dark and wet. Bravado. There was rubble on the floor and barely room to walk upright. The walls pressed, brushing David's shoulders on both sides. No one liked the passages—wormholes networking the major tunnels of Little Saigo. They were the poorest efforts of the construction workers— access routes, hammered out quickly and not meant to last.

David sneezed. Dust rose in thin swirls around his ankles, turning his shoes greyish white. The air smelled musty and worse. He was closer here, to the sump at the bottom level. The smell of old sewage was faint—not, thank God, the overpowering stench that permeated the lowest level. But he knew the odor would cling to his hair and clothes.

It was the rubble that made him nervous, indicating movement in the rock and possible structural damage. Just how safe it was down in Little Saigo was never a burning social issue, but the wormholes were unquestionably dangerous. Few people used them. He could count on being alone here. He hoped.

He remembered the old routes pretty well, as long as he went by instinct, and didn't think too hard. Some of the wormholes crossed behind major tunnels rather than going through, and some of them dead-ended into solid rock.

He smelled food—grease, garlic, fish—so he must be close to the family units. He wished he'd had dinner. Murmurs and snippets of conversation filtered through the ventilation shafts.

David moved carefully, but quickly. Light filtered into the darkness, and David veered toward it. He heard voices, activity. He clicked the red penlight off and slipped it in his pocket.

David ducked out of the wormhole and into the main corridor. A woman looked at him, then turned away. Anyone coming out of the wormholes was up to something. She flashed her wrist at David, the toogim glowing green. He raised his hands in what he hoped was a gesture of benevolence. The woman took her two daughters by the arm and walked, her gait careful. Not too fast,

David remembered. Don't stampede the predator, or throw him a scent of fear and the chase. But not too slow, either, if you want to get away.

Marion's apartment was empty and untouched, everything in order, or what passed for order in Little Saigo. The dry wall had never been installed, and the walls were a roughed-in skeleton of wires and studs. An extension cord snaked out of the apartment in the usual jury-rigged effort to bring in electricity. A chipped plastic faucet stuck out at knee level on one side wall. The original plumbing had been intended for a toilet, but it was Marion's only source of water. Water, power, and sewage were controlled by the tunnel rats. Even Marion paid.

David heard a shoe heel on concrete. His shadow, large and spidery in the lamplight, was dwarfed by another shadow.

"This here's Marion's place," a man said. The voice was deep and slow-moving, the words carefully enunciated.

David took a deep breath and waited for his heart to slow. The lined face was familiar—high cheekbones, overlarge ears, pale complexion. The man wore stained corduroy pants, heavy work shoes, and a wrinkled blue shirt. He was large, seven feet tall, and bent forward in a permanent stoop caused by years spent in cramped passageways. His hair, black and oily, was touched with grey, and his eyes were small, dark, and sleepy-looking.

"Bertie?" David said. "That you?"

The man leaned forward menacingly. "You know Bertie?"

David stepped back instinctively, showing the toogim on his wrist. "Don't you remember me? It's Silver, David Silver."

"Silver . . . Davie? Davie Silver? Mrs. Silver's boy, that right?"

David's knees felt weak. "Right. That's right."

Bertie extended a moist, callused palm. "Davie Silver! I can't believe it!" Bertie slapped his leg. "I just can't believe it's you!"

"How've you been, Bertie?"

"Okay, Davie, getting along. Hey, you remember Bennie Howitzer? That kid you used to hang around with?"

"Yeah, sure, I remember Bennie."

"He's in prison, did you know that? Long time now, he's been locked away."

David thought for a minute. "What about Gregorio?"

"Gregorio Alonso?"

"Yeah, Mrs. Alonso's boy."

"He's dead, Davie. Killed in a turf fight with those tunnel rats. And Maybelle Riverton, she's gone."

"Got out?"

"No, gone. She's a hummer now."

"Maybelle?"

"You wouldn't recognize her, Davie. Not anymore. And that girl that was so little, that Keri—"

"So, *Bertie*, how's the old toe?"

"The toe? Gosh, it's the same, Davie. Good as ever."

"Still reliable? Give me a report, Bertie."

Bertie's face went red, the blush creeping from his cheeks, down the lined and weathered neck, to the V of skin at the top of his shirt.

"Naw, now, Davie."

"Come on, Bertie. Me and Gregorio, we always used to say you should be on TV."

"Aw, Davie." The shoe was a lace-up, but Bertie had it off in no time. "There she is! The weather toe." Bertie's grin was huge and happy. "Never did think when that auto door crushed it that a accident could turn out good."

"What's it say?"

"Storm, David. Real bad weather."

"On the money, every time."

Bertie sat on the floor and admired the toe. "This old thing, on the TV?" He smiled, and worked the shoe back on.

David sat down beside him. "Listen, Bertie. I'm worried about Marion. I'm afraid something's happened."

Bertie slowly worked the lace on his shoe. "Me on TV!"

"Listen to me, Bertie. Have you seen Marion?"

"Marion?"

"I need to listen to the tapes. She may have said something that would—"

"Nobody can listen to the tapes, Davie, you know that."

"I know, Bertie, but this time I have to. I think Marion's in trouble. She may have said something—"

"Nobody can listen to the tapes."

"Bertie, *listen* to me. Marion's in trouble. She could get hurt."

"Who would hurt Marion? Nobody bothers her, Davie, *you* know that."

"Somebody has."

"Hurt Marion?"

"I think so."

"Who . . . a prowler, David? I seen one in the hall there. A prowler got Marion?"

"Who are the prowlers, Bertie?"

"Bad ones. They take people. Marion's people. Even tunnel rats.

They got that girl that had the toy box."

"Toy box. Magic box? You mean Naomi Chessfield?"

"I don't know her name. She hides a lot. But she's got big—"

"That's her. We got to find her, Bertie, find her fast."

"Got a knot here, Davie. Give old Bertie time to get the knot."

David watched Bertie's thick fingers pick at the worn rawhide lace. The urge to push Bertie's hands away and tie the shoe himself was almost more than he could bear.

David stuck his hands in his pockets.

FORTY-THREE

DAVID HEARD A WOMAN SINGING.

"Is that Marion?"

Bertie stopped, his bulk plugging the passageway. The man's sweaty musk was pungent in the constricted tunnel. "What, Davie?"

"The singing, Bertie. It sounds like Marion."

"Aw, no, Davie, that's Miz Brendon. She's got her grandbaby back from her son-in-law. He's no good, that son-in-law, so she's hiding out."

"Okay, Bertie, okay. Let's find Marion."

It was amazing, David thought, what he could hear, back in the wormholes. Bertie lumbered ahead, bent forward at the waist, moving with easy familiarity. What things had Bertie heard, coming through the ventilation shafts?

"Shhhh. Here, Davie. See that? A prowler. But he hain't got Marion."

David stood on tiptoe to peer over Bertie's shoulder. A man stood with his back to them, keeping lookout down the tunnels. The light was dim, but David could see tattoos laced across the man's forearms. A tunnel rat. Some kind of cooperation going on.

"Bertie," David whispered. "Can we get out farther down this way?" He jerked a thumb in the direction opposite where the man kept watch.

"Comes out near them tunnel rats, Davie. Not a good place. Them down there, they don't even like Marion getting into these parts. Kind of off-limits."

"It's a good place for the prowlers, Bertie. It's got an exit large enough for a car. That's where I need to go."

There wasn't room to swap places. Bertie pointed. "Go back, Davie. Go . . . um . . . that way when the floor makes a hill."

David was aware, suddenly, of the rhythmic groan of powerful machinery.

"What is that?"

Bertie laid a heavy hand on his shoulder. "Don't be 'fraid of that, David. That's the pump. The city got it working again, I guess. They been at it a couple days."

David nodded. The sump had been leaking into the city water supply for years. "Didn't know they finally got around to pumping it out."

Bertie shrugged. "Don't do 'em much good. Tunnel rats keep breaking it when no one's around. Marion told them down at the government how much to pay them rats. Had some kind of agreement, but then they said—"

"No extortion for wiseguys and riffraff," David said. "I remember reading about it."

The sound of voices was faint over the low rumble of the pump.

" . . . it up. We don't need this. You'll cost us everything, Santana, if you haven't already."

Winston's voice.

"But why here? They expected you to come here, this was stupid."

"Winston, the words, please." The Elaki. "For the control group. It is research project, you know of parameters, Winston."

"The control group isn't *needed* now."

"*Winston.* For your phase two. P.H."

"*P.H.?* That's not ready to try on *people.*"

"Oh, but it is." The voice was slow, silky. "P.H. is beautiful, Winston. It sets us apart in the marketplace. It's the whole point."

"But we can't control the *reaction* yet. My God, you let it out now, everything just gets that much worse. I need *time.* Can't you people understand that? What's a few more months? We can give people what they want, *exactly* what they want. No addiction, no side effects, no . . . no goddamn scummy drug dealers—"

Winston cried out and David heard the sibilant hiss of a distressed Elaki.

"You *will* cease. For to kill him, most stupid."

Light diffused the darkness as David and Bertie neared the main tunnel. David put his penlight away, and pulled his gun out of the holster. Bertie's breath was warm on the back of his neck.

"What are you going to do with these women?" Winston sounded ill.

"Don't you idiots know who you're dealing with?" Naomi Chessfield's voice was incredulous. "That's the Maid. *Marion.* Nobody touches her. Her people will rise up and—"

"The only thing keeps the tunnel rats in hand be me," Marion said dryly. "He ugly, but not stupid. Don't be worrying, Naomi."

"They'll rise up and kill each and every—"

Marion sighed. "She harmless. And under my protection."

"That's between you and the rats." The low silky voice again. David crept closer.

"Turn your back, Winston. Think of your work."

"That old lady's *blind* for Christ's sake!"

"Ah, Winston."

"Don't *touch* me. You people are sick. Come on, Tester, let's get out of this."

David wondered if he could get close enough to see without being spotted.

"Load the whacko."

David moved to the edge of the tunnel. Someone was moving off to the left, toward the mag lev entrance. Marion and Naomi were huddled close together, next to the wall. Two men bent over them. There was no sign of Winston or the Elaki.

"Marion!"

David clamped a hand over Bertie's mouth. "Quiet. Quiet."

Marion was rising slowly to her feet. "You come into my place. You take this girl under my protection. You get trouble, from me and the rats."

David came out of the wormhole quietly, then slipped on a loose rock.

"Don't move," David said. Bertie lumbered out behind him.

Both men stood up. Their forearms were covered with iridescent tattoos that shone in the dim light of the tunnel.

"I said don't move." The men were still. "Marion, it's David. Naomi, I want you to take Marion's arm and move away. Don't get between me and the gun. *Bertie*, stay put."

"Heigh ho, Silver!" Marion shook her head. "And you all too young to know what I mean."

She moved slowly, and David wondered if she was hurt. Come on, he thought. Come on. He pictured the man keeping watch in the tunnel behind them. Two with Santana, the Elaki had said. And three who hunt.

"Bertie, take Marion and Naomi and get out of here. Not *that* way. There are other prowlers in the tunnels. Go back the way we came. Find a safe place and stay put till I find you."

"Be careful, Davie."

Bertie and Marion disappeared into the wormhole. Naomi stopped at the entrance, then turned back around.

"Go on," David said.

"They've got my box."

She stood so close he could hear the quick intake of her breath, the loud gulps when she swallowed. David didn't like the way the men looked at her. He wished she had a shirt on, under the vest.

"Naomi." David clenched his teeth. "Go."

Tears slipped down her cheeks.

"That *one*," she said. "He . . . she. It's got my box. *You know what's in there, Silver.*"

"Naomi, *go. Now. Move.*"

He heard something behind him.

"Go, go, go!"

A shot flicked sparks along the wall beside him, and echoed through the tunnel.

"Throw it behind you, cop."

David dropped the gun.

"Up against the wall."

David backed into the cold stone wall. A man in a red sweatshirt waved the barrel of a gun. The lookout. David's knees felt weak.

Naomi was trembling. She had a cigarette between her fingers, but her hand shook so badly she dropped it.

One of the men against the wall, one with a heavy handlebar mustache and a trim narrow waist, lit a cigarette. He licked the end of it and offered it to Naomi. Her mouth popped open, making David think of a hungry baby bird.

She took a small puff of the cigarette.

"Move away, Quintero," the lookout man said.

Quintero stepped back, but kept his eyes on Naomi.

David didn't hear anything, but saw Naomi shift her attention to the well of darkness on his right. Both Quintero and the fat-necked man beside him turned to look.

David checked the lookout man. The man's gaze was cool, and still focused on him. David squinted into the darkness.

The figure moved closer and David caught his breath. Santana was tall and impossibly thin, soft brown skin covering a build that was lean to excess, thin wires of muscle strung over bone. Two women moved stealthily behind him—a matched pair of cats with a dangerous aura of confidence.

"I see you, all my babies." The melodious voice was marred by a slight childish lisp. Santana paused under the light, and David studied him, as he was meant to.

Santana's eyes were deep brown, the whites so clear they were almost blue. The lashes were black and long, girlish. He wore black boots that had silver over the toe, black jeans, and a white silk shirt. A silver buckle glinted on a leather belt that encircled a slender waist.

His fingers were long and supple. The cheekbones on the face were high and pronounced, the skin smooth and luminous. A beautiful man/woman—mesmerizing as a snake. Small rosebud breasts swelled under the white shirt, nipples erect, prominent.

"Give it to me," Naomi said. "*You've* got it!"

Quintero turned to Santana. "That box she was carrying. That's what she means."

Santana smiled. From nowhere, it seemed, the box appeared in the long brown fingers.

Naomi bared her teeth. David felt her move just as she screamed. She hurled toward Santana with the lit cigarette.

The women behind Santana strained forward, then settled back at a small movement of Santana's hand. The box smashed on the stone floor.

Santana held his arms wide, welcoming Naomi like a lover. He swept her off her feet, and pulled her arms behind her back. David heard the pop when both shoulders dislocated. Santana put his mouth on Naomi's, stifling her cry of pain. He bent her to him, pressing until her neck snapped. David flinched.

Santana rounded his lips over Naomi's mouth, like a dog sucking marrow from a bone.

The tunnel was silent. Quintero took a deep breath.

Santana's mouth slipped wetly off Naomi's lips. He let her go and she slid down his chest, her chin catching his belt buckle before her weight pulled her to the floor. David stared at the crumpled body, the glassy eyes, the magic box that lay an inch from the lifeless hand.

"David Silver," Santana said softly, and the warm promising voice sent ice up David's spine. "I been wanting to know you for some time now." Santana held out a hand. David felt the flesh on his cheek tighten and twitch, though Santana was not close enough to touch.

"I know Rose." The voice implied a peculiar intimacy. "She and I go way back. So I been curious about you. Her husband. A cop." The voice was lilting, sweet and slightly southern. "And the weather, you know, is in our favor. We have time to kill." Santana motioned to Quintero. "Hold him."

Quintero grabbed David's arms, and the coat bunched and strained, pulling across David's back, clumping over his shoulders. He was hot, suddenly, cramped, the coat holding him like a straitjacket.

Santana was smiling, face luminous and soft.

"I will love you." The rich timbre of the voice promised him pleasure. "I will hurt you." The voice throbbed, promising pain.

Santana moved toward him in the dark passageway, body flowing, sinuous, rippling ever close. David feared the proximity, yet felt a fascination that was almost desire. Get it over, he thought. Get it done.

The seductive slowness became a blur of motion, and a well-calculated blow caught David on the left side, breaking two ribs and bruising a third. He heard the chuff of his breath as it escaped his throat, felt Quintero's grip tighten on his arms and take his weight as his legs jelled and collapsed beneath him. And he knew, in a small working part of his mind, that Santana had pulled a punch that could have gone right through him.

Santana touched David's cheek with fingers that smelled faintly of lilac. He cupped David's chin in the sweet-smelling hands and bent close, licking David's lower lip with a fleshy wet red tongue.

David closed his eyes and groaned, clenching his teeth against the tongue that strained between his lips.

Santana pulled away, sighing softly. "Sweet. So sweet."

David lifted his head, his voice a guttural hiss. "Stick to the pain, Santana."

FORTY-FOUR

DAVID'S MOUTH WAS PULPY AND WET, AND BLOOD TRICKLED down the back of his throat. He coughed, thinking he should roll over on his stomach.

"He's still moving."

David coughed again, and strained sideways.

"More like *trying* to move."

"We been here too long." Santana's voice. "Beller, check for weather. See if it's safe to go out."

"What about her?"

"Leave it."

"We taking the cop?"

"I have something in mind."

Someone was lifting him—firm hands under his armpits, propping him against the wall. He slid sideways. Santana straightened him up again.

David couldn't remember being hurt this bad before, couldn't remember feeling such hot brokenness inside.

"*Silver.*" Santana patted his cheeks affectionately. "Look at me, Silver. Focus. Still there? I have something for you."

Why did he keep on? David wondered.

"I wish I had time to take you with me," Santana said, voice soft, regretful.

David wanted to lay down, but there was a reason—wasn't there?—that he needed to sit up.

"Pay attention." Santana opened his fist. "See this?"

David squinted. Fine black dust laced the cracks and crevices of Santana's moist palm.

"This is it, my friend. My *cop.* Black Diamond. It will make you feel better, so much better. And it's the new and improved version. Programmable, Silver, do you know what that means?"

David wanted to say something, but the words wouldn't come.

"Easy, Silver, take it slow. This is just a taste. Five minutes. Five intense beautiful minutes. But if you like it, Silver—and you will—and if you ask me nice, I'll give you something that will

198

keep you up for seven hours. That's *hours*—seven. And just the beginning of what we can do, Silver, think of that. Programmable highs. The drug has no limits, only people do."

Santana stroked David's shoulder and David flinched backward, the pain hot and electric. Broken collarbone, David decided. Christ.

Santana smiled. "I'm afraid, the shape you're in, you may not survive. And then, maybe you will. Either way, the word will get out. From the coroner's office, or the hospital grapevine. And the cops will shiver, and gear up their guys—ready to battle my Diamond. But the customers, Silver, *my* customers, will line up for miles.

"So this is for you, my cop." Santana blew Black Diamond from the palm of his hand. The black dust settled with soft finality over David's face.

FORTY-FIVE

IT WAS OVER TOO SOON—A MEMORY WHILE HE WAS STILL TRYing to hold it. The pain seeped back, waves and waves, intense, grinding, taking his breath away.

Tears trickled from the corners of his eyes.

Clothing rustled—there was someone in the passageway. Someone had watched. Boot heels clicked on the stone floor, getting closer and closer.

"Come on, Quintero, we need you right now. The van's on its side and we need everybody to get it up."

"On its side!"

"Man, you should see it. We had a blow like you wouldn't believe. Whole side of the street's wiped out."

"What about him?"

"He ain't going nowhere. Santana said come."

Their footsteps were loud, then soft. They would be back, David knew.

He rolled sideways and tried to get up on his knees. He couldn't raise his left arm, so he pushed with his right, rocking back and forth, trying to keep his balance. He remembered when his daughters were babies, how they had swayed back and forth on their knees, trying to crawl. Had they been this frustrated?

His legs went, pitching him facedown on the floor. His fingers brushed something soft and feathery. Naomi's hair. David stared into her sad, wary face.

He pushed with his toes, pulled with his right elbow, and inched across the floor. Sweat ran down his temples and seeped across his back, drenching his shirt and raincoat.

He stopped at the edge of the wormhole. He wanted the raincoat off. He wiggled out of it, keeping the left arm straight, setting up hot runnels of pain. The broken ribs kept his breathing shallow, but he was able, finally, to crawl away from the bloody, sweat-stained coat, into the cold dusty blackness of the wormhole.

He kept moving, going slowly, treasuring every inch of progress that took him farther away from Santana. He understood Rose's nightmares, her fears, her memories. He didn't know where he was heading. He could die in the black twists and turns, like a mouse behind kitchen walls.

There were worse things than solitude and darkness.

The temptation to press close to the wall and rest was getting stronger. He was cold, and shivers ran through him in bursts of agony. He stopped moving, resting his cheek on the gritty rock floor.

He wished he had kissed the girls good-bye. Which one of them had been crying?

So few of his friends had made it out of Little Saigo. Why him and not them? He thought of the woman he'd heard singing when he and Bertie had made their way behind the walls. Had Ruth sung to him when he was a baby? Had his mother?

How wasteful it was, to throw away Ruth's affection for his children.

He heard singing again—a man's voice, baritone and pure. "Hatikvah." Jews in the tunnel. The voice washed over him with the comfort of his father's affection.

His father had taught him so many things—his prayers, his duties, how to tie knots, how to hammer a nail. But he had not taught him how to keep Lavinia happy.

He wondered if his father was really dead.

David crawled. He would keep moving until he found a way out of the wormhole. He would kiss his daughters.

A large cockroach wandered past his cheek.

His breath came quickly, and the broken ribs circled his chest with a deep hot ache. Best not to think, he decided. Bertie would stay put, as ordered. Mel would never find him behind the dark stone walls. Santana might.

Definitely better not to think.

The top of his head bumped solid rock. David stretched his hand forward and sideways. The wormhole had ended. No twists, no turns, definitely the end. He reached upward, felt rock, and realized the ceiling pressed two inches over his head.

The sump pump throbbed beneath the rock.

David squirmed sideways, but there was no room to turn. His elbow wedged him in tight. He could not breathe, or go forward. He yanked his elbow loose and squeezed his eyes shut. Slow, easy breaths, Silver. Slow, easy breaths.

He inched backward, his left toe hitting rock. Fear made him cold, and he sobbed. There could not be rock behind him. *Think.* He'd crawled in, he could crawl back out.

He prodded backward with his foot. He'd turned a corner without being aware of it. He moved backward slowly, keeping his mind strictly on the task at hand.

The jog in the tunnel was a short one. David squirmed back into the open wormhole.

His shoulder was swelling and aching with mounting intensity. He thrashed from side to side, trying to get away from the pain. Moving hurt more, and he forced himself to lay still. If he kept going, he chanced working himself into unknown depths of rock that did not open into any tunnels, but instead drove him deeper into the earth.

Behind was Santana.

David laid his head down on the cold rock floor.

Somewhere a dog was barking. David opened his eyes. He heard the scrape and scuffle of dirt underfoot. A rock hit the wall, setting up reverberations in the wormhole behind him.

"What the *fuck* is going on here?" The voice came through the ventilation shaft, echoing oddly.

David closed his eyes and smiled. Mel's voice. A dog barked, then whined, scrabbling at the rock on the other side of the wall. Dead Meat? Leave it to Mel.

David frowned. The scuffling noises had come from behind. If Mel and the dog were on the other side of the wall, what was in the passage behind him?

Something—someone?—was in the tunnel, heading his way. David held his breath and listened. Whoever it was moved steadily and swiftly. His best bet was to stay quiet.

Pale yellow light wavered across his foot, and striped his leg and hip. David winced when the light hit his eyes.

"Silver." The voice caressed him, and the light went out.

David's cry amounted to little more than a moan, and Santana's hand was across his mouth before he could call out. Santana crouched over him, his silky lips warm on David's ear.

"Did you forget that I promised you pleasure, my cop? A taste was all you had. I have a programmed pleasure for you, if you want it."

David bit hard, teeth latching onto Santana's soft palm. He tasted sweat and dirt. Santana slammed his fist into David's side. David gagged.

Dead Meat barked frantically on the other side of the wall.

"What the fuck, you stupid dog! He ain't in the goddamn rock!"

David closed his eyes.

"Shhh, now, shhhh, Silver. I'll give you a choice. Call for help, if you like. Or take the Diamond. I have it right here."

Santana rattled a packet.

"What will it be, my cop?"

He took his hand away from David's mouth.

David licked his lips. He needed to call out, warn Mel. But the Diamond would take the pain away, let him breathe. He could go back to that good place, and get out of this one, just one more time . . .

He raised a hand to hit the wall when he yelled. But he did not yell. He dropped his hand slowly, curling the fingers into a fist.

Santana laughed softly. "I thought so. You are no different, my cop. No different."

He opened the packet, and David felt the warmth of Santana's breath as the black dust misted in his face.

FORTY-SIX

SANTANA HAD DAVID'S ANKLES, AND WAS DRAGGING HIM backward through the wormhole. Santana held a flash in his mouth, and David watched the patterns of light on the wall.

His hearing was suddenly very acute. He could hear the shift and groan of rock in the tunnel.

Santana stopped, easing David's legs gently to the floor.

"They have to find you, Silver, before you decompose." Santana kissed him gently. "Good-bye, my cop."

David squinted his eyes. Santana had left him at the end of the wormhole, and he had a clear view of the main tunnel. He heard the echo of voices.

"It was close to here. Davie sent us out through the wormhole."

"How many of these prowlers were there?"

David frowned, wondering if he was imagining his wife's voice. Maybe not. Rose and Haas were getting too tangled up in this case. Why had Mel let them come? Why hadn't he gotten backup from Halliday?

"I don't think I remember how many. Lots of them."

David heard their footsteps, their breath moving through their lungs, the hiss of blood that moved through their veins like liquid silk.

"Ah. This is bad." Haas's voice. "Who is this?"

David closed his eyes, watching himself spin in the darkness.

"Her neck's been snapped," Rose said. "So Santana's here."

"You can't be sure it's Santana, Rosy."

"I'm sure. *Where* is Mel?"

"Back a ways, fooling with Hilde."

"She's as likely to be on the trail of a rat as she is to be after David."

"Bertie, where does this tunnel lead?"

David rolled his head to one side. Painful. It wasn't supposed to hurt.

"It leads outside," Bertie said. "The tunnel rats use it a lot. Davie wouldn't go back there. Davie knows better."

The voices receded. David opened his mouth and watched a clear silver bell escape between his lips.

Rose's voice drifted back.

"I don't *know* what I heard. No, go on. We need to cover as much as we can, as fast as we can."

Rose was moving cautiously. David saw shadows, too many shadows. Somebody else was out there.

"Hello, Rose."

David heard her intake of breath.

"Hello, Santana."

"Enjoying your retirement? Been a long time since . . . the old days. God, the memories. You, me, and Monolo. Pretty Monolo. Not so pretty there at the end, eh? Now I wonder, Rose, why you married a cop. No, don't do that. Don't rush me. Kill me, and you won't find him. I'm the only one who knows where your Silver is."

David listened, but Rose didn't say anything. He could hear her breath coming in deep gulps.

Something flapped, like a sail in the wind.

"See what I have, Rose? Do you recognize his coat?"

Rose had stopped breathing so hard, David realized. He couldn't hear her breathing at all.

"You could give it away, maybe, after you get the bloodstains out. I'm afraid there are a lot of those. But I got to know him, your husband. A man in pain is so revealing. He is funny, your David. Laughs at odd things and . . ."

Rose screamed, and screamed again, and the shrill echoes shattered the silence of the tunnels and brought a chill to David's back.

Footsteps pounded through the passageways. A dog barked and snarled, toenails sliding on the stone floor. David inched forward, turning his head so he could see.

Haas rounded the bend. David saw figures moving behind him.

"*Rose!* Rosy, what—"

Haas straightened suddenly, his expression oddly bland and uncaring. Light glinted on a metal handle that protruded from his back. He crumpled and fell forward.

David looked for Santana, but couldn't find him. Rose cradled Haas in her lap, oblivious to the women who moved swiftly and silently toward her. David started to crawl. He had his head and shoulders out of the wormhole when he heard a bark and a snarl. Dead Meat tore into the tunnel, hurling herself at one of the women—the blonde.

Mel was right behind the dog, holding an empty leash.

"*Rose? Rose!* Jesus Christ."

The dark-haired woman went for him.

"*There's* Davie!" Bertie lumbered into view. "Boy, Davie, you sure are trouble, just like the old days."

Dead Meat yelped and fell. Blondie aimed a kick at the dog's head and Bertie grabbed her arm. She moved sideways. Bertie's eyes widened and he crumpled.

Mel's gun went off and the dark-haired woman hit the floor. Blondie picked herself up off Bertie's chest.

"Shit," Mel said. He fired and missed, and she grabbed him in a headlock, knocking his gun to the floor and bringing her knife to his throat. Dead Meat snarled and snapped, biting the woman's calf.

"*R-Rose,*" Mel sounded almost annoyed.

The woman twisted sideways, away from the dog's teeth. Mel broke her hold, and slammed a fist into her stomach. She staggered backward, tripped over Dead Meat, and hit the floor. Mel kicked her savagely, the sweet spot on the side of her head. She quit moving.

Mel leaned against the wall, breathing hard. He shook his head and looked at David. "You weren't kidding, huh? When you said your neighborhood was tough?"

Dead Meat whimpered and licked Haas's ear. She circled three times, settled beside him, and put her head between her paws.

FORTY-SEVEN

THE TUNNELS WERE RIFE WITH MOVEMENT. DAVID OPENED HIS eyes, then closed them. Mel was lifting him up.

"Come on," Mel said, "over you go. *God.*" Mel groaned.

"Leave him, son, put him back down there." Marion's voice. "I want a look."

Soft, cool hands.

"There's a radio in my car," Mel said. "But I'm not leaving them down here while—"

"You ain't got a car, by now. And even if you call, last ambulance come down here got stripped in fifteen minutes, driver beaten to death."

"They got to meet us," Mel said. "Violation of the Critical Personnel Act of 2036, we're talking big fines and prison terms. And cops are right at the top of the list."

"They won't come, son. And it's your friend, the Hun, here, I be worried about. Can you pass him off—teacher, doctor, social worker—"

"Liquor store owner," someone said.

"Just don't say lawyer," came another voice. "Then he couldn't get buried."

There was a ripple of laughter.

"His name is Haas," Mel said. "Can we move him?"

"I got the bleeding stopped. He's a big boy, ain't he? And I got a good pulse. But this knife wound is bad. Severed nerves right along the spine. He needs critical care, but I don't rate his chances. We *shouldn't* move him, but we got no choice."

"I can *get* somebody down here, lady."

"You know what medical supplies bring on the black market in Little Saigo? Ain't no phones working, either. City's full of looters right now. Which is good, friend, 'cause otherwise the tunnel rats would have been here by now. But it ain't safe to stay here, so get out the way of my people."

"I can carry him. My partner needs—"

"Hospital. I *see* that, son. Broken clavicle, broken ribs, possible skull fracture, probably internal bleeding and lacerated organs. Not to mention his vitals are a mess. His heart don't slow down, he going to explode. So we take him up to the surface, there's *private* tunnels, lead surprising places. Maybe we can get the medics to meet us there. If they meet us at all. Okay?"

"Okay."

"Now here's the way it's gon' be. Bertie's mine. He be okay, I'll look after him. That blond prowler who hit him stays here too, and no question. The brunette one dead, so we leave her."

"I can't do that."

"I ain't asking permission, son."

David heard clothing rustle and old bones pop. "You two. Take this one here."

"Look, lady, Miss Marion, the best—"

"Hush, boy, I'm busy." David felt hands under his arms, lifting him. "Kiff, you and Ben take the big guy. Keep him facedown, and gentle as you can."

A dog snarled.

"Whoa. Hey, get your hands off."

"What?" Mel's voice again. "You want to bring this place down around your ears?"

"For shooting a dog? I eat dog."

"Don't brag in front of my sister. And don't mess with the dog. Come on, girl, we're not going to hurt him. Come on. That's good. Okay, baby, good dog, good girl. All right I got her, I got her. Come on, Rose, get your dog. Hold her for me, okay? Rose, wake up, will ya?"

David twisted sideways, but the men carrying him held him still.

"Get it moving, folks."

Light glared in his eyes, then faded. David grimaced, and the man holding his shoulders tightened his grip. They were moving through the passages, and David's left foot kept catching the wall. He wished the two men carrying him would get their rhythm coordinated.

He sang "Hatikvah" very quietly.

The man carrying his shoulders peered at him. "Why you singing, friend? What you on?"

"He got the *pretty*, he does."

David felt indignant. "*People* sing," he said. "It's Elaki can't carry a tune." He heard String's voice suddenly, loud in his head.

Who is this Jack Cracker?

" 'Take me out to the ball game,' " David sang.

"That's one I know," said the man at his feet. "Daddy taught me that one."

He joined in, their voices mixing with the scuffle of feet on stone. " 'Take me out to the park. Buy me some peanuts . . . ' "

David stopped singing, not noticing that the other man carried on without him. Peanuts. Peanuts? And the memories collided—the strange male voice in the Ambassador. "Not your problem, *Peanut*." Myer down at vice—"I ain't interested in what you want to do with *peanut* butter." The voices were one and the same. Myer had been in the Ambassador. *Myer*.

"Myer," David said.

"Say what?"

"Peanuts."

"Song makes you hungry, don't it? Sounds good to me too. Surprised *you* want anything. I get beat up like you, lose my appetite for a long time." The man sighed. "Wish I knew what you *on*."

FORTY-EIGHT

THE BARN HAD EXPLODED DURING THE TORNADO, AND PILES of splintered grey wood were strewn across the field. One of the trees had been uprooted and tossed on its side, and loose branches lay like broken arms.

The old barn was a landmark, a haven. David had expected to care when it went. He did not feel sorry that the barn was gone, and he did not feel grateful that his house, and the newer barn beside it, still stood.

He sat down in the grass and rested. Even a short walk tired him. The afternoon naps would be difficult to give up. He rubbed his shoulder. He was a new man—literally. Nano machines had rebuilt the broken bones; reknit the cracked ribs, the chipped teeth. He still ached a lot—phantom pain, the doctors insisted, like when people used to lose limbs. Which didn't make it hurt any less.

He would be careful not to break anything ever again. Five days in the hospital had been tedious as hell, even in a private room with police priority and medical science at his disposal.

Haas still waited on critical hold, at the bottom of the medical priority list, losing more and more physical function with each passing hour. His right leg was paralyzed, he could not sit up, and the now limited mobility of the left leg was fading. He drifted in and out of consciousness, and the last time David had checked, Haas had settled into a light coma.

David envied the coma. He himself had suffered too many visitors. People had found the opportunity to drop in and inquire, oh, so casually, about the "programmed" high Santana had given him. The word was out.

He still had headaches. Aftermath of the drug and the concussion, according to the Elaki neurologist. Sometimes, when his head was tight and pounding, he heard weird sounds, odd roaring. Thinking about it made his head ache. He got up and headed home.

The storm had taken shingles off the roof of his house, and ripped a drainpipe from one side. More problems that he did not have the energy to see to. His footsteps thumped the wood porch. The front door was unlocked.

Rose was sitting in the living room, reading to the girls. The house smelled like lemony detergent. The rooms were silent and neat—books put away, papers gone, everything dusted. David wasn't sure, but it looked like Rose had vacuumed the cushions on the couch.

Sunlight blazed through squeaky clean windows.

The girls were wide-eyed, but quiet. Dead Meat put her paws on his waist and whined softly.

"How are my girls?" he wanted to shout. He wished they would run to him, hug him, demand to be picked up. He would lift little Mattie up on his shoulders, swing Kendra off her feet, swoop Lisa up for a piggyback ride. He wanted to touch the baby chubbiness of Mattie's smooth cheeks; but somehow, he could not lift a hand to release that small affection, could not make the gesture that had once been as natural as air.

The girls stared at him. It was odd, how quiet they were. Dead Meat went back to the couch. Her tail hung low, and she put her head on her paws and whined.

Mattie reached down and stroked the dog's back.

David left the bedroom door open while he hung up his jacket. Rose was reading again, answering with unwonted patience when Lisa interrupted and asked questions. Rose spoke to the children with infinite kindness now, as if they would shatter at a raised or angry voice. She had found the time to clean every surface in the house. She had not found time to visit Haas in the hospital.

David sat on the bed. He should be on his way. Halliday would have picked Winston up hours ago.

Even the work—the work that framed his world—even that tasted stale now. Surely, if he kept going through the motions, things would get better.

Could he bear another dinner where he watched Rose sit before an empty plate, smile at the girls, and stare at the walls?

He stretched out on the crisply made bed. He was sleeping alone now. Rose spent her nights on the couch, sitting upright and silent in the darkness. Sometimes he got up and looked at her. She was never asleep. As far as he knew, she had not slept since that night in the tunnels.

And he knew, while he stared at her and she ignored him, that she needed him now more than she ever had. In his dreams he heard her screams, echoing through the tunnels.

David called Halliday from the bedroom phone.

"Silver here."

"David? How are you?"

"You got him?"

"In custody since eight o'clock this morning."

David checked his watch. Two P.M.

"I'm coming in," David said. "Have you fed him?"

"No."

"Wait, then."

"You insist. David, are you up to this?"

"I'm fine, Roger."

"The miracles of modern medicine."

"Something else, too. At the Ambassador, when Mel and I found Dyer's coat. There was somebody in the storeroom, talking to that Elaki—Slyde. And I think it was Myer."

"*Myer?* You saw him?"

"I heard him."

"David—"

"Roger, he said, 'Not your problem, *Peanut*.' It's the way he said it. Peanut. And when I was down at vice, he was on the phone talking about *peanut* butter. I know it was him, Roger."

"We'll see, David."

"Look, Roger, I've got a feeling about this. Get Della to check up on an ex-cop named Nimenz. Works as a bouncer at the Arrongi."

"The Arrongi, huh? Will do."

David sighed. "Thanks, Roger. See you."

His shoes were muddy. David changed into another pair, an old, shabby pair of Eagles. Best to be comfortable. The days just got longer and longer.

FORTY-NINE

"HEY, SILVER, HOW'S IT GOING?"

"You come down yet, Silver? Or you still flying?"

"¿*Que pasa,* Davidolo?"

"Bahm bah bahm—the *interrogator* is here. He vill make you talk, und you vill like eet!"

"Did you hear how he spilled the garter belt strangler?"

"That's nothing, man, one of Valeri's gang named him in his will. Talk about establishing rapport."

David ignored them. He wanted to talk to Della, but she had a civilian at her desk. The man held his head in his hands.

"I mean I was completely, totally dependent on the *kindness,* the *charity,* of a total stranger. No one's going to help me—that's what I thought." The man's voice was hoarse. He looked to be in his forties, well fed, expensive suit. "My own coworkers—I've worked with these people, off and on, maybe nine years! They won't let me in the door. Said it was *procedure*—I'd have to work it out."

David stopped by Mel's desk. He inclined his head.

"Stolen identity?"

Mel nodded.

"What's he doing here?"

Mel shrugged. "Ought to be down on Minton, spraying his spit at the Hacker patrol."

The man threw up his hands. "I couldn't even get back in my house! My kids will let me in, but they're not home from school yet. And this man, this perfect stranger, comes shuffling up while I'm digging in my pockets—for *what* I don't know, I got no credit now and who the hell carries cash? And he says, 'Man, can I help you?' This . . . this *fellow* is unshaven and I had taken him for some kind of Little Saigo derelict." Expensive suit leaned back in his chair. "I said I got to get somewhere and I got no credit. He says where you need to go? I mean, he *knows* just by looking I'm desperate. So I say, the police, I need the cops. And he tells the car the cops, and the car says *which* cops, and starts reeling off—city cop? County cop? Missing persons, homicide? And it hits me." The man leaned close suddenly and Della flinched. "They killed

213

me. Some computer just as good as *killed* me."

"Sir, this is stolen identity, covered by CCP—"

"Who?"

"CCP. They have jurisdiction on all computer crimes. They're on Minton Avenue. I can—"

"No! I want homicide! I want—"

"Come on, David," Mel said. "Roger's waving."

David followed Mel into the office. Halliday was on the phone, but he motioned them in. Mel sat on the table, swinging his legs.

"Look, I'll get back to you." Halliday put the phone down and gave David a wary smile.

"How's the shoulder, David?" Roger said.

"Okay. Where is he?"

"We put him in two."

Mel grinned. "You're a mean bastard, David. Guy didn't even get breakfast. I feed *my* prisoners."

"Not two," David said. "I don't want the mirror. Even the dumb ones know it's two-way. This guy is smart and self-conscious. And I want his undivided attention."

"Okay. I'll have—"

"No, I'll move him. Just get three set up to record."

"Going to tell him he's in the movies?"

"No. We're after other fish. That okay with you, Roger?"

Halliday nodded. "You'll need this." He handed David a file folder. "See what you can get on that business in the tunnels. We got Santana for the assault, torture, and attempted murder of a police officer. You." Halliday stretched backward over his chair. "Can we make it stick? *Probably.* Didn't get the usual crime-scene evidence, but Christ, the city was downed by a tornado. May be your word against his. Jury will go with you."

"Got to find him first."

"Matter of time." Halliday looked thoughtful. "I want him for Dyer. See if you can get Winston to help you there."

Mel scratched his thigh. "I don't know about connecting him to Dyer. So far we got nothing to connect Santana with Machete Man. Nothing since prison. No prints in Clinton's apartment, no testimony from appliances. In fact, nothing at all in there. Somebody ran nano machines over the whole thing. We didn't get a loose DNA molecule." Mel shook his head. "Hell, that alone should do it. Convict him on obvious lack of evidence. Admission of guilt."

"Yeah," Halliday said. "And vice can make a morals charge stick when somebody blushes."

"We got nothing from the street either." Mel tipped his chair back. "Nobody admits seeing Santana and Clinton together, which is shit. Thing is, nobody wants to cross Santana, for which I can't blame them. Even if they did, these losers never go down good with a jury."

David nodded and looked at Halliday. "Lab ever get any more testimony from Dyer's car?"

Halliday shook his head. "Just complaints about maintenance. It was a '29, they were bad about that. Nothing from the appliances in Judith Rawley's apartment either, about anybody but the guys you saw. And they're dead." Halliday scratched his cheek. "So Winston's our best bet. Did some checking on that guy, Nimenz— bouncer at the Arrongi? Used to work the Organized Crime Task Force, back in '31. Along with another hotshot who came in off the robbery unit."

"Myer."

"Yeah. Good hunch, David. You going to use Winston to get to Myer?"

"It's the only thing we've got that might hold up."

Roger nodded. "Try to keep everything admissible. You never know."

David looked at Mel. "Do me a favor. Give me some time with him, then walk by with some sandwiches—roast beef, with onions, pickles, and fries. The works. Make sure you get us something to drink, too."

"Done."

David rubbed his shoulder. "Wish me luck."

He tried to clear his mind and relax as he went down the hallway. No hostility, he told himself. Forget that this guy's been working with Santana, that he left you in the tunnels, that he's a cowardly sniveling little shit.

Great, David thought. I'm sounding like Mel. Real detached.

He took deep even breaths.

He stared through the two-way mirror. Winston's arms were folded and he was slumped in his seat, muscles rigid. He's pissed, David thought.

David tucked the file under his arm and pushed the door just a little too hard. Winston jumped.

"Hello, Dennis," David said. He glanced around the tight little room. "Where's your paralegal?"

"I . . . they just said questions. Aid in the investigation."

"Dennis, you have the right to legal representation during questioning that might incriminate you. And you don't *have* to talk to me. You know that?"

"Yeah, I . . . I know. Look, maybe we can do this some other time, okay? I should go home now. Alex needs to be fed."

"You can't go home."

"But you said—"

"I said you can have a paralegal. You're in custody, Dennis."

"But when . . . when can I go home?" Winston glanced at the mirror.

David opened the door and looked down the hallway. "Let's go," he said.

"Go where?"

"Come on."

Dennis was handcuffed. Good touch, Mel, David thought. He took hold of Winston's arm and led him into the hallway.

Winston ducked his head, avoiding the eyes of the cops behind their desks. Shame, David thought, would work well on Dennis Winston. It was worth changing interrogation rooms just to parade the man up and down the precinct.

"Dennis, you need to make a pit stop? Men's room?"

"Uh, yeah."

"Here." He let go of Winston's arm and stuck his head through the doorway of the men's room. One of the stalls was occupied. Somebody was spinning a roll of toilet paper.

David lowered his voice. "I wish I could take the handcuffs off you. But there's a rule."

Winston nodded and stumbled in. He stopped in front of a urinal and fumbled with his zipper. A toilet flushed and the stall door swung open.

Vic Junn came out and headed for the sinks. David folded his arms. Junn was a looker, the prick. A stroke of luck.

Junn chose the towel dispenser next to Winston. He dried his hands and peered over Winston's shoulder. Winston hung his head, shoulders hunched forward.

" 'Lo, Silver."

David nodded.

"Ought to at least take the poor bastard's cuffs off," Junn muttered on his way out the door.

Winston stayed in front of the urinal, but nothing happened. He zipped his pants and looked at David in the mirror.

"Look, this is silly," David said. He put his thumb on the release button of the handcuffs. The print registered, and the cuffs sprang open.

"There. I'll be right outside, okay?"

Winston nodded.

David stood in front of the scarred metal door. Definitely against the rules, this time.

A few minutes later Winston tapped on the door. David took his elbow.

"This way."

The interrogation room was small, cell-like, the green tile floor battered and dirty. The only furniture was a scarred wood table and two metal chairs, side by side. Mel had set it up just the way David liked. The ashtray was gone, and a pitcher of water and a glass were in the center of the table. A new Miranda-Pro sat to one side.

"Have a seat," David said.

He pulled the Miranda-Pro close to his end of the table. Then he turned his chair so he faced Winston, almost knee to knee. For the average white middle-class American male, twenty-seven inches was the limit of comfortable proximity. David made sure he was closer.

"Your full name is Dennis Jacob Winston. Is that correct?"

"Yes."

The Miranda-Pro clicked, recording the voices, as well as printing a written copy.

David checked the voice registers. Fine.

"Can you speak up?" he said.

Winston leaned forward. "My name is Dennis Jacob Winston."

"You are thirty-eight years old, and were born in Greenspier, Ohio. Is this correct?"

"Correct."

"Your social security number is 2-770-999-321."

"Yes."

"Your address is 32 Cliffdale Road, Rainbow Townhomes, zip code 43226-99345-89."

"Yes."

"And you live alone?"

"Well, I . . . have Alex."

"We usually don't put cats into the official record, Dennis, but . . . if you like. You live alone, though you share your home with a cat named Alex. Correct?"

Winston straightened in his chair. "I do."

"Mr. Winston, has anyone Mirandized you? Advised you of your rights?"

"Your partner. That . . . Mel."

"Detective Burnett?"

"Yes, Detective Burnett."

"Let's go through it again. You have the right to remain silent. Anything you say can and will be used against you in court. You have the right to talk to a paralegal for advice before we ask you any questions, and to have the paralegal with you during questioning.

"You will be appointed a paralegal from the Gucci County Public Defender's Office, but you are free to hire a paralegal from the private sector, if you so desire.

"If you decide to answer questions without a paralegal present, you retain the right to stop answering questions, at any time. You also have the right to stop answering at any time until you talk to a paralegal. Do you understand these rights?"

"Yes, I do."

"Is there any language you need explained? Any questions concerning these rights?"

"No. No questions."

"Place your thumb here." David guided Winston's hand. The Miranda-Pro beeped. "Good. Now." David tore the printed copy across the perforation. As usual, the left-hand corner pulled a ragged hunk from the next page.

"Sign this, please. Right *there*." David handed Winston a pen. "Do you want a paralegal?"

"I don't know. What am I being charged with?"

"There are, so far, no official charges lodged. My captain and the DA are working on conspiracy to commit murder, conspiracy to sell class-A illegal substances, and obstruction of justice."

"But that . . . that's no fair. I'm not the one . . ."

"Mr. Winston, are you waiving your rights to a paralegal?"

"Look, let's talk about this. *I'm* not the one you want."

David activated the Miranda-Pro. "Mr. Winston, you will have to sign this waiver, if you want to discuss this."

Winston took the pen.

"Read it," David said. "Out loud."

Winston cleared his throat and read.

David leaned back in his chair. "You're thirty-eight years old."

Winston sighed loudly.

"Is that right, Dennis? Thirty-eight?"

"Why do you ask, if you already know?"

David folded his arms and waited. Winston sat quietly for three minutes. He swallowed and shifted in his seat. He looked up at David.

"Well?"

David stared at him.

"All right, yes, I'm thirty-eight years old."

"You got a B.S. in chemical engineering at Georgia Tech."

"Chem E and pharmacology."

"And an M.S. in computer science. At Virginia Pol."

"Virginia Polytechnical Institute."

"You graduated Phi Beta Kappa with Highest Distinction. From Georgia Tech."

"So?"

"You spent six years working for Procter and Gamble, then three years at Kaypon Pharmaceuticals. Then you moved to Washington, D.C., and spent two years working on a government project called Ferrus. What was your job title on that project?"

"I was . . . you would have to have a security clearance for me to talk about that. You have no 'need to know.' "

Della had been told exactly that when she'd tried to get some background on Project Ferrus.

"And then you transferred here to Saigo City. To work on Project Horizon."

"Yeah."

"How long have you known Santana?"

"Not . . . not long."

"A week?"

"Yeah. Yeah, 'bout that." Winston's muscles were rigid.

David poured water in the glass and pushed it toward him. Winston took it gratefully, draining it halfway.

"Maybe a month," David said.

"Maybe."

"Maybe, Winston, more like three years. Maybe since you started on Project Horizon."

"No, I didn't know him then. I only just . . . only just met him."

David shook his head sadly. "Don't lie to me, Dennis."

"I'm not lying."

"Dennis, I've been a cop a long time. I can spot the *good* ones."

"I'm telling you the truth."

David sat back in his chair and folded his arms.

It was strange, but unmistakable, that the smarter they were, the more physiological changes when they lied. Unless, of course, you were dealing with a psychopath. Someone like Santana.

It would be fatal to let Winston get away with even a small lie.

David was aware of footsteps in the hallway.

"Look at you, Dennis. Your mouth is dry—go ahead, have some more water. Your face is red. Feel how hot your cheeks are. Your

muscles are stiff as a board. You're not going to get anywhere,
unless you tell the truth. You're going to jail. For murder. For
dealing."

"That's not fair!"

David softened his tone. "No, of course it's not fair. You were
trying to do your job."

"I was."

"You wanted to help people."

"But the thing is, *I do*. I *really* do!"

"Hey, Dennis, I understand that. It's the other people, the
Santanas, who ought to be locked up. But I don't have anything
on Santana. And I do have a lot on you."

"Like what?"

David smiled sadly.

"Honest to *God*, Silver, you got to believe me. I do not know
anything about that end."

"What end?"

"The . . . the dealing."

"And the killing."

"And the killing." A drop of sweat rolled down Winston's temple.

"See, Dennis," David leaned close. "See, what *I'm* saying is,
maybe you weren't a part of it. You're not the kind of man who
murders young women, who kills policemen. But you know some
things that can help me get the ones who did. What I'm trying
to find out here is . . . are you the kind of guy who doesn't care?
Who can turn away when a young girl's neck gets snapped by a
drug dealer?"

Winston flinched.

David opened the file. "Here she is. Not too pretty. Want to
look at this?"

"No."

"You don't like it?"

"Of course not!"

"No, of course not. Decent people don't look at things like this.
They're not used to it. And, Dennis, I think you're a decent guy.
Santana—he's not a decent guy. You and I both know that. When
did you first meet him?"

"I met him . . . one summer. 2037. Right after I started on Horizon."

"Did you ever see *this* man?"

David held up a picture.

"I don't know. I don't think so."

"Do you know who he is?"

Winston shrugged.

"This is Vernon Ray Clinton. Machete Man. I thought you would have recognized him from the newspapers. They printed his picture several times."

"I guess . . . yeah, he does look familiar. I didn't read the articles."

"Too upsetting, Dennis? Weren't you curious? Didn't you want a look at the guy who broke into your grandmother's home?"

"Look, Silver, I . . ."

"The guy who crept through her house. She heard him come in, Dennis. Think about that. She lay in her bed. An old woman, heart beating like a scared rabbit, up against a man who has already hacked five people to death. Against a guy who was going to cut her up, and enjoy it. Have fantasies, Dennis—sexual fantasies— about cutting up your grandmother. He masturbated all over her bedspread, Dennis."

"For God's *sake*, Silver."

"Not for God's sake, Dennis. For her sake. For your grandmother. Who would still be alive, if she hadn't been a convenient tool for guys like Clinton and Santana!"

"Look." Winston licked his lips. "You got to understand. I don't want you going out to the lab. I want to keep working. I don't want this in the news!"

"It's too late for all that, Dennis. Don't you see, this has gotten out of hand? I can give you one thing. I can keep this out of the media. For a while. So your people out there can finish up, and make their announcements, before they get blown away by a hostile press."

"I . . . but what about me?"

"We'll protect you."

"But my work—"

"No go. We can't let them get at you. Maybe you can pick it up after this all blows over. Maybe it will be a good thing—clean out all the bad elements."

"They'll close the whole thing down."

"That might be a good idea. You could get a fresh start. No crooks. No dealers. No scum."

Dennis was right, David knew that. Once the project got closed down, it would never be funded again. But he told Winston what he wanted to hear. It always worked, telling people what they wanted to hear.

"You're not one of them, Dennis. Are you?"

"No."

"Look at this picture again. You sure you've never seen him with Santana?"

"That summer . . . when I first signed on. I saw them together a couple of times in the lab. After that, no. They were getting careful."

"What were they doing when you saw them?"

"Talking."

"You overhear what they said?"

"No. Just that they laughed a lot. They looked at us funny. The staff."

The footsteps outside got heavier.

"You hungry, Dennis? I didn't get lunch so I sent for something."

David opened the door. Mel handed him a grease-specked bag.

"Thanks, Mel."

"Wait. Don't forget the drinks."

David shut the door. "Come on, Dennis. Grab a sandwich. Orange Crush or Coke? Here, don't forget fries." David handed him a napkin, and waited for him to take a bite. "Okay, now, when did they first start raiding Little Saigo?"

Winston stopped chewing.

"When, Dennis?"

Winston spoke around a mouthful of food. "Two years ago."

David took half a sandwich. The roast beef was hot, shaved thin, piled generously on fresh, soft bread. He chewed mechanically and swallowed, the food settling in his stomach like sawdust.

He listened.

Dennis Winston talked between bites until he'd eaten all the sandwiches, fries, and pickles. Winston was one of the ones who needed the right opportunity. He talked until dinner, and between slices of a large pepperoni and onion pizza. He talked through three pots of coffee, five glazed doughnuts, and four trips to the men's room.

When it was over, David went to Halliday's office and sat at the table. His fingers shook—too little sleep and too much caffeine. He was barely able to hold his cup of coffee. Which was just as well, he'd had enough.

Halliday's face was grey with fatigue and worry. His tie was off—hanging over the lamp. The precinct outside was dark, lights on at Mel's desk and David's.

"Where's Mel?" Halliday asked.

"Seeing Winston safely tucked up. He'll be along. Della and

Pete will look after Dennis for tonight."

"Marathon session."

David looked at his hands. "I didn't want to give him time to sleep on it and change his mind. This guy blows with the wind."

"How'd it go?"

David stared at the floor. He saw Judith Rawley's bloody throat. Naomi Chessfield's dead face. Dyer, in pieces, at the morgue.

"Went well," David said. "We got Santana connected to Clinton. We got Clinton connected to Dyer, and *maybe* Santana, too. And we got Myer." David heard the note of satisfaction in his voice. "We got Myer for arranging the murder of Judith Rawley."

"God *damn*, David. God damn."

FIFTY

DAVID KNEW HE SHOULD BE WORKING—THERE WERE FILES TO update, a case to build against Myer. Della and Pete were on the streets, talking to informers, trying to connect Myer to Judith Rawley's killer. Warrants were being prepared. They could search Santana's van, if they ever found it.

Della came through the door, walking like her feet hurt. She put a cold can of Coke to her cheek and eased herself down in her chair. She rubbed her eyes.

"Anything?" Mel said.

"Not yet. Maybe Pete will get something."

"Maybe."

David wiped sweat off his forehead. Della leaned back in her chair and held the Coke to her lips while she studied a printout. David could hear her breath echoing in the can.

"God, Della, *drink* it or put it down."

She looked up, eyes narrowed.

David rubbed the back of his neck. The fluorescent lights were humming. So were the terminals. The room was a snarl of tiny mechanical noises. David knew his breath was coming too fast. His head hurt. He needed to get out of the precinct. Get some air.

Halliday's door slammed open.

"In my office," Halliday looked at David and Mel. "Both of you. You too, Della."

The precinct quieted suddenly, as it always did when String came in. Halliday glanced over his shoulder.

The Elaki looked like he'd been chewed by a dog. His mid-section sagged. He shed scales as he walked.

"How you been, Gumby?" Mel said.

"Most involved. I have news that is not good."

Halliday crooked a finger at him. "In my office."

Everyone sat down, except String. Halliday turned on the TV. A red dot flashed, signifying an emergency broadcast. The familiar face of Enid West, WKBC's news reporter, filled the screen. Her voice rasped unmercifully on the ear, but her information, as always, was current and correct.

" . . . and sources close to the investigation confirm that the Elaki involved in Project Horizon have used people in their laboratory experiments, committing murder in the name of science. As word spreads, Elaki are being stopped in the street by angry bystanders. We go now to the office of Shula Boyo, otherwise known as Topguy."

An Elaki face filled half the screen.

"Mr. Topguy. You are in charge of Project Horizon?"

"Yesss. I run the Horizon Project. It is a joint Elaki-Human endeavor."

"And do you use people as so-called guinea pigs in experiments?"

"But most emphasis not. We treasure life, which is why we have the involvement. Horizon is to find cure for human addictive behavior. Drug abuse, eating disorder, alcohol abuse. These things which tear so bad the life of you good people."

"Mr. Topguy, do you think you'll ever find such a cure?"

"Most yes. We are close to this. Soon to announce."

"Sir, we have witnesses who say known criminals, associated with your project, kidnapped people from the disadvantaged area known as Little Saigo, and delivered them to *your* lab, for use as guinea pigs. What do you say to that?"

"Nonsense most complete."

"Would you allow us to go into the lab and take a look around?"

"I am afraid that possibility is not in the cards of the question. I will not have such important work disruptured."

"I understand the Homicide Task Force of Saigo City is preparing a warrant to search your facilities."

"We will comply with local laws. Please to understand that diplomatic status has recently been granted to this project. Notification came through this morning. Such status includes all personnel and facilities."

"Why won't you let us take a look, Mr. Topguy? What are you hiding?"

The Elaki quivered. "We will soon make our announcement. Until then, I have no need of further comment."

The Elaki's image faded from the screen.

David stood up and kicked his chair over.

"This," said the voice from the TV, "is the scene outside the office of the Elaki ambassador."

"Nothing," David said. "All for *nothing*."

The phone rang. Halliday turned the sound down on the television.

"Halliday. Yes." Halliday rubbed the back of his neck. "When? What do you mean you're not sure? Don't waste my time with excuses. Find him before Santana does."

David closed his eyes. "Winston's gone."

Halliday nodded.

David looked at String. "And suddenly Project Horizon's got diplomatic status."

"Unidentified sources," Della said.

"String." David glared at Mel. "Got to be." David turned to the Elaki. "My friend, the Elaki cop. Working with Project Horizon the whole time. The mind probe, String, that was a good stroke. That way I *knew* Puzzle was afraid of you. I *knew* you weren't in with him. Just plant what you want me to know—"

"But, no, Detective—"

David grabbed him. String was slippery and zipped backward, but David was expecting it. The mind probe would backfire on String after all—it had taught David to wrestle, Elaki style.

David grabbed the Elaki beneath his fins and butted him with his head. The Elaki would sag and fall and—

String contracted and slid out from under David's grasp. Someone grabbed his shoulder and David swung wildly, clipping Mel's ear.

"Ow. *David*. It ain't him."

"It *is* him."

Halliday stood up. "Sit down, Silver!"

"Tell me, Mel, how do you *know* it isn't String?"

"You know it's not him, David. And you know who spilled it. Rose did."

"Rose?"

"Think, will you?"

"Rose wouldn't *do* that, Mel. She promised me . . ."

"David, she won't even talk to me when I call. She's in trouble, she—"

"Rose is fine."

"No, David, she ain't fine. I never known my sister to crap out like that. Like she did down in that tunnel."

David took a deep breath. *"Crap out?"*

"She freaked, David, you were there. She damn near got Haas killed."

"Are you blaming *Rose* for that?"

"Face it. She got scared. It ain't like her, I know, but this Santana has a weird effect on her."

David stepped close enough to feel Mel's breath on his face. "You got a big mouth, Mel, you know that?"

"Take it easy, David. She's *my* sister."

David hit Mel as hard as he could. Mel fell backward across the desk.

"*Out*, Silver." Halliday's fists were clenched. "Walk it off."

Della crouched beside Mel. "You okay, Burnett?"

Mel staggered to his feet and Della steadied him. He wiped blood off his mouth with the back of his hand.

"I'll give you one, David. Touch me again, and I'll wipe the floor with your ass."

"Please, Detectives." String swayed from side to side. "I do not wish to cause these tensions. I did not betray the confidence. I have been in the area for Los Angeles—grey cloudy skies and short smiling humans. I must tell you—"

"This ain't about you, String."

"Both of you *sit*, or get out," Halliday said.

David looked at Mel. "You always have so much to *say*." He spoke softly, barely a whisper. "What can you *do*?"

String moved to Halliday's desk. "I must inform you, sir . . ."

Mel watched David warily. "You want this, David, okay. Come back when your bones are solid, the glue gets absorbed, and you got all your bandages off."

David scooted forward and slammed a fist into Mel's belly. It didn't connect. He had a glimpse of Mel's knuckles before they smashed his nose. He hit the wall, jamming his sore shoulder. The pain in his nose made his eyes tear. He staggered forward, swinging. Someone grabbed his collar and pulled him back.

"*Enough.*" Halliday's voice.

David surged forward halfheartedly. Pain took the edge off intent. Halliday pushed him into a chair. David held his nose with one hand, and kept his left arm close to his body. His shoulder throbbed.

Halliday loosened his tie and sat down behind his desk.

"Detective Silver, have you compromised this investigation by providing your wife with confidential information?"

"No sir." David held his head back and blood trickled from his nose. "Any information my wife had, she found out without any help from me."

"And how is your wife involved?"

"She was once employed by the DEA. She's run into Santana before."

"I think it's time I talked to her."

"Good luck. She'll stand mute." David closed his eyes.

"Then you and I will talk. In depth."

The phone rang.

"Yeah," Halliday said. "Yeah, he's here. David."

David picked up the phone. "Silver." His nose hurt. "Yeah, it's me. Who is . . . Winston?"

Halliday hit the speaker option and Winston's invective filled the office.

" . . . scummy son of a bitch. You promised me. You promised! I don't care if you put me in jail for the rest of my life, I wouldn't help—"

"Winston. *Dennis*. I didn't know this was going to happen. Look, you're a target. *Think*, will you? Santana will come for you. Tell me where you are, we can talk."

"Yeah, and then I can go to the john in handcuffs!"

"Winston?"

The dial tone buzzed.

Mel handed David a handkerchief. "Your nose is bleeding."

"You bastard, I think you broke it."

"Good."

"Get him some ice," Halliday said.

Mel went for the door.

"No, wait." Halliday looked around the office. "Before we clear this room, you better all know what we're up against. According to Mr. String, Santana is branching out. He's sent out feelers to West Coast associates—*Elaki* associates. Black Diamond is going national."

FIFTY-ONE

GRAVEL CRUNCHED UNDER DAVID'S FEET. THE LIGHTS OF
Saigo City glowed and sparkled on his right. Someone had been
burning leaves—illegally—and the dark smokiness was strong in
the air. It was a clear night, the moon nearly full. They were far
enough out of the city to see a few stars.

He was wearing his favorite jacket for the first time since
last spring. He'd lost weight and the jacket hung loosely from
his shoulders. Years of wear had softened the brown leather to
butterlike pliancy. The silken pockets were tattered with holes.
There was a deep scar over the right shoulder, where one of
Mickey Sifuente's hired pistoleros had shot at him. That had
been over on Bell Avenue, behind Ollie Ramey's little bar and
restaurant.

He walked through purple darkness toward the floodlit wreck-
age.

A Jeep, front end broken and crumpled, was smashed into a
walnut tree. David had seen the Jeep before, parked in Dennis
Winston's driveway.

David, careful of broken glass, squatted down on his haunches,
studying the stretch of road in front of the tree. One of the uniforms
started to say something, then noted the ID hanging from David's
belt. David crooked a finger.

"Find any skid marks?"

"No sir."

David nodded. He stood up slowly. Quick movements still hurt.

Mel was bent over a body on a stretcher. He had the sheet pulled
up at the bottom. A naked white foot dangled over the side, the
elastic cuff of the sweatpants soaked in blood. David noted the
medics leaning against the van, one of them smoking. No live
ones here.

One of the uniforms, a woman, held a running shoe out to Mel.
She pointed behind the walnut tree. Mel studied the bottom of the
shoe and grimaced. He motioned David over.

"Look at this."

David took the bloodstained shoe. The webbed imprint of a car accelerator was molded into the sole.

Mel scratched the back of his neck.

"Okay, good," he said to the uniform. "I want that accelerator. Better collect all the floor controls—brake, dimmer switch, whatever. And go to the hospital with him. Make sure we get the clothes."

"Yes sir."

Mel turned to David. "What you think? Suicide? He kept his foot on the gas all the way."

"No skid marks."

Mel rubbed his chin. "Went right for the tree. Never tried to stop."

"Could have been murder," David said. "Santana. Or Myer."

Mel shrugged. "There's easier ways, David. I don't doubt they'd have got him eventually. But you and I both know he was being pulled apart."

"You think he was consumed with guilt over the way things turned out? And decided to end it? It is Winston, isn't it? You ID'd him?"

Mel pulled back the top of the sheet. Winston had gone through the windshield. David had to study the face before he was sure.

"He wasn't finished, Mel. With his work."

"Santana had him coming and going, David. There wasn't going to be any more work."

David looked away from Winston to the dark field on the right.

"One way to make sure," he said.

A month ago it would have been unthinkable for Mel not to have asked what that way was.

"I got some things to finish up here," Mel said. "Let me know what you come up with."

David headed up the gravel road toward his car.

Winston's townhouse was locked up tight. David kicked in the bottom panel of the door. An alarm went off.

David went back to the car and called Halliday, requesting that he be squared away with the local precinct. Halliday agreed, but David felt his disapproval.

The apartment was silent now, dark. One light blazed in the kitchen. David checked the home programmer. Winston had not made any recent changes. Alex's food bowl was empty and sticky with saliva. Licked clean. There was no more than an eighth of an inch of liquid in the water bowl.

David felt a presence.

Alex stood in the doorway, muscles tense, tail high.

"Hello, kitty," David said.

Alex flitted across the floor and rubbed against his legs.

"Hungry, boy? Hungry?"

Alex purred.

David rinsed and filled the water bowl. Alex sniffed it and looked back at David. David found a piece of cooked fish in the refrigerator. He sniffed it, gagged, and set the dish back on the shelf.

David went through the cabinets. In a low corner compartment he found three kinds of cereal, saltine crackers, a jar of peanut butter, a can of peaches that looked decades old, and a new box of dry cat food. David poured some on a plate and set it down beside the water bowl.

Alex wound in and out of David's legs, his furry back rippling like an accordion under David's palm.

"Good kitty," David said. "Lonesome huh? Missing your buddy?"

Alex purred and crunched delicately. David stretched. No doubt, then, that Winston's suicide was contrived. Winston would have seen to Alex, no matter how desperate he was.

David chewed his lip. The method was more Myer's style than Santana's. And Myer had a lot to gain. Without Winston's testimony, Myer would be next to impossible to prosecute.

David knew what would happen. They would go through the drill, sweat the physical evidence, but in the end, they would cut Myer a deal. He was going to have to turn Myer loose to get Santana.

David poked through the apartment while the cat ate. The unmade bed was coated with cat hair. He was fighting the urge to straighten the sheets when Alex appeared in the doorway.

The cat regarded him seriously, then lifted a paw, licking, with practiced dexterity, the rough pads on the bottom.

"I guess you better come home with me," David said.

Alex looked at him with sad, intelligent eyes.

"No handcuffs," David said. "You'll come peacefully, won't you?"

He lifted the cat and tucked him under his arm. Alex shifted and settled in comfortably.

"I hope you like children," David said. "Not to mention dogs, bunnies, and God knows what else."

He went through the kitchen on his way out, picking up the cat food and the water bowl.

FIFTY-TWO

THE COOLING SYSTEM IN THE OFFICE WAS FLUBBED. IT WAS late Sunday afternoon, and the electrician had gone home. Mel, Halliday, and Myer were crammed into interrogation room one. Halliday had refused to let David conduct the interview.

"You'll lose it, David," he had said. "Don't even ask."

Halliday being right didn't make David any the less angry. He sat out in the hall, perched on a stepladder the electrician had left behind.

The precinct was boiling. The weather had turned hot and humid—the last punch of summer. The windows were open, but covered by Venetian blinds. Bars of sunlight baked the tile floor and the empty desks.

David ran a finger around the collar of his T-shirt. A waft of hot air from the open window blew across his face.

Roger had shed his coat and tie, as had Myer. Sweat ran down their flushed cheeks. Myer was laughing, Mel smiling.

They were getting it—everything they needed. And Myer would go to jail, but not for long. Not bad, for a guy who had committed murder and protected drug dealers.

Myer waved at David through the two-way glass.

David took a deep breath and looked away. Mel came out in the hallway, shutting the door behind him.

"I'm going to get some hot dogs, David. What you want?"

"I'll get them."

"Naw. I want out for a while. What can I get you?"

"I don't want a hot dog. I want a taco."

"Okay. I'll be going by Hoi's place anyway."

"I don't want it from Hoi's place. I want one from that place on Mill."

"Mill's all the way across town, David." Mel pulled his shirt up and wiped the sweat off his face. The hairs on his stomach glistened with dampness.

"Tacos on Mill are better."

Mel dropped the shirt and it hung in a wad over his belt. He scratched his neck.

"They're not so bad at Hoi's place."

"*God* damn it, Mel. Will you quit?"

"Quit what?"

"Quit being so *nice* to me. Just stop it, okay? Quit pretending you don't know what I did."

"What, David?" Mel frowned and leaned against the wall. "It's not just this business with Rose, is it?"

David applauded. "You're *good* at it, Mel."

"Good at what?"

"Playing dumb."

"Jesus Christ, this is just the kind of stupid ass conversation I have with women."

"Don't you ever think, Mel, about why I laid in that tunnel and kept my mouth shut, while you and Rose and Haas walked right into Santana."

"That's what's bugging you? You were *hurt*, David. Guy beat the crap out of you. You probably blacked out."

"*No*. Not blacked out. I laid there and I heard you coming. I heard you and I didn't yell."

"So that's it. Jesus. Okay, David. Why didn't you yell?"

"He had me pinned down."

"Okay then. You couldn't."

"But I could." David rubbed his eyes. "I'd already had one hit. And he gave me a choice. Call out . . . or take the Diamond. And I was hurting and I wanted just to fade away, so I . . . took it."

"That's it? That's your big sin?" Mel put a hand on David's shoulder. "Forget it, pal. You weren't thinking straight. You were out of it, David."

"Don't you *do* that, Mel. Treat me like I'm some kind of junkie. I could have warned you."

Mel tightened his grip on David's arm. "You know better than this, David. Now look it. I've seen you pick those junkies up in alleys, sit them up, try to feed them, go after the little pricks that beat them bloody. I've seen you give them money that they say they need for their kids, and I know you knew better. Think who you're talking to. I've *seen* you. All these years, you watch their nasty, desperate lives, and you never get so hard you see them anything less than human, even though every hit they take might be a bullet in your back." Mel took a breath. "You're good at cutting other people slack. Cut some for yourself."

David sat down on the ladder.

"Now I want to know something." Mel scratched his thigh. "You taken any hits since Santana?"

David glared at him. "No."

"Thought about it?"

"Maybe."

"But you haven't?"

"I *said* not."

"Good. I been wanting to ask you that."

"Why didn't you?"

"Why didn't you bring this up earlier? Tell me what was wrong? All these years we been partners, we been friends, you couldn't bring this up? Would have saved your nose." Mel turned away, then looked back over his shoulder. "Haas any better?"

David shook his head. "Still on critical hold, and getting worse. No neural response now, from the waist down."

FIFTY-THREE

THE WEATHER HAD TURNED SUDDENLY CHILLY, AS IF THE SUN had worn itself thin with the last wave of heat. David's eyes watered. The wind made his ears ache.

He took out a handkerchief. "Nothing more irritating than a runny nose on a stakeout."

Mel cocked his head. "Lots of things more irritating. Take, oh, take diarrhea for instance, or just plain . . . you know Ridgway? I was in a car with Ridgway all night one time and—"

"Mel, would you shut up?"

"This reminds me of an incident," String said. "We too are similar, in our jobs the stake up."

"Stake*out*," Mel said.

"Yes. There are times when an Elaki must . . ."

David focused on the pavement as it disappeared under the wheels of the shuttle.

Rose was leaving him.

He had gone home early yesterday to a silent house, and wandered from room to room, looking for his children. Their beds were made. The animals that usually lounged among the pillows were gone. The night-light was missing.

He heard Rose's soft tread in the hallway. It took him two tries to summon his voice.

"Where are they?"

"In Chicago, with Ruth."

He turned back to the empty room. He had wanted to see them. He had *needed* to see them. "Won't they miss school?"

"Yes."

"Are you . . . going somewhere?"

"Yes."

He wanted to ask when she'd be back. He wanted to ask *if* she'd be back. Why had she gone to the press without talking to him first? Did she understand what she'd done to him? Did she know she had cost him Myer?

His mouth was dry, his throat tight. In the end it had been easier to say nothing at all.

Mel sent the car away. The parking lot was huge and empty. They caught a bright red shuttle to take them to the main buildings. The shuttle had open sides, and the wind whistled through. They were the only ones aboard, and Mel kept changing seats.

"Rose okay?" Mel asked.

"Fine," David said.

Something snapped in the wind, catching David's attention. A large multicolored banner hung across red and blue turnstiles. CARNIVAL PLANET. Rose hated this place. They'd brought the kids two or three times before on what usually turned out to be the hottest day of the summer.

Santana would be here, so Myer had told them, completing an initial contact with the head of a West Coast organization. It was a first meet, head to head, the wheeler-dealers. Afterward, they would both send employees, but this was the initial exchange. Large samples of Black Diamond swapped for one million in earnest money. Santana was setting up.

Myer didn't know who the West Coast dealer was. Just that the exchange would be made in NEW HOLLAND.

"I do not understand the business with that one, the Myer." String's left eye stalk was drooping more than usual. "I can tell you that the Myer is a bad cop. Guilty of much and deserving of cho."

"We know that," Mel said. "What we needed was evidence."

"Knowledge of the officer is not enough?"

"Got to prove it to a whole *bunch* of people."

"Does this prevent the mistake from being made?"

"No, but it spreads the blame around."

"Ah."

"You can't tell me, String, that you Elaki secret police—"

"Izicho, please."

"That you Izicho please never make mistakes. Suppose you cho off the wrong guy? You telling me that never happens?"

"It happens rare. And then, of course, the Izicho officer is sanctioned."

"Cho?" David asked.

"Cho."

Mel looked at David. "Interesting system."

David thought of Myer, laughing and joking his way through the interrogation, a cagey old cop who knew the business before any of them had been out of diapers. David had glared through the two-way, fists clenching and unclenching.

When it was over, Myer had gotten slowly to his feet, carefully draping the worn suit coat and the cheap tie over one arm.

Where? David wondered. Where had the money gone—the drug money that Myer had betrayed and killed for? Gambling? Women? Drug habit? Something to do with his kids?

Myer had stopped in the hall and looked at him.

"Hey, Silver."

Myer's face was grooved with age and fatigue. His eyes were old. Knowing.

Never me, David thought. Never me.

"How's it happen, Myer? What goes wrong?"

Myer shrugged and spread his arms. "Who knows? There's so much, you know? Maybe it's just my feet hurt."

David nodded, waiting for Myer to look away, to refuse to meet his gaze. It didn't happen.

"I used to be pretty good," Myer said.

"So I heard."

"Yeah. See you, Silver."

Myer walked down the hallway, wedged between Mel and Halliday. A tired, bent cop, whose feet hurt.

David adjusted his earpiece.

"Silver, Burnett, and String, checking in."

"Copy." Halliday's voice was soft in his ear. "No sign yet of Santana. Take your positions."

They avoided the empty turnstiles at the entrance, ducking through a door marked "Employees Only."

"We go this way?"

"No. Over here," David said.

The park was empty, except for the occasional employee in bright yellow overalls. Most of them were cops—the ready team. They would be called when things got hot. Santana wasn't going to duck out of this one.

The paved walkways were exquisitely clean. The fountains were already running. Fur-covered robots wandered around on all fours, offering rides to the air. Organ music blasted from speakers.

"Creepy," Mel said. "Looks weird without people."

"People would not subtract from the weirdness," String said.

Mel grinned at him.

NEW HOLLAND was a boat ride beneath a glaring white dome. Canals snaked through fabricated darkness, touring interactive exhibits that told the tale of the mysterious island. Survivalists had built up a sandbar in the middle of the Caribbean and declared it a sovereign nation—New Holland. Then, after a typhoon in 2024, all the New Hollanders had disappeared. Theories about their demise were meat to tabloid journalists. Rumors had them murdered, taken away by submarine, living in a secret underwater city. Some of the missing islanders had been sighted by relatives, and from time to time, island currency would surface.

It was dark and cold under the dome. David and Mel and String waited inside the doorway, Mel and David letting their eyes adjust. Water lapped at the edges of the canal, and the air inside smelled dank and musty.

"We're in," David said.

"You should be alone," Halliday told him. "Sensors are in place and they haven't picked anything up. We do not, repeat, *not* have them on constant feed. We'll query at intervals, and upon your request. Copy?"

"Copy," said Mel.

Power cables snaked across the aisles between the canals and the story exhibits.

"Stay out of the front passages," Halliday warned them. "At least until people start coming through. Your presence will trigger the exhibits. Anybody coming in will know you're there."

"Copy," David said.

"How we going to get in position?" Mel said. "We want that little side inlet, and the only way there is past the exhibits."

"A downward wiggle will be necessary," String said.

"Crawl, Mel."

Mel went first, with David squirming behind him, and String following. The floor was gritty and there were wet spots. David felt them soak into his shirt. He wished he'd gone first. Mel had stepped in pink bubble gum, and black mud was encrusted in the ridges on the bottom of his right shoe.

They elbowed their way along the floor of the passage until they passed the partition and could stand up. A boat bobbed gently in the small section of canal behind the canvas.

"This the one?" Mel asked.

"Got a motor on it," David said. "None of the others do."

"An interesting implement," String said. "Is this necessary to make a human waterborne?"

"Waterborne at no more than fifteen miles an hour, going flat out. Maybe twenty with a wave behind it. And a stiff breeze."

"It gives you maneuverability, Mel. You expect a speedboat in this bathtub?"

"This does not look to provide maneuverability."

"Makes it easier to mow down the tourists, though. What you think, David? In the boat, or out?"

"If somebody spots us inside, we're going to look pretty weird just sitting. Three men in a tub."

"With Gumby here, we're weird enough."

"Outside then."

"Out it is. Try and make it look like we're fixing something." Mel took a pocketknife and made a hole in the canvas partition.

"Welcome," a voice boomed. "To the island of New Holland." Reggae music echoed across the water.

"Too early for customers," Mel said. "Query, Halliday."

String quivered and swayed from side to side. "Sometime I would very much like to come here from the front."

FIFTY-FOUR

DAVID AND MEL HAD SHED THEIR JACKETS. THE WIND OUTSIDE had died, and the sun was bright again. It was cool inside NEW HOLLAND, but people were coming through in shorts.

There had been no sign of Santana or his people. Nothing but regular customers since the park employee had tripped the first exhibit early that morning.

Mel looked at String, who was sleeping.

"I don't understand how he can relax standing up like that." He poked the Elaki's shoulder.

"Quit it, Mel, you'll knock him over."

The winds of the typhoon scene echoed through the dome.

"What *really* happened?" a voice boomed.

Mel screwed up his face, matching his words to those on the speaker.

"Were they swept away by the storm, picked up by a Japanese submarine . . . or have they gone . . . somewhere else?" Music filled the air.

"Or maybe," Mel continued, "maybe the stupid fuckers killed each other off."

"Ate each other," David said. "That's why there weren't any bodies."

"What happened to the bones?"

"What are you, forensics?" David checked his watch. One-thirty. "I thought this was set for noon. Twelve-ten, supposedly."

"Wonder when Halliday will call it off?"

String's eye stalks twitched. "Increase the patience."

David shrugged, trying not to give way to the heavy disappointment settling in his stomach.

"There," Mel said. "Look at *her*. Will she warn the guy about the crocodile, or let him get eaten?"

David looked through the peephole. A woman sat in a boat, keeping a hand on the smallest of the four children around her.

"There will be good lessons here, for the young ones," String said.

"She'll let him get eaten," David said.

Mel peeped out. "I don't know, she looks pretty nice. Got good legs, too. She'll warn him. Five bucks?"

"Done."

David smiled. He'd watched Rose with the girls in this park. He knew the mother's frame of mind.

String leaned backward. An Elaki stretch.

"May I be in for the bet? Five dollars also. I agree with Detective David."

Mel shrugged. "Easy money, guys."

The exhibition-two robot wandered down a sandy beach. The robot wore khaki shorts and a loose shirt and looked extremely lifelike.

"How'd they get crocs on New Holland, anyway?"

"Brought them in," David said. "To guard."

"Jesus. *That* explains what happened to them."

The robot cast a fishing line into ocean ripples. The children in the boat squealed. Must see the croc, David decided.

"Mommy, *look*. Hey, mister—"

"Shhh." The woman clamped a hand over the child's mouth.

The croc opened huge jaws and lunged. The robot screamed and struggled while he was pulled underwater. The children squealed, the youngest watching in shocked silence.

"Quite lifelike," String said. "Are the woman and children real?"

"I don't believe it!" Mel shook his head. "Put her hand over the kid's mouth! Why would anybody bring their children in here, anyway?"

"The bigger ones love it."

"It's sick."

"David?"

Halliday's voice made him jump.

"Copy."

"Two subjects. One female, one male. In through the south employee entrance."

"Copy."

"Here we go," said Mel.

They sweated it until two-ten. Then Halliday's voice was back in their ears.

"Santana has been spotted. Wearing a short denim skirt, white tennis shoes, red cotton shirt, and a straw hat with a yellow scarf."

"Nice legs?" Mel asked.

"Pay attention, Burnett. Santana is accompanied by a male subject, approximately six-three, wearing jeans and a blue flannel shirt. Both have gotten into the back of a boat with an *Elaki* subject in a plaid vest."

String's belly rippled.

"Elaki?"

"Copy."

"It is as I told you," String said.

"Query check on subjects A and B behind exhibition."

"Subjects A and B on the move. Heading for exhibition three."

"Copy."

Mel frowned. "Three. That's the orgy scene, isn't it? Where they're eating and carrying on?"

"Split up," David said. "You and String on the boat. I'll stay back here and go this way."

"What about the street soldiers?"

"I'll be careful. Go on, you need to be ahead of them. Stay on the Elaki. We don't want him getting out with the stuff. I'll get Santana."

"I foresee a possible complication," String said.

"Don't sweat it, Gumby, we'll handle it. David, you be sure and call in the troops."

"You bet."

Mel climbed in the boat. "An Elaki crime wave. God help us."

"Move it, Mel."

David ducked through a door, taking a short cut to the maintenance entrance near exhibition three. He dodged props, boxes, cables. It was dark, and he used a penlight to make his way.

"Halliday. Query on subjects A and B."

"Both subjects have converged on exhibition three. Out in the open, north side of exhibition, visible to people in boats. Readiness team has been alerted. Exits are being covered. Will send backup your way."

"Make sure they keep good distance. I don't want them in too soon."

"Don't wait too long."

"Copy."

David went through the door and positioned himself on the side aisle, opposite Santana's street soldiers. He crawled halfway to the canal, stopping when he heard voices.

"You fugley today, Elmer?"

The voice was female, youthful.

"What?"

"You fugley?"

"I don't know."

"You are. You're fugley."

"What's fugley?"

"Fucking ugly."

The woman laughed. A muscle spasmed in David's leg.

"Bitch," the man muttered. "Hey. Here they come."

David ducked back in the shadows, maneuvering to get a view. A red boat bobbed near the edge of the exhibit. Santana sat in the prow, and the Elaki stood in the stern, balancing easily.

Elmer grabbed the side of the boat and held it steady. Santana and the man in the blue flannel shirt climbed out. The Elaki shifted toward the center of the boat.

The typhoon winds from exhibit six triggered.

"Shit," David said. He leaned forward, trying to hear.

Santana pointed to a blue case and opened his arms. The Elaki made an odd, high-pitched noise. David heard a splash. Something surfaced in the water. A slick, dripping Elaki rose between the boat and the edge of the canal and handed a sealed package to Santana.

David grimaced. Elaki don't swim, eh, String?

Santana was laughing. David could see the open mouth, the delighted features. An earring dangled from Santana's right ear, catching the light. David knew without looking that it would have a unicorn on it, with a blue eye made of turquoise.

The woman handed the plastic case to the Elaki in the boat. The Elaki said something to Santana, then dived into the water.

"*Now,*" David said. "Backup. Two Elaki, one holding a blue plastic case, en route, *underwater.*"

"In the canal?"

"That's right, damn it, *move*. I'm going after Santana. Backup in place?"

"Backup *is* in place."

"Copy."

The boat, empty now, drifted gently to the next exhibit.

"Jesus Christ!" Mel's voice was loud in his ear and David winced.

"What?"

"He's gone after them. Underwater."

"Who?"

"*Gumby*. Look at that sucker go!"

Five cops in yellow coveralls burst through the south door, cutting off Santana's escape. David saw Pete and Della.

David stood up, pointing his gun. "Stop. Police. Everybody take it easy and nobody move."

Pete and Della were yelling. The man in the blue flannel shirt threw the package of money at David, and Della fired.

Santana leaped into the canal. The package hit David's elbow, throwing his aim as he pulled the trigger. David peered into the canal. Had Santana been hit? David took a breath and jumped.

The water was cold and David came up shivering. He rubbed his eyes and shook his head, slinging droplets of water out of his hair. There was movement in the water ahead of him. Something red floated by. He grabbed it and held it up. A red shirt. Santana's.

"Mama, look, there's a man in the water."

"Just part of the exhibit, honey. See if it'll talk to you."

The typhoon noises were going again. David swam toward them, bumping softly into the edge of the partition. There were puddles of water in the aisle in front of the exhibit. He pulled himself up over the side, stopping to catch his breath.

"Pursuit," he took a breath. "Pursuit into exhibition six. Halliday?"

No answer.

He checked his earpiece. Gone. David crept down the aisle-way, following a line of water. His gun was useless. And Santana didn't need to be armed.

This time, David thought, there won't be anybody holding me down.

There were blood splats next to the drips of water. Santana was wounded. David took a deep breath.

The blood trail led him past the exhibit and into the dark hallway. Santana would head for the emergency exit. He'd be wet, bleeding—conspicuous, even without the red shirt.

David saw a shadow move just as an arm went around his neck.

"Got you, my cop." Santana, wet and warm, pinned David's hands and pressed him close. He wrapped his hand around David's throat.

An alarm shrilled and the emergency door slammed open. Rose paused in the doorway, illuminated by a blinking red light. She was dressed like an exhibit robot, in brown khaki shorts and a T-shirt, and David was sorry to see that she did not have a gun.

Santana laughed softly. "Rose. I should have known you would come. How is Haas?"

Rose stopped in the aisle-way, and stood very still. David felt sweat roll down the small of his back. Rose smiled, a look David rarely saw, and did not like. Rose moved closer, but without the usual assurance. David bit his lip.

Santana's hand moved down David's spine. David's muscles tensed so tightly he ached.

"Don't, Rose. I'll cripple him, just like Haas." Santana shrugged. "If you care. You could sit them side by side—start your own vegetable garden."

She was hesitating. Abnormally quiet. Not in control.

David swallowed. "Rose," he said. "You took Clinton. You can take Santana."

She looked at David and frowned. As if she didn't know who he was.

"Hurt him if you want to," David said. "But please, don't kill him."

One corner of her mouth lifted slightly. But still she hesitated. David felt the pressure of Santana's thumbs on his spine. Blood ran in a steady stream down Santana's thin, tautly muscled arm. Sweat filmed his upper lip, and he smelled strongly of fear. Afraid of Rose? If so, she'd be the one he'd be watching.

David let his muscles go limp, dead weight sagging. Santana's grip tightened, then released. David hit the floor and rolled out of the way.

Rose and Santana faced each other, both of them crouched forward, chins tucked down, balancing on the balls of their feet. Had he been right? David wondered. Could Rose take him? Maybe he should—

"Stay," Rose said.

David settled back. Advantages, he thought, in being married awhile.

Rose and Santana circled each other warily. Santana grabbed for Rose, but she slipped away, exposing her throat. The side of Santana's hand moved like a knife edge. David lunged forward, but Rose was gone before the blow connected.

It seemed to David that it came down to balance. Santana veered sideways, trying to catch Rose in a headlock. He aimed a blow to her temple. Rose grabbed his wounded arm and pulled him forward, taking advantage of his momentum. She twisted the arm backward and dislocated the shoulder, slowly and cruelly. Santana arched his back and cried out. He sagged, but stayed on his feet.

"This is for David," Rose said. There was sweat on her upper lip, and her eyes had taken on a peculiar glaze. She brought her elbow down hard on Santana's shoulder, breaking the collarbone. Santana crumpled, and fell on his back, knees drawn up. Rose kicked him hard, on the right side, over the liver, and David felt a twinge of pain in his own ribs.

Santana groaned deeply and rolled to his belly.

"And this," Rose said, "is for Haas."

David lurched forward. "Rose, *no*—"

She brought her heel down with deadly force two inches over Santana's belt line. David heard the snap of vertebrae. Santana went limp. David sagged backward, sitting down suddenly.

Rose's chest heaved as she caught her breath. She wiped sweat off her forehead. David stared at her.

"He's *alive*, David. Like you asked." Her smile made him sad. "But he isn't going to walk away."

FIFTY-FIVE

DAVID AND ROSE SAT SIDE BY SIDE. ROGER HALLIDAY PACED in front of them.

"I suppose you're going to call it self-defense again."

The medics were carefully strapping Santana belly down on a stretcher.

"He isn't dead, Captain," David said softly. His hands were shaking.

"He's damn near close to it." Halliday turned to Rose. "How the hell is it you happen to be here?"

Rose pursed her lips and glared at Halliday.

"I've been on David's tail since last night. No, he did not spill what he was up to, but it doesn't take a mental giant to know you were setting something up with Santana. Sorry, Captain, but the local Homicide Task Force is no match for somebody like Santana."

Halliday stopped pacing and scratched his chin. When he spoke, it was with unwonted softness and intensity.

"I've done some research on you, Mrs. Silver. I want it understood. I will not let my . . . association . . . with David gloss over your use of *my* investigation to carry on a personal blood feud."

"And I will not let your inept and inefficient operation cost my husband—or my children—their lives. Is that understood?"

David put his head in his hands.

"Roger?" Della's voice. David took a deep breath and made a mental note to buy her dozens of blueberry muffins. "Roger, can you come over here?"

Keep him awhile, David prayed. Give *him* time to cool down. Rose sure wasn't going to.

Roger took his suit coat off and draped it with careful deliberation over his arm. "Excuse me."

David looked at Rose. "You've been here all morning?"

At first he thought she wasn't going to answer; then she nodded.

"Listening in to your transmissions. I've been blending in—

247

the orgy-on-the-beach exhibit. Dodging a robot who was trying
to feed me plastic pineapple and feel up my shirt. You went right
past me two times."

"God damn it, I thought you'd taken the kids and left me."

"Glad to see me, weren't you?"

David smiled sadly. "For more than one reason." His smile
faded. "I don't like what you did."

"I know," she said. "You still want to stay married?"

"Yes. You?"

"For now."

"For—"

"I'm kidding. Yes."

He gave her an uncertain smile. She brushed his cheek with
blue, swollen knuckles. She didn't wince, and David realized she
was still a long way away.

"We're going," David said.

"Can't until we settle with Halliday."

"Later, when the two of you cool off. Right now you have to
come with me."

"Where?"

"Hospital. Time to face it, Rose. Time to see Haas."

The ward for medical hold was in a grey concrete wing of
Southern Medical. The corridor leading to the ICU ward was
narrow and poorly lit. No one stared at Rose or David as they
passed a waiting room. Their air of shock and upset were not out
of place.

They passed through grey double doors. A woman in a green
cotton jumpsuit and a plastic hair net glared at them.

"*No* visitors," she snapped.

David flashed his police ID.

"That doesn't buy you one thing," the woman said. "Get out
or I'll call security."

Rose's hand shot out so quickly that David felt the air whiz.
She held the woman brutally, two fingers pinching her throat.

"When your voice comes back," Rose said softly, "call anybody
you want."

David felt his face turn red. He went past the desk, looking at
the names over the doors. Rose walked past him.

"Over here," she said.

The light was off and the room was greyish and dim. There
was just enough space for the two of them to stand beside the
bed. Haas had his eyes closed.

"Haas?" Rose spoke quietly, barely a whisper.

His eyes opened.

"Hello, Rosy." Haas's face was pale, lined and weary. His legs were oddly still under the sheets. "David. You bring beer?"

David smiled thinly. The man could be counted on to be good-natured and heroic. Haas turned his head to Rose, then caught his breath, eyes shutting tightly. His face turned ashen, then he relaxed and opened his eyes.

"The doctor says such pain is psychosomatic. Just in the head."

David remembered Haas in the kitchen, gratefully accepting whiskey and aspirin. Tall, strong, capable.

"I am learning doctors say many irritating things."

Rose was crying. David watched the tears roll down her chin and neck before they soaked into the top of her shirt. Haas watched her helplessly, then turned to David.

"Please." He looked back at Rose. "I will heal, Rose. I believe this and so must you. Be patient, and we will track the Santana together."

"No need," David said. "She got him."

Haas's eyes widened. "Is dead?"

"No." David swallowed. "He won't walk again."

Haas turned his head on the pillow so he could see Rose's face. "This is good."

They were two of a kind, David thought. "I'll be outside," he said, and left them alone in the room.

EPILOGUE

DAVID DIPPED A CORN CHIP IN SALSA, GETTING THE HOT SAUCE by mistake. He took a deep drink of water, and caught sight of String from the corner of one eye. The Elaki dipped chips in the hot sauce and ate without flinching. There were pieces of tortilla embedded in his pink belly scales.

He had turned out to be quite a swimmer, though it was worth your life to mention it to him. The canals, as it turned out, had been full of Elaki. The ready team had netted nine in all.

The Elaki swimming ability came as a surprise to David, though he supposed it shouldn't have. The Elaki were equipped with an aquatic lung, a balloonlike sack at their top ridges that they could fill with air. They had whipped through the canals like greased pigs on satin.

David watched Lisa drink her Coke—sip, sip, ignoring the food.

They were going after the permanent incarceration penalty for Santana. The plaid-vested Elaki had escaped with the Diamond. Project Horizon had been shut down and the Elaki had announced their cure for human addictive behavior—a carefully constructed societal cure, involving careful nurturing during childhood, job opportunities, support of the family unit. Public reaction was negative. The Elaki were telling people what they already knew. No magic pill? No easy solutions? Maybe Black Diamond *could* be a safe outlet, but right now it was a killer. And if the Elaki had humanity's well-being at heart, why did they kidnap people and use them in their laboratories?

David wondered if Dennis Winston would ever have been able to engineer the Black Diamond not to hurt. What had Winston said? It would sure make a cop's job easier.

Lisa shredded her napkin. "Daddy. They're bringing food to people who came in after us."

"I'm hungry," Mattie said.

"Eat another chip." David looked at his watch. Even accounting for the size of the group—Rose, the girls, Mel, and String—even so, the wait for a table had been ridiculous, and their order was taking forever.

"You ever come here by yourself?" Mel asked String.

"Twice."

"Food come quick? Good service?"

"But very much so."

Mel looked at David, then back at String. "Your mistake, Gumby. Mixing with humans."

String turned an eye stalk toward Mattie, who was cramming chips in her mouth. "You have a tiny food pouch. Keep room in it for the taco."

"Don't need room for taco," Mattie said, studying the Elaki's eye stalks. "I'm getting a burrito."

Mel distributed the last of the pitcher of beer.

"A toast," he said. "To Dyer. And to Haas."

David felt Rose take his hand under the table. He squeezed her fingers.

"And to all his animal friends," David said with resignation. "And their temporary home with the Silvers." David grimaced. "May they all go away soon."

Mel grinned. "What's the tally, David?"

"One pregnant horse, an incredibly obnoxious goose, who does not get along with Alex—"

"Alex that cat?"

David nodded. "On the good side, the goose has motivated Alex to team up with Dead Meat—"

"*Daddy*. Not Dead Meat. Hilde."

"Hilde."

String wiped salsa from a belly scale. "I once knew an Elaki with certain zoological fascinations . . ."

David glared at Mel, who shrugged.

"Why you always blame *me* when he does this?"